A Forget-Me-Not Summer

About the author

Sophie Claire writes emotional stories set in England and in sunny Provence, where she spent her summers as a child. She has a French mother and a Scottish father, but was born in Africa and grew up in Manchester, England, where she still lives with her husband and two sons.

Previously, she worked in marketing and proofreading academic papers, but writing is what she always considered her 'real job' and now she's delighted to spend her days dreaming up heartwarming contemporary romance stories set in beautiful places.

You can find out more at www.sophieclaire.co.uk and on Twitter @sclairewriter.

Also by Sophie Claire

The Christmas Holiday

sophie claire

A Forget-Me-Not Summer

HODDER

First published in Great Britain in 2015 as
Her Forget-Me-Not Ex by Accent Press
First published in Great Britain in 2019 by Hodder & Stoughton
An Hachette UK company

1

A CIP catalogue record for this title is available from the British Library

Paperback ISBN 9781529392814
eBook ISBN 9781529392821

Typeset in Plantin Light 11.25/14.75 pt by
Palimpsest Book Production Limited, Falkirk, Stirlingshire

Printed and bound in Great Britain by Clays Ltd, Elcograf S.p.A.

Hodder & Stoughton policy is to use papers that are natural,
renewable and recyclable products and made from wood grown in
sustainable forests. The logging and manufacturing processes are expected
to conform to the environmental regulations of the country of origin.

Hodder & Stoughton Ltd
Carmelite House
50 Victoria Embankment
London EC4Y 0DZ

www.hodder.co.uk

To Ian, Mum and Dad, and Maureen and Robert,
for your encouragement and support

Prologue

London, three years ago

'Is there anyone we can call for you?'

Natasha blinked. The nurse smiled kindly. Her eyes were the rich blue of hyacinths, filled with concern and pity.

'Your husband maybe?' The nurse looked at the ring on her left hand.

'I left him a message. He's abroad.'

'A family member?'

She shook her head.

'You're going to need a D and C. Dilation and curettage. It's a minor operation, but necessary. Do you understand, Natasha?'

She nodded. The baby was gone. Her heart folded up on itself and she squeezed her eyes shut against the pain.

Afterwards, she lay staring at the white ceiling. The fluorescent lights tinged everything violet. Losing the baby still felt too enormous, too violent to think about so she turned her mind to Luc instead. She had to make a plan.

What would happen when he came? Would he come at all? His work was so important, after all, she thought bitterly. She knew she ranked very low in his life and he'd only married her for the baby. She held up her left hand. The platinum ring was a silver blur that swam and swayed. When he'd proposed she'd hoped it would be the start of something new, that he'd put his freedom-loving days behind him, and they'd work to become a family. She'd hoped they'd both share the same goal, and the baby would bring them together. She'd hoped so hard.

The nurse appeared. 'Did you have a name for the baby?' she asked gently.

Natasha nodded. She hadn't discussed it with Luc – they were barely talking – but it was certain in her mind. 'Hope. Her name was Hope.'

Now Hope had died there was nothing left, no reason for her to stay. The pain was crushing, intense.

The sound of quick, heavy footsteps in the corridor made them both look up. There were raised voices, then Luc appeared, breathless. She was surprised.

'I got here as fast as I could,' he said.

Her heartbeat picked up at the sight of him. His dark hair, his treacle eyes. She wondered if she'd ever stop loving him. *He doesn't love you, though.*

He stayed with her as she drifted off, welcoming the anaesthetic of sleep. He was still there when she woke and the nurses told her she could be discharged. He took her back to his penthouse, and she didn't have the energy to argue.

Back at his flat, he looked worried, couldn't do enough

for her. It was as if he was speaking to her through a funnel: his words were muffled and distant. 'Are you hungry?' he asked. 'What can I get you?'

Too little, too late, she thought. He wasn't the man he'd been the last few weeks. Since she'd told him about the baby, resentment had filled this big flat, pressing against the glass walls.

He left the room. She heard the front door shut, and a memory resurfaced of when she'd left her great-aunt's house at sixteen. She'd made a promise to herself then that she'd never allow herself to be in that situation again: unwanted, resented. A plan was assembling in her mind.

It didn't take long to pack her clothes, toothbrush, and the tiny framed photograph of her parents. She was waiting by the door, ready to leave, when he came back from the shops.

'What are you doing?' He stared at her.

He had a pint of milk in his hand. She looked at it. 'I'm going home.'

She thanked her lucky stars that she'd kept the lease for her bedsit these last two months. Perhaps a part of her had always known it would end this way.

'But you've only just come out of hospital.'

'I'm going,' she repeated firmly.

'Why?'

Her head was fuzzy: the room tilted left, then right. She put out her hand and touched the wall to steady herself. He doesn't love you, she reminded herself silently.

'You're not strong enough—' he began.

'Because it's over. The pregnancy was a mistake. We

only married because of the baby, and now . . .' She couldn't stay where she wasn't wanted. Self-preservation kicked in and she lifted her head, looked him in the eye. 'Now we can both get on with our lives.'

He didn't argue. He didn't say anything at all. His silence sliced through her, killing any doubts she'd still carried.

The intercom buzzed. Her taxi had arrived. She bent to pick up her case. Tears welled, salty and hot. She wished she wasn't so weak. She wished she didn't love him so much, so fiercely and completely.

'I'll take that,' he said, nodding at her suitcase.

Their hands collided. He snatched the case away from her and she mumbled something about divorce papers, then left.

He didn't try to stop her. Far from it. He saw her to the taxi, lifted her luggage into the boot, then stood back, hands in his pockets, his mouth a flat line, and watched as the taxi drove away.

He didn't love her, he never had. And that was why she had to go.

Chapter One

Present day

When he came in, Natasha was slicing the thorns off a marshmallow-pink rose. The door chimed and she glanced up, ready to smile, then froze. The flower in her hand was forgotten and she stared. There, in her shop, was Luc.

Her heart thumped. The shop flooded with cold air, as if it were a winter morning, not a bright June afternoon. His tall figure and broad shoulders filled the door and his dark eyes fixed on her but gave nothing away. She swallowed, feeling a sharp twist in her chest, and glanced at the back room. But, of course, Debbie had already gone home, so she was alone.

'Natasha,' he said, stepping forward and closing the door. 'Good to see you.'

The sound of his voice was as unsettling as an earthquake. Deep. Sure of himself.

'Luc,' she said. She couldn't disguise her shock. It had been – how long? – three years since she'd last seen him. 'Why are you here?'

He didn't answer immediately but glanced around her

tiny shop, taking in his surroundings. She followed his gaze from the sunflowers to the gerberas and, for a moment, she hoped this might be an accident. That by some bizarre coincidence he'd arrived in her tiny village and walked in to buy a bouquet. But then he turned back to her and his eyes fixed on her with such fierce determination that she knew it was no accident. Her fingers gripped the rose a little tighter.

'You could at least pretend to look pleased to see me,' he said.

He was right, she thought. She might feel like she'd just been plunged back in time to a dark place of violent emotions, but she didn't want him to know how much he was affecting her. Not when, in the past, he'd been so cool with her.

Pretend, she told herself. Act as if you're totally indifferent to him.

'I'm just – just surprised, that's all. I wasn't expecting you. You should have called.' As she spoke, she noticed that he'd changed. The details were subtle: small lines around his eyes, a few greys at his temples. He was still good-looking, though, she noted grudgingly, and effortlessly stylish, even in a simple cream T-shirt and jeans. Suddenly she felt self-conscious. No doubt he would disapprove of her new quirky style: he'd think her outfit was eccentric and too bright, not sophisticated like his. She fought the urge to hide her fingernails, painted pale blue with tiny daisies, telling herself it didn't matter what he thought. She might have tried to please him in the past, but those days were over.

'There wasn't time,' he said, and looked at the flower in her hand, but there was an uncharacteristically distant expression in his eyes. 'It was quicker to come straight here.'

Natasha frowned. Really? How much time would it have taken to call her from the train or the car or however he'd arrived? 'Don't tell me – you urgently need a bunch of flowers?'

He shook his head and the corner of his mouth tilted. It was almost a smile and impossibly sexy. She was certain that no woman could look at him without feeling a little weak in the legs.

'No. Not flowers. I need you.'

She put the rose down What did he mean? And why did her mind instantly fill with heated images? Memories of him and her. Naked.

She struggled to think straight. 'Me? What on earth would you need me for?'

'I need your help.'

As he held her gaze steadily, she realised he was being serious and a spike of emotion shot through her, something between fear and anger. 'Luc, I'm your ex-wife. We're not usually top of the list for being keen to help.'

'I wouldn't ask if it wasn't necessary. Besides, I have faith in you to help, ex-wife or not.'

Did he now? She eyed him suspiciously. Did he mean she was a pushover? But then she noticed he was pale, and now she wondered if the lines around his eyes were signs of ageing or something else – strain possibly, or tiredness. Though she tried to prevent it, she felt a tug of concern. 'What's wrong, Luc? What's happened?'

She saw pain in his eyes.

'You're not on the run from the police, are you?' she joked, then wished she hadn't said anything. She was just nervous, rattled by his unexpected appearance, by the desperation now etched into his handsome features.

'Is there somewhere we could talk?' he asked.

She glanced at the clock. 'I suppose I could close a little early . . .' Then she threw him a stern warning look. 'But whatever you've got to say, you'll have to say it here.'

'OK.'

He was so quick to accept that she knew something was seriously wrong and anxiety needled her. He was her ex-husband but that didn't prevent her from feeling sympathy for him. But she was wary too.

She locked the shop door, flipped the sign to 'Closed', and dropped the roses she'd been trimming into a bucket of water. Then she returned to stand behind the counter. She felt safer with a bit of space between them. It seemed incredible that, after three years apart, he still had the power to set her on edge.

'So, what's the problem?' she asked, trying to sound detached and efficient, though her hands were unsteady as she swept up the thorns and leaves scattered across the counter.

'My father is ill,' he said. 'Very ill, in fact.'

She stopped tidying and looked up. 'Oh, Luc, I'm sorry.' She'd never met his parents but her heart went out to him.

'He collapsed, it's his heart, and the next few weeks – days – are critical.'

She nodded cautiously, unclear how this had anything to do with her or how she could help.

Luc ran his tongue across his lips. 'I've just been to visit. All the family are there . . .' He swallowed again, then met her gaze. Steadily. '. . . but he was asking for you.'

'Me?' She laughed, a high-pitched sound. 'Why me? I've never even met him.' Her cheeks coloured and she turned to deposit the cuttings in a bin behind the counter, then briskly dusted off her hands.

'Exactly.' He picked up a leaf she'd missed and absently rolled it between his fingers. 'He was unhappy when he learned that we got married without inviting anyone. Now he's asking that we spend some time with him. In France.'

'We? I don't understand.'

'You and me,' he said.

She frowned. 'There is no "you and me" any more. Anyway, why on earth would he want me to—'

'Because he believes we're still married.'

There was a long pause. In the street outside, a car rumbled past. Natasha blinked, not sure she'd heard properly, but the words settled around her, like a handful of rose petals fluttering to the ground. *He believes we're still married.*

After three years? Why? She'd assumed his family didn't know about her: Luc certainly hadn't told them about his marriage at the time. He'd behaved as if he were ashamed of it. Of her.

Confusion made her head spin, and she felt a sharp point of irritation too. Let's face it, what did any of this have to do with her?

'Why on earth would he believe that, Luc?'

He ducked his head. When he'd appeared in her shop, she'd thought Luc didn't seem quite himself, but this was new: the man who was never anything but a hundred per cent certain of himself now looked sheepish.

He said quietly, 'I haven't told him about the divorce.'

There was a long pause. 'Haven't told him?' she repeated incredulously.

He shook his head.

Luc wasn't a man to hide from the truth. He was bold and strong, with a core of steel. 'Why not?'

His shoulders went back, his chin up, and there was hardness in his eyes, which warned her this was not safe territory. 'It's complicated. Now isn't the time to go into it.'

Fine. Two could play at that game, she thought, raising barriers of her own. Because she needed them. She hung up her apron and ran her palms over her dress, smoothing the rosebud-patterned cotton skirt. She adjusted the small red scarf around her neck and touched her hairband. Everything was in place, yet she felt ruffled. Irrational though it might be, seeing him made her feel vulnerable, as she had been when they were married, and scared that the pain of that dark time might return.

'Well, it sounds like it's time to have an honest conversation with your father,' she said briskly, then turned and lifted her jacket off the hook behind the door, hoping he'd take the hint and leave, vanish back out of her life as suddenly as he'd appeared.

'Natasha . . .' he said, but she walked past him, keys jangling in her hand, and held the door open for him.

She shook her head. 'No way. I'm not getting involved in this.'

Reluctantly, he moved past her and stopped in the street outside. With his skin the colour of caramel and his glossy dark hair, he was as conspicuous in the English country village as an exotic flower. 'I wouldn't ask you if I had any alternative.'

'I'm sure you wouldn't. There's a reason why we got divorced.' She locked the door.

'It's just two weeks.'

'No!' she said. Then, more calmly, 'I don't owe you anything, Luc.'

'I know you don't. That's why I'm asking – appealing to you.'

She could see the worry in his eyes, and guilt stabbed at her: he'd come here clearly counting on her help. Then her friend drove past them and waved. It was Suzie, on her way home from the village primary school. Seeing her was a reminder of all Natasha held dear. She'd built a life for herself here and she was happy. She thought of her shop and all the friends she'd made. She was part of this community now. She belonged. As she waved back, she contrasted that with the turmoil she'd lived through when she was married to Luc, and her instinct for self-preservation kicked in.

'No,' she said firmly, and began to walk quickly, taking a left off the high street – it would be quieter on the back roads. Suzie's eyes had widened with curiosity at the sight of Luc, and Natasha didn't want anyone else to see her with him. 'It would be a lie. I won't do it.'

'My father is seriously ill, and this is his wish – what am I supposed to tell him?'

'The truth?'

It wasn't far to her flat, just a couple of hundred yards, but today it seemed like miles. Her sandals tapped along the pavement, and it irritated her that he kept up effortlessly with his long strides.

'That our marriage lasted three months and we applied for a divorce as soon as was legally possible?' His tone was biting. Vicious. 'The truth would kill him. He's hanging on to life by a thread.'

She tried to ignore the guilt she knew he'd intended her to feel. 'Then stall. Play for time. Tell him . . . I'm travelling.'

'How do you think I've explained your absence until now?' He sighed and raked the hair back from his eyes. 'We don't know how long he has left. He wants to meet you.'

She stopped beside a red letterbox and planted her hands on her hips. 'Why?'

'He wants to know who I married. He wants to see for himself that I'm happy.'

She snorted. 'Well, that's asking the impossible! Even if I came with you to France, we couldn't pretend to be a happily married couple.'

'We could.' His tone was resolute.

And a shiver touched her spine. What Luc wanted, he always got. Like a bulldozer, once he was on course, he was difficult to block.

She set off again, her stomach churning. For heaven's

sake, shouldn't their divorce have made her immune to him?

He blew out a long breath. 'Listen, if there's something you want – anything – I'll pay for it. In return for your time.'

She flinched and glared at him. 'You always thought money motivated me, didn't you? Well, you were wrong, Luc. Then and now. I have everything I need.'

There was only one thing that might make things even more perfect, but she wasn't about to tell her ex what it was. It was nothing to do with him, her private dream. Her fingers automatically reached inside her pocket, checking for her phone as she thought of the call she was expecting.

'Then you're lucky,' he said.

They reached her flat and she stopped. 'Yes, I am. Or maybe I don't want much. Not the things money can buy, anyway.'

She marched up the steps to her door. She was settled now, but it hadn't always been like that. After their brief marriage, it had taken her months to get her life back on track. He had no right to come barging in, demanding favours of her. She owed him nothing. Nothing at all.

She opened the door and faced him one last time. 'I'm not doing it, Luc.'

'Natasha—'

She waved away his protest. 'I'm very sorry about your father, and for what you're going through right now, but I can't help you.'

She went in, tempted to say goodbye, then push the

door firmly shut on him and the tornado of emotions that was spinning through her – but he held the door open.

'Wait,' he said. 'Aren't you going to invite me in?'

She couldn't believe he'd even ask. And the thought of his tall figure filling her tiny flat, of being alone with him in such a private place, made her skin tingle. It went against the grain to be so rude, but to let him in would be too . . . intimate. 'No.'

'I've come all this way – and we haven't seen each other in a long time. Let me buy you dinner, at least.'

'So we can catch up?' she asked drily. 'Reminisce on old times?'

'So we can catch up, yes.'

She realised how bitter she'd sounded and regretted it. After all, she was over him, wasn't she? She looked at her watch. He *had* driven a long way to get there, and it would be rude to send him packing without so much as a cup of tea.

'We could go to the pub,' she said. 'The Dog and Partridge is just down the road. They do good food.' She'd hoped they wouldn't be seen, but perhaps being surrounded by other people would calm her nerves and the buzz she'd been feeling since he'd walked into the shop.

He nodded. 'Sounds good.'

'But don't think this is another chance to persuade me,' she warned, as they set off again. 'I won't change my mind.'

'I just want to eat and spend a little time with you,' he said quietly.

Thankfully, the Dog and Partridge was busy and she

was reassured to see friendly faces all around. Gary the landlord greeted her, and when he cast Luc a curious look, Natasha introduced him. 'This is Luc. He's . . .' she hesitated '. . . an old friend.'

'Friend?' Luc shot her a fierce look. 'We were married.'

Her cheeks burned as Gary, wide-eyed, turned to her and said, 'I didn't know you'd been married. You dark horse.'

'Well, we all make mistakes,' she said, darting Luc a sideways glance. But his expression remained grim. This wasn't the time to make jokes, not when he was clearly worried sick about his father.

They got their drinks and ordered food, and Luc produced his wallet. Natasha shook her head.

'I'm perfectly capable of buying my own drink.' She pulled out her purse. After their wedding, he'd said, *I suppose you'll want your own credit card now you're my wife.* From the moment they'd been married he'd behaved as if she were a parasite.

'No,' said Luc. 'I offered to buy you dinner.'

'Tell you what. We'll each buy our own.'

His nose wrinkled. 'And have to split the bill in half? I don't think so.'

Her chin went up. 'Then I'll leave now. I pay my own way, Luc. I don't want anything from you.'

His phone rang and he scrabbled to answer it. 'Excuse me,' he said, his accent suddenly pronounced. 'This might be important.'

He walked away, his phone to his ear, and Natasha handed a note to Gary, who was still a little wide-eyed from watching them. 'He really presses your buttons, doesn't he? I've never seen you like this before, Natasha.'

She knew Luc didn't bring out the best in her. But, then, how many ex-husbands did? 'He's only here because he wants my help,' she said. Then added, 'But he's not going to get it.'

She carried their drinks to a small table beside the window and sat down, then checked her phone. There were no missed calls, but she was still expecting one so she left it on the table. The pub was noisy and she couldn't be sure she'd hear it if it rang. A few moments later, Luc joined her.

'Everything all right?' she asked, taking a sip of her lemonade.

'That was my sister. She's at the hospital – there's been no change.'

He lifted the pint of beer to his lips and his throat worked as he swallowed. His eyes were clouded as he gazed out of the window, his mind evidently elsewhere.

Luc thought of his father as he'd last seen him that morning, lying in the hospital bed, pale and shrunken beneath the thin white sheet. The life had been sucked out of him, and it seemed as if only the tubes attached to his wrists were keeping him going. The doctors were worried. They'd done all they could. Now Luc could only hope that his father's fighting spirit would kick in. There was no sign of it yet.

Strange how things changed so quickly. He and his

father hadn't spoken properly in years – not counting their brief conversation last year, when Luc should have put him straight and told him about the divorce. Now the rift that had kept them apart seemed petty and trivial in comparison with his father's suffering. The threat of death had sharpened Luc's focus. Things that had seemed important in the past no longer were, and others had been magnified.

Especially his father's wish. Luc didn't understand why it was important to Jean-Pierre to see his three children all happily married, but he was prepared to go to any lengths to give the old man something to live for. It was the only thing left that he could do, now that he'd made sure his father was receiving the best care and the most advanced treatment. Of course, he wasn't happy at having to ask his ex-wife for help but Jean-Pierre had been blunt: 'I want her here, at my bedside. And you're going to arrange it.'

He couldn't go home without her. The fear of doing so, of disappointing his father – losing him – brought a film of sweat to his brow. He pressed a finger to the bridge of his nose.

If he didn't return with Natasha, how would it look to his family? As if he hadn't tried. As if Natasha was heartless.

As if she didn't exist.

He'd never felt the need to conceal the truth in any other area of his life, but with his father . . .

Regret and shame tightened his chest. He knew he'd made mistakes and now he was trapped in this knot of misunderstanding and distorted truth. But there wasn't time to dwell on how it had come to this. The urgency of the situation meant he had to stay focused on the immediate problem.

Luc took another sip of beer, and eyed Natasha warily, his eyes drawn to her curves, her small waist, in a way that discomfited him. Her white-blonde head was dipped and her slim shoulders bent as she checked her phone yet again. Ever since they'd sat down, she'd seemed distracted. He needed her cooperation, but she was completely disinterested. He'd hoped she would listen, that she'd appreciate the gravity of the situation, have some compassion. But her hostility shouldn't have come as a surprise. Memories fired at him, ugly and bitter, of when she'd left him. Simply packed her case and gone, then refused to answer his calls or messages.

She was the only person who could help right now, but her mind was clearly on something else.

Something or someone?

'Is there someone else in your life, Natasha?' he asked brusquely. He'd known this was a risk. His hand pressed hard against his glass. 'A boyfriend? Partner?'

Her blue eyes flashed, as if he'd crossed a barrier he'd had no right to penetrate. He stilled, waiting for her answer. Acutely aware of her. She was so familiar that the last three years might never have happened. Yet so much about her had changed. Her hair, which had been long, was now cut in a neat bob. Her pale skin glowed brighter against the vivid red and green of her fitted dress. But the most marked difference was in her air of confidence.

She was bright, she was attractive. The chances of her being single were slim.

Very slim.

Then she lifted her chin. 'No,' she said, meeting his gaze squarely. 'Not at the moment.'

He almost smiled. With relief? If she was single, that was one less obstacle to surmount in persuading her to come with him to France. Yet relief didn't explain the soaring sensation in his chest.

He brushed aside the thought as inconsequential. All that mattered now was his father's health, and getting Natasha to return with him to France. He gazed out of the window at the picturesque village, with its tidy streets and friendly faces.

Persuasion was getting him nowhere. He'd try a different tactic. He thought of his business: in the construction industry he frequently encountered problems. People were reluctant to sell their patch of land, or there were environmental constraints. He was well used to working round hurdles and getting results. He just needed to lay aside thoughts of his family and approach this with a clear head.

There were two ways he could play it – appeal to her sense of compassion, which hadn't worked or buy her. Offer her compensation that would make it worth her while. She'd said she didn't want for anything, but there must be something.

There was always something.

Natasha took advantage of the lull to sneak a closer look at her ex, drinking in his familiar features. Those long lashes, the strong line of his jaw. She wondered if he was in a relationship, but she was certain she knew the answer: undoubtedly there would have been dozens of women since her. He had been trapped into marriage, as he would have seen it, which would have made him revert to type. She could easily imagine he'd celebrated his freedom by enjoying a stream of short-lived, mindless affairs, which she didn't want to hear about. She didn't care what he did now. After this meal he would walk back out of her life.

Yet, try as she might to keep her distance, the shadows beneath his eyes were getting under her skin.

'How long has your father been ill?' she asked gently.

He turned to her. 'Not long. It came completely out of the blue. One minute he was fit and strong, the next in hospital fighting for his life.'

His voice was thin with pain.

'That must have been a shock.'

'It was. These things make you rethink everything. What's important, what isn't . . .'

'They do,' she agreed, and glanced at her phone, remembering the call she was expecting. She hoped it would be good news. The estate agent had assured her everything was hopeful.

'Your company was everything to you,' she said bitterly. 'Is it still?' He'd made it clear when they'd begun dating that his work came first: it took him all over the world, and he wasn't looking for a serious relationship to tether him.

That was why her accidental pregnancy hadn't gone down well.

He straightened in his seat. 'Right now, helping my father is my priority. Nothing else matters.'

She raised a brow, intrigued and, though she didn't want to be, impressed by his new attitude. Hearing him say that, she could relate to him more. Families, relationships – they were important. If he'd been able to see that before, maybe their marriage would have had a chance . . .

The waitress brought their food, traditional steak pies and vegetables, and she noticed that Luc, who had always had a good appetite, picked at his. Natasha tucked into her own; she'd had such a busy day and hadn't had time to stop for lunch.

Just then her phone lit up and began to ring, the estate agent's number flashing.

'Excuse me,' she said to Luc, and snatched it up.

'Bad news, I'm afraid,' the estate agent told her. 'The owners have rejected your offer. Another interested buyer's put in a higher bid.'

Her heart sank, and she pressed the phone tighter to her ear. 'A higher bid? I thought there'd been hardly any interest.'

'A local builder viewed the property yesterday. It was always a risk with a piece of land like that. It's a good size and in a fantastic location. They could easily fit two, even three new houses on the plot and, with it being by the road, access wouldn't be a problem.'

She sucked in air. 'You mean they'll knock down the cottage?'

Across the table, Luc glanced at her. She ignored him. This was too important for anything else to distract her.

'Er – yes. That's likely.'

Something curled up inside her. As if the estate agent was trampling on her childhood memories, on her mother's dearest wishes. 'They can't do that,' she said, knowing that of course they could. 'That cottage is old – and it's beautiful.'

Her words were met with silence. And, of course, the cottage wasn't beautiful. But it had been once.

Then the agent asked, in her sing-song voice, 'So would you like to raise your offer?'

'I can't,' she confessed. Her throat felt raw. 'That was the maximum I could afford.'

'I see. Well, if anything changes, we'll let you know,' the estate agent said, but it was clear from her tone that that was unlikely to happen.

Natasha put away her phone and tried hard to swallow her disappointment, to keep her composure in front of Luc.

'Something wrong?' he asked.

'Nothing,' she said, and looked at her half-eaten food. Her appetite had vanished, along with the dream she'd been nurturing. She'd stupidly – naively – thought she had it in the bag, that all her years of working and saving hard had paid off and that the cottage would be her reward, that she would finally be able to make good her promise. To lose it all now to someone with no personal interest in the place, who regarded it merely as a patch of soil on which to build . . .

She pictured the slate roof, the clotted-cream walls smashed to the ground, and felt a squeeze of pain coupled with guilt. She'd promised her mother . . .

'It doesn't seem like nothing. You're upset, Natasha.'

When she'd first met Luc she'd loved the way he said her name with all the French stresses and pronunciation. But then she'd become pregnant. After that he hadn't spoken her name in the same way. He'd barely spoken to her at all. She certainly wasn't about to confide in him now.

'I just got some bad news, that's all,' she said briskly, and nodded at his untouched food. 'Have you finished? Only I think we've both got other things on our minds. Perhaps we could catch up another time. What do you think?'

It was pointless sitting here with her ex-husband. They didn't really have anything to talk about, and her mood had nose-dived.

He gave a tight nod. 'OK.'

They turned left out of the pub and walked back past the old stone church and along the only main road in and out of the village. There was no way of avoiding the house and, as they walked past it, Natasha couldn't help looking at the 'For Sale' sign she supposed would soon read 'Sold'. A knot formed in her chest and she blinked back tears. She was silly, getting all sentimental about it. It was just a cottage, after all, and she'd still have her memories. But she'd come so close to making it hers that losing it now was painful. It had been her home. She could hear her mother as she'd pleaded with Aunt Thelma: *Keep the cottage. Don't tear Natasha away from her home. Her father worked so hard on that place. He rebuilt the house and planted those trees. It meant so much to him – to us. His ashes are scattered there – he's part of the place.*

Aunt Thelma had been tight-lipped. *We'll see*, she'd said. And Natasha had naively taken that to mean yes.

Then Natasha's mother had turned to her: *I love you so much. And your father did, too.* She was seven, old enough to remember having lost her father and to know she was about to feel the bite of grief all over again.

She hadn't been old enough, though, to grasp that adults didn't always live up to expectations. *I know, Mum. I'll look after Poppy Cottage.*

'Is this the place you were hoping to buy?' Luc asked, and stopped outside it.

She spun round to him. 'How did you know?'

'I learned enough from your side of the conversation to understand you'd had your offer refused on a house, and it's a small village, there aren't many places for sale.' The corner of his mouth lifted. 'And the way you're glaring at it, with smoke coming out of your ears, is a bit of a giveaway.'

'Yes,' she said quietly. 'This is it.'

'Is it empty?' he asked, his hand on the gate.

'Yes, but . . .'

He'd already disappeared round the side of the cottage.

What was he playing at? Natasha sighed. She thought about following him, but what was the point when she couldn't afford it? Instead, she folded her arms and waited for him to return.

When he did, she asked him impatiently, 'What are you doing?'

'Just looking.'

'Why?' she said tersely. Quite frankly, she'd had enough. It had been a long day.

'Construction is my field. I'm interested.' He stepped back and squinted up at the roof. The tiles were mostly twisted and loose, and the chimney was smothered in ivy. 'It's very run-down,' he said, grimacing.

'It's a complete wreck.' The place had stood empty for years before the owners had finally put it on the market.

He came back towards her, his gaze still on the house. 'Why would you want to buy a place like that?' he asked, clearly unimpressed.

What was the point in trying to explain it to him? A man who had a family but never saw them, hadn't even told them about his divorce. He'd never understand.

'I thought it had potential,' she said, running her gaze over the grubby walls, the rotten window-frames. Remembering. 'With some work it could be . . . special.'

But Fate had decided it wasn't to be. She had to accept that, even if it was hard to swallow.

'Poppy Cottage,' he said, reading the sign beside the door. Then he turned and watched her closely. 'Is it true that you can't afford to make a higher offer or were you just saying that?'

'It's true.' Had her offer been accepted, she would have had no money left to make the necessary repairs. She would have had to do her best to improve the house herself, and save up for the structural work. She pushed her hands into her pockets and walked away. When she realised Luc wasn't with her, she turned and looked back: he was still standing outside the cottage, talking into his phone. Presuming it was his family again, she carried on. A few minutes later he caught up with her. They walked back to her home in silence, brooding.

When they arrived, she said wearily, 'I'm not going to invite you in, Luc. We've said all there is to say.'

His jaw looked as solid as wood. 'I'm disappointed. I thought you would at least consider my request. As I said, I'll make it worth your while.'

'I don't want to get involved in a lie.' She took a deep breath, then decided to be brave and tell him honestly. 'And I don't want to get involved with you again, Luc. It was too painful last time.'

Somewhere in the distance a blackbird called, its song high-pitched and disconcertingly cheerful.

'It was.'

She blinked, surprised by his quiet admission. He'd found it painful too? He'd been so hard-nosed about – about everything that it came as a shock to hear him say that. Yet the look in his eyes suggested he was sincere.

'I lost a baby, too,' he said quietly.

She couldn't hold off the invasive memories of the hospital's white walls and bright lights. Her throat constricted. There had been bandages and padding, but nothing had lessened the pain. 'Yes, well – I don't want to go there again . . .'

His phone rang, and he lifted it to his ear immediately. After a few moments, he smiled. 'Great news. I'll get the paperwork sent through urgently and I expect to have the keys as soon as it's finalised. Tell me the address again.'

Natasha watched, vaguely irritated by the interruption, as he pulled out a notebook and jotted a few words.

But as she saw what he was writing, understanding dawned and a chill crept over her.

The call ended and he snapped his phone shut. She could tell from the look in his eyes that she wasn't going to like what he said before he'd even uttered a word.

This was the Luc she had known before. All hint of emotion was gone and his features were as hard as bronze. Instinctively, she took half a step back.

'I've just bought your cottage,' he said coolly.

'Bought it? What do you mean?'

'I made an offer. A very high offer that the other guy can't match. They accepted it.'

'No . . .' she began. 'How—'

'Come with me to France,' he cut in. 'And it's yours.'

Her throat closed. He'd deliberately bought the cottage so he could hold her to ransom with it.

Why had she agreed to go for a drink with him? She should have shut her front door in his face instead of being civil to him. *He* hadn't behaved in a civil way. In less than two hours he'd managed to pinpoint the one thing that mattered most to her, then use the knowledge to his advantage. She should have seen it coming: there was a reason why he was such a successful businessman.

'You can't do that.'

'I just did.'

He held her gaze, but she couldn't tell if he was ashamed of what he'd done or triumphant. He should be ashamed. It was plain wrong.

Her nails were digging into her palms. 'How could you, Luc?' This was so typical: he wanted something, he got it.

'How could I not? You couldn't afford the place yourself. Now you can own it.'

Because he'd snapped his fingers and bought it. It was a reminder that he was wealthy and she was just an ordinary girl. Their backgrounds were so different, they might as well have been raised on different planets.

'You make it sound like you've done me a favour!'

'I have. Without me you were out of the picture. A higher offer, remember? The house was going to be demolished.'

The fact that he was right made her even angrier.

'How much did you pay?' Part of her didn't want to hear the answer. It must have been a huge amount to have eliminated the other bidder.

'Irrelevant,' Luc said, in that cutting, ultra-decisive manner of his. It made her bristle. 'All that matters is that the cottage will be yours if you agree to come with me.'

Chapter Two

'I can't believe you've done this to me.' Natasha bit the words out.

Luc saw the fire sparking from her eyes and felt a ripple of satisfaction that he'd finally got her attention. His pulse upped its pace. But fury wasn't what he'd expected from her, and an unsettling sense of misgiving stole through him. Had he misjudged this?

She'd looked so upset when she'd taken that call. Distraught, even. Then they'd walked past the cottage and he'd simply seized the opportunity to jump in and help.

And, yes, he expected her to help him in return.

His teeth clenched. That was why he was here. He'd done what he had to do – the only thing left within his power – for his father. He'd paid a ridiculously high sum for the cottage, but he would have paid a lot more to keep his father alive. He'd failed so spectacularly as a son, he couldn't fail him again in this one simple request to bring Natasha home.

'Your family has never even met me,' she said. 'You could take anyone home – anyone! If you're so desperate to buy someone's cooperation, then why not pick a girl who's willing? It doesn't have to be me.'

'It does.'

'Why?'

His gaze flickered away. She was right. He could have approached – or employed – any woman to play the part. An actress he knew would have relished the role.

But that idea was unthinkable. It had to be Natasha.

Why? The thought circled in his mind.

Because there had already been too many lies. Because to bring someone else would be a deception too far and he couldn't do that to his family.

Because Natasha was the woman he'd married. Only she could do this.

'It just does,' he said finally. He pushed out of his mind all the times in the last three years when he'd glimpsed a head of blonde hair in the street and his breath had caught.

'No,' she said, through gritted teeth.

The quiet country air vibrated with tension as their eyes met, and his muscles tightened, memories stirring of when passion had overwhelmed them and she'd spoken his name as if he was everything to her.

'Here's my number,' he said, dropping a black business card into her hand. She looked at the red logo of Solo Construction Ltd. 'I'm going to find a place to stay for the night and I'll be back to see you in the morning, first thing. Think about it, and if you want to do it, call me – any time. It doesn't matter how late.'

She glared at him. 'Do you really think you can force me like this – that I'll just roll over and accept it?'

'I think we can help each other.'

She lifted her chin and looked straight into his eyes. 'Don't wait up, because I won't be calling you, Luc.'

'Think about it,' he repeated, and left.

Natasha punched the numbers into her calculator and sighed with exasperation as, yet again, the figures didn't tally with the printout in front of her. Starting again, she tried to concentrate on the shop's accounts, but she knew she was making mistakes because she was thinking of Luc and his offer.

She wasn't going to do it. She wasn't even going to think about it. He'd crashed back into her life like a demolition ball and had manipulated her into complying with his demands or losing the thing that meant so much to her. Well, she wouldn't give him the satisfaction.

Sighing, she gave up on the accounts. She gathered together the papers, slotted them back into their file and looked at her watch. Still early. She could ring a friend and meet at the pub for a drink, but after her earlier visit, Gary the landlord would have questions, and she couldn't face them right now. She needed to work off her anger. Spotting her trainers by the door, she decided to go for a run.

Poppy Cottage wasn't the only thing that meant a lot to her, she reassured herself, as she set off at a fast jog on the country lane heading out of the village: she still had her shop, the business she'd worked so hard to establish in just three years. That wasn't much consolation, though, because she'd done it all with one goal in mind: buying the cottage. Today she'd lost it a second time. Luc was offering her another chance to own it, she conceded, but he was also using it to twist her arm. Now he owned Poppy Cottage he was in a position of power over her, which made her all the more determined to refuse his demands. He needed to be taught that some people could not be bought or bullied, and what better way to do that than to turn him down? Tell him he could keep the bloody cottage. Her feet pounded the tarmac, and her muscles pumped with energy and adrenalin.

But if she did that, she would lose out. She'd lose her only link to her parents. She dropped her speed a little and settled into a comfortable rhythm.

Perhaps she should consider Luc's proposal. If he could be so ruthless, why not be mercenary herself and accept? She took a left turn. A rabbit darted across the road and disappeared into the hedgerow with an urgent rustle. If she did, it would confirm to Luc that she could be bought, that material possessions meant more to her than her principles and pride.

But that house was her only link with the past, with the two people who had loved her. And with her future, too. Although she hadn't met the right man yet, she'd always hoped that one day she would raise her own family there. If she didn't do as Luc asked, if she let him leave tomorrow, would she spend the rest of her life regretting it?

She slowed again as another left turn brought her onto the road heading back towards the village.

She was torn: if she accepted his offer, she'd be sucked back into his life and let herself in for two weeks of hell. If she refused, she'd be letting down her parents. What was more important: her pride, or the promise she'd made to her mum?

Natasha arrived back at home, stretched her muscles, then climbed the concrete steps to her flat. Once inside, she kicked off her shoes and switched on the shower. She was going round in circles, thinking about Luc. She needed to get an early night. Hopefully everything would be clearer in the morning.

In her dream the banging was the clatter of the Dutch delivery van reversing into her shop. She wanted to cry out as it smashed through the door, bricks tumbling, glass splintering, but no sound came from her mouth and it kept on moving, the enormous trailer looming over her as she raised her arms to protect herself—

Waking up, she realised the noise was coming from her door. Someone was thumping on it. As she jumped out of bed and ran to answer it, the possibilities ran through her head: was it her neighbour in the flat next door? Or Debbie? She heard her name being called and flung the door open.

'Luc! What are you doing here?'

In the dim yellow light that hung above her, he looked even more stressed than when she'd seen him earlier. There were shadows under his eyes, and his hair was ruffled, as if he'd jumped out of bed and pulled on the nearest pair of jeans and a T-shirt. She glanced down at her pyjamas, suddenly feeling exposed, and wished she'd had time to grab her dressing-gown. But he wasn't looking at what she was wearing; he was obviously beside himself with worry.

'It's my father,' he said hoarsely. 'He's worse. The hospital, they told me to get back there straight away. *Sans délai*,' he said, apparently unaware that he'd slipped into French.

She swallowed and tucked her hair behind one ear. Her brain was still foggy with sleep, but her skin prickled as she anticipated what was coming next. She stepped back, but that was a mistake because it allowed him to come into her apartment. He filled the tiny hall.

'Natasha,' he said. 'Please come with me to France.'

Mutely, she shook her head, feeling cruel but telling herself she had to harden her heart to protect it. She had to say no, stick to her guns, and tell him what she'd said all along: that she wanted nothing to do with him and he should leave now.

'I gave my word I would bring you back with me – I can't disappoint him!'

'Keep your voice down!' she said, and closed the door. 'You'll wake the whole village. It's four o'clock in the morning.'

'Sorry,' he said, and rubbed a hand across his stubble-dark jaw. 'Can't you see how important it is – to have made a promise to someone?'

Memories of their wedding vows, so quickly forgotten, sprang to mind and she wanted to laugh at the irony of his question. But she'd made a promise to her mother. And Natasha was the only one left to preserve Poppy Cottage, her father's resting place, and prevent it being bulldozed.

'*You* made a promise – not me,' she said, though even

she could see the holes in that argument. His father was desperately ill – what else was he to have done?

Absently she noted that he was wearing shoes but no socks. She didn't know where he was staying and didn't want to. She'd done everything she could to distance herself from Luc, and now he was in her flat in the middle of the night, with a life-and-death situation he expected her to resolve.

'Please, Natasha – don't let me down.'

His ragged words made her insides twist. She didn't like to turn her back on someone in need, no matter what had happened in the past. When he'd first walked into her shop, she'd wanted him to walk straight back out, but now she realised he wasn't going to do that. His father was too sick. Too much was at stake for him.

'You thought you could bribe me, blackmail me, by buying the cottage.' She hugged herself, not liking how prickly and hot she was feeling.

'I only bought it because you refused to help. You left me no option. You could have considered it, at least. And knowing you're the only person in a position to help . . .' His lips clamped shut. Then he said, 'If you turn your back on this, he could give up.'

Guilt surfaced again, only this time it was stronger. She was aware that her defences were weakening, like the stem of a wilting gerbera. 'If all else fails, send me on a guilt trip, why don't you?' He frowned and, though his English was good, she wasn't sure he'd understood. 'You make it sound like your father's life is at my feet.'

'It *is*!' he cried. He closed his eyes briefly and shook his head. 'I wish it wasn't, but it is. If he doesn't come through this, my mother will be – will be broken. My sisters too. My nephews and nieces will grow up not knowing their grandfather.'

'All because of me? That's not fair, Luc. Even if I agreed to come with you, it doesn't mean he would recover. You must see that.'

She was trying to harden her heart, to will him out of her life, but his words had snared her – because she knew about death. The thought of children losing a loved one was too close to home, and she couldn't shut it out of her mind.

Children shouldn't have to know grief or loss. They should be protected from it. She couldn't live with herself knowing she might have helped another family avoid the pain she had known as a little girl.

'You're right.' Luc ran his fingers through his hair and turned as if to pace, but found himself face to face with a coat rack and no space to move. He spun back to her. 'But I have to do everything I can for him. This isn't about you and me, Natasha. What happened between us – you have to put it out of your mind.'

'I don't think you'd be saying that if I needed your help.'

'You're wrong.' Their eyes locked.

'Really? The man who doesn't commit to anyone but himself would have helped his ex-wife? Yeah, right.'

'I would,' he ground out, and she could see his frustration. 'Why won't you do this?' His brow creased and he studied her, perplexed. 'You're angry with me.'

'Too right I'm angry.' She pushed away the memories

from when they'd been married – the hurtful things he'd said, the way he'd made her feel so small, so unwelcome – and forced herself to focus on the here and now. 'You bought my cottage. That was – it was underhand.'

'But there's something else, too,' he said, studying her. She blinked. What did he mean? She looked away, shuffled her feet, uncomfortable with such close scrutiny. 'What are you scared of, Natasha?'

Her head flew up. 'I'm not scared. Why would I be?'

But as she spoke, she answered her own question: she was scared of the person she might become around him. Attracted to him. Vulnerable to him. Not in control. Just as she had been three years ago.

'I'm uncomfortable with the idea of deceiving someone,' she said quickly. 'Especially a man in poor health who – who's so fragile.'

Better to throw this back at him than to admit she was afraid of being hurt again. Her shoulders straightened. Besides, that was irrational: she didn't love him any more, so how could he hurt her? She wouldn't allow herself to be afraid of her ex-husband.

So, if she wasn't afraid, what was stopping her?

'But can't you see?' His voice was raw. 'It's the only thing that might help him. It's what matters most to him. If I can do this one thing for him, satisfy his desire to meet my wife . . .'

There was so much pain in his voice. She felt as if she was clinging to a cliff-edge, her grip loosening, strength draining. Deceiving Luc's family would be wrong, but that was his concern, not hers. Even if they found out, she would simply return home and get back to her own life. As he'd said, if she agreed to this, she would be helping his father, and Luc seemed to believe it was the only hope left. Plus, she might not be needed for more than a few days: if the hospital had rung and told him to get there quickly, his father might not live much longer, but she didn't want to add to his trauma by pointing it out.

'Think of it as a business arrangement, Natasha. You do this for me, you get the cottage in return.'

A business arrangement sounded so simple. No emotion involved – except, of course, the feelings she attached to Poppy Cottage.

So, why not? She took a deep breath. Detach yourself. Think of Mum and Dad. Think of the promise you made, of what the place could be in the future. She closed her eyes and thoughts swam around her head: *This isn't about you and me . . . I'll look after Poppy Cottage . . .*

She knew she was mad to do this, but she clung to the thought that she'd made a promise to her mother. 'OK,' she said softly.

Luc opened his mouth to carry on, then belatedly registered her answer and blinked. He looked too stunned to speak. Exhaustion was catching up with him, slowing his reaction time, she realised, with a tug of sympathy she most definitely didn't want to feel.

'I'll do it. I'll come with you.'

A look of relief flashed across his face, he smiled and threw his arms around her. It was so unexpected, so fierce with emotion that she momentarily froze. Her face pressed against the soft cotton of his T-shirt and she could feel his heat, his heartbeat. Her own pulse thumped. Then he seemed to remember who she was and pulled back. Cleared his throat.

Breathing fast, she told herself it was the night air that was making her feel quivery, nothing more.

'In return for the cottage,' she said, as if to reassure herself. 'That's the only reason I'm doing this.'

His expression darkened and his lips thinned. 'Of course,' he said. 'We'll have to leave as soon as possible. How long do you need to pack, to make arrangements for your shop?'

'Give me a couple of hours. Debbie – she works for me – will be getting up at six to receive a delivery.' He nodded. 'She'll take care of the shop for a couple of days until I get back.'

The steely look in his eyes was unnervingly familiar. It plunged her back in time to the moment she'd told him she was pregnant. He'd transformed from lover to hostile enemy.

'No,' he said. 'Two weeks, like we agreed. Two weeks and the cottage is yours in return.'

'Why two weeks? Surely a few days will be enough to set your father's mind at rest.' It was a time of crisis for Luc's family, of private pain. They wouldn't want her hanging around.

'Don't try to negotiate it down. My offer is very generous.'

'I'm not negotiating. I'm asking you a question. Why drag this out longer than necessary?'

'Two weeks is nothing.'

He might believe that, but for her, two weeks in his company would feel like a year.

Chapter Three

Luc arrived twenty minutes earlier than they'd agreed, but she brushed off his offer to help her pack. 'I'm ready to go.'

He bent to pick up her case and she locked her flat, then followed him out to the street where a rental car was parked. As he lifted her case into the boot she noticed there were still shadows beneath his eyes and he'd cut himself shaving. She felt a twist of compassion and reached to remove the piece of blood-stained tissue – then thought better of it and pointed instead. 'You've left a piece of tissue there,' she said.

His hand flew to his face and he smiled ruefully. 'My mind was elsewhere.'

Yes, she could imagine. Receiving a call from the hospital at four o'clock in the morning telling you to get back to your sick father wouldn't do much for anyone's nerves. She thought of when her mother had died. If she could wish for one thing – anything – she would ask for more time with her.

'Have you heard any more from the hospital?'

'I rang them. He's still in intensive care.'

In other words, he was still alive.

They got into the car. Luc drove a little too fast for

her, but she didn't say anything. The roads were empty, and it was obvious he just wanted to get to the hospital as soon as possible. She could understand that. It was the rest – like why his father thought they were still married – that baffled her.

'Did you manage to make arrangements for your shop?' he asked, as they joined the motorway.

She nodded. 'Debbie's going to ask Shauna to come and help. She's our Saturday girl and she'll cover for Debbie when she goes on maternity leave later this year. The experience will be useful for her – if she can do it.'

'And if she can't?'

'Then Debbie will manage. We sometimes have to if one of us is sick, but it's less than ideal. Debbie's five months pregnant, and summer is a busy time of year for us – we're inundated with weddings and christenings.'

'I appreciate you doing this.' He sounded like he meant it.

She nodded, terrified at what she'd committed herself to. She wanted to be angry with him for pressuring her to do it, but that wouldn't be fair – he was thinking only of his father, she could see that now. Anyway, she'd made her decision, and now she was committed to it, however much she was dreading the next fourteen days.

At the airport they slipped past all the queues and went directly to his private jet, which was ready with a full complement of staff waiting to usher them in. She'd never travelled like that before, although once upon a time they had planned a trip away . . . Then she'd become pregnant and he'd never mentioned it again.

Once they were settled in their seats, a steward brought coffee, then laid a tray of bread and French pastries on the table between them. Natasha accepted the coffee gratefully and hoped the caffeine would do its work. She'd never felt a greater need to be alert.

'So, come on, then,' she said, once she and Luc were alone again. 'What's my brief?'

He looked at her, one brow arched. 'It's very straightforward – just pretend we're happily married.'

The plane climbed up through dense white cloud, emerging into bright sunshine that bounced off the metal coffee pot and flooded the cabin with daffodil-yellow light.

'As simple as that?' She'd expected pages of instructions. He was a man in control at the best of times, but surely he wanted to get this right.

Shrugging, he took a croissant, broke off a piece, and spread butter over it. 'As simple as that.'

'Do they speak English? Because I don't remember much French from school.'

He considered this. 'They all speak English. Enough to have a conversation, anyway.' He gave a dry laugh. 'My sisters watched a lot of American television growing up, and my father had lessons so he could communicate with his customers. He loves showing off how well he speaks English. So, you don't need to worry about that.'

She believed him. If Luc's proficiency in English was anything to go by, they were probably all fluent. 'Won't they think it's strange that I'm married to you but haven't picked up any French at all?'

'You're worrying too much. They won't be testing you. Though they'll probably want to get to know you.'

'How did you explain my absence in the past? What did you say about me?'

He put the piece of croissant into his mouth but, like yesterday in the pub, he seemed to be forcing himself to eat. The navy T-shirt he was wearing hugged his broad chest, but now he'd shaved she could see he'd lost some weight, in his face, his neck. And she didn't like the rush of concern that provoked in her. She took another sip of her coffee and wrapped both hands around the cup to warm her fingers. There was an uncomfortable chill in the air and she wished she'd worn a warmer outfit, rather than the green and yellow sundress and light cardigan chosen in readiness for the South of France.

'I didn't have to explain your absence – until now I hadn't been home since we got married.'

'Not at all?'

He shook his head. She knew his relationship with his family wasn't close: when they'd first met it had been clear he wasn't in touch with them much, but when she'd asked him about it he'd been reluctant to discuss it, touchy and tight-lipped. And because she hadn't known him long and didn't want to rock the boat, she hadn't pressed him. She'd been so timid then, so afraid to stand up to him. With hindsight, she should have asked more questions. It had worried her at the time but, looking back, it should have raised a red flag. It had been a blatant clue that he was selfish and didn't value relationships. Even blood ties.

'You have a family but you don't see them?' Although

she couldn't be too critical: blood relations didn't always live up to the romantic notion of being loving and supportive, she thought, reminded of Aunt Thelma.

'I see them occasionally.'

'When was the last time you saw them before your father became ill?'

'There was a christening in Paris last year for my niece, Élodie.'

'And you didn't mention the divorce then?'

He barely looked at her before answering. 'I flew in and out between meetings. There wasn't time to talk properly.'

'That's it? In the three years since we got married you've seen them once?'

'Sometimes I meet my sisters – but we're all busy. You know how it is.'

Natasha didn't know because she had no siblings of her own, and if she had, she couldn't imagine going months or years without seeing them and shrugging it off so casually.

The coffee tasted bitter and she reached for the bread and jam, needing something sweet. There must have been a terrible rift for him to be so distant from his family. Perhaps they were difficult to get on with, she thought, picturing a bunch of haughty French aristocrats – the Addams family, but without the comedy.

Whatever the cause of their disagreement, things were bound to be strained between them and Luc after he'd been away so long. And she was going to enter into all of this. What was she letting herself in for?

Mind you, he didn't seem worried, and that shouldn't

come as a surprise to her: he'd always been emotionally cool. When she'd become pregnant and they'd got married he'd been positively Arctic with her. He was always happiest working, giving his all to his business.

And yet he seemed cut up about his dad.

She wondered how his family had felt to hear from a stranger that he'd got married. Were they hurt or had they met the news with indifference? After she'd left home at sixteen, she hadn't kept in touch with Thelma, and she was certain her great-aunt would have shown no reaction if she'd heard that Natasha had got married. Even now that indifference still had the power to wound her.

'I need to know the background to all this, Luc. Why have you had so little contact with them?'

His features sharpened in a way she recognised. It told her clearly this wasn't a subject he liked to discuss. But, unlike three years ago, she wasn't easily deterred.

'Did you argue?' she persisted.

A muscle flickered in his jaw. 'Yes.'

She took a bite of bread and jam, and waited for him to go on.

His eyes narrowed, became shards of dark metal glinting in the sunlight. 'With my father.'

'When?'

'I was twenty-four.' He made a mental calculation. 'About eight years ago.'

'That long?' She tried to hide her surprise. 'What did you argue about?'

'It doesn't matter now. *C'est fini*,' he said, and his hand sliced through the air in a dismissive gesture.

He flipped open his iPad and began scrolling through email messages.

'So, because you had a row with your father, you cut all contact with your entire family?'

He tipped his head to one side, not disagreeing with her but not forthcoming either. A flush of irritation touched the back of her neck. She wasn't prying or being nosy: she needed to know the background to the situation she was about to get involved in.

'Luc, talk to me. You're expecting me to pretend we've been married for the last three years. There are things I need to understand if we're to be plausible.'

His eyes barely moved from his iPad. 'You know enough.'

'What if your mother or sisters ask me questions?'

'They won't. They're too busy thinking about my father.'

'But if they do?'

'I don't want to discuss this, OK? If they ask you anything, you just tell them you don't know because I don't like to talk about it.' He pulled out his phone and punched in a number.

She stared because she hadn't known that mobile phones could work in a plane – but, then, she'd never been in a private jet before – and because she couldn't believe his nerve. Her fists balled.

'You're not making this easy for me. If I screw up, it's your fault!'

When he didn't want to talk about something it was like a metal shutter had come down. She could see how three years ago she'd found it intimidating, but she wasn't in love with him now. And she was older, wiser.

'It's better for you not to get embroiled in my life,' he said.

He'd put his phone on speakerphone and the sound of it making a call filled the cabin. A clear signal that for him this conversation was over, but she refused to be dismissed so easily.

'I'm already embroiled in it,' she said, over the ringtone. 'By coming here, I'm in the thick of it.' Her voice was rough with anger.

God, this was going to be impossible. Two weeks with her ex-husband, posing as his happily married wife. She'd have to keep all this blood-boiling irritation hidden. She'd have to smile and pretend she was in love with him. She wasn't sure her acting skills were up to that.

'You sound as if you want an apology from me, but you won't get it. If I'd had any other option, if there'd been any way of avoiding this situation, I promise you I would have chosen the alternative. I didn't want to do this any more than you.'

'Well, thanks.' It was confirmation that he didn't want her with him. She didn't know why this hurt but it did. 'It sounds to me like you and your family should have worked on your relationship a long time ago. If you had, then you wouldn't be in this ridiculous position where he thinks you're still married!'

'Don't judge me, Natasha,' he said quietly. 'You know nothing about my family.'

The phone was answered with a woman's cheerful greeting, and Luc turned away to focus on his conversation.

Natasha glared at him. Maybe he was right. She knew

47

nothing about his family – but she knew that relationships were of little value to him except for short-term gratification. Growing his business and making money were his priorities. The perfect example being how he was now fully engaged in a discussion about planning permission, having refused to prepare her for what was to come.

Luc waited for his colleague to find the information he needed, glad of the chance to escape Natasha's questioning. There wasn't time in a one-hour flight to fill her in on the background: he wouldn't know where to start. There had been friction between him and his father from as far back as he could remember. He wasn't proud of his failed personal relationships – with his family, with Natasha. In every other area of his life he was successful: work and business relationships he had no issues with. Present him with a financial meltdown or a PR crisis and he was able to think calmly and take control: others described him as a born leader. But he and his father had always had a turbulent relationship. He didn't want to talk about their blazing rows, the clashes, the rift. Truth be told, he was ashamed.

Eight years ago, he'd stormed out of his family home so angry, so convinced he was right and his father was wrong. Black and white. Now he saw things differently, and not just because his father was sick. With time, perhaps also with age, his perspective had shifted, and a couple of years ago he'd begun to make tentative steps towards reconciliation. Which was why, at Élodie's christening, he and his father had spoken for the first time in years. Luc had been aware of his mother watching them, her eyes shimmering with happy tears.

But it had been difficult. Strained. Pride had got in the way for both men. And although he'd thought about it many times afterwards, Luc had put off repairing their relationship.

He'd never imagined that time would suddenly run out.

Now he just hoped they'd have the chance to put things right. He'd asked his mother to tell Jean-Pierre that he was on his way and Natasha was with him. Hopefully, his father would cling on until they arrived and Luc had fulfilled his wish. It was a fragile hope, but he clung to it.

He finished the call and put his phone down. Natasha sat straight-backed, glaring at him. She wore a pretty knee-length dress and a sunny yellow cardigan that lit up her blonde hair, but her expression was thunderous, her bare legs tightly crossed.

He wasn't enjoying this any more than she was. But needs must. He was doing the best he could in the worst of circumstances.

'Do they think we still live together in London?' she asked, stubbornly refusing to let the subject drop. 'Will I have to lie about that too?'

'They know we're based in two different places.' He felt a little calmer after speaking to his colleague. His business kept him grounded, reminding him of his strengths, his successes. 'They know you're a florist and you have your own shop in the country.'

Her blue eyes widened. 'And they think that's normal? That we live separately?'

'Lots of people work in the city and have a bolthole for weekends. It's not much different in terms of set-up.'

'I've never thought of my poky little flat as a bolthole.' She gave a dry laugh. 'You make it sound so romantic, you working in London, coming home to your darling wife at the weekends.'

He imagined himself climbing out of his car on a Friday night and greeting her with a kiss, then hastily wiped the picture from his mind. 'It may not be romantic, but it's pragmatic. I travel all over the world with my work.'

'Yes,' she said. 'I have such fond memories of meals eaten alone while admiring the view from your penthouse apartment.'

Her tone made Luc look up in surprise. Her brow pulled into a frown as she smoothed out a pleat in the skirt of her dress. She'd been lonely? That was news to him. He'd felt he'd capitulated when she'd moved in with him. That she'd got what she'd hoped for.

He said evenly, 'I warned you from the start what it would be like. What I'm like. I was always honest with you.'

'Yes. Honest is one word for it,' she said. 'Cruel is another. Heartless too.'

Cruel? Heartless? 'What are you accusing me of, Natasha?'

'Nothing,' she said, mouth pinched with resentment.

'I have no time for tiptoeing around the truth. If you have something to say, say it.' As he spoke, he wondered if he had disturbed a wasps' nest, stirring up all the old resentments and problems that had culminated in their divorce.

'There's nothing to say, Luc. I'm just glad it ended. That pregnancy and our marriage were big mistakes, and the miscarriage was a blessing in disguise. We could never have made it work. Our relationship was a train wreck.' The words tumbled from her mouth, and she turned away, chin lifted.

He stared at her, and the atmosphere in the cabin grew taut. 'A blessing?' he asked.

His words were cold and quiet, and when she looked at him he saw hesitation in her eyes. Good. She couldn't really have meant that.

Then her expression hardened. 'Yes. It freed us both. Weren't you relieved to walk away from that sham of a marriage?' She folded her arms. 'Of course you were. I know I was.'

Luc stared at his ex-wife, petite and pretty enough to waken every male instinct in him, yet the words she'd spoken made him recoil.

Her phone trilled loudly, making her jump, and she pulled it out of her bag.

'Debs, hi,' she said, and hugged her right arm around her waist. 'Yes, everything's fine. Has the delivery come?'

How could she speak about their baby like that – refer to the miscarriage as a blessing? Pain corkscrewed through him and his fists curled. It hadn't been a blessing. It hadn't solved their problems. Well, perhaps it had superficially, but he would have given anything to be able to reverse what had happened, to preserve their child's life.

He'd just been coming to terms with the idea of becoming a father when their baby had died, and although it was only tiny and undeveloped, though he'd never seen it or even felt it kick, it was a loss. A loss that would stay with him, he knew. Hearing Natasha dismiss it made him feel as if he'd been alone in mourning their child.

And yet he shouldn't have been surprised because he'd seen this side of her before. Callous. Detached. When she'd left him, walked out on their marriage, abandoning it before it had even begun.

She'd only been home from hospital a few hours, pale, exhausted and quiet. She'd answered his questions with monosyllables, and their strained, tense attempts at conversation had echoed around his penthouse apartment. He didn't know what to do. She'd looked so unhappy, so washed out, and she'd said she didn't want anything. She looked as if she'd prefer him not to be there. And at the same time he'd been swallowing the pain of having lost their baby.

He'd felt helpless and useless – so he'd gone to make her a cup of tea. That was what English people always did at a time of crisis, wasn't it? Except there was no milk in the fridge so he'd told her he was nipping down to the corner shop.

He was only gone five minutes. When he came back, she was standing in the hall, a suitcase at her feet.

'I'm going home,' she'd said.

He was stunned. That was the last thing he'd expected. 'Why?'

Her face was grey-white and her eyes were blood-shot. 'You're not strong enough,' he began, but she interrupted.

'Because it's over,' she said. 'The pregnancy was a mistake. We only married because of the baby, and now . . .' She'd looked away briefly. 'Now we can both get on with our lives.'

Was that really how she saw it? Everything she'd said was logical: the pregnancy *had* been a mistake. It shouldn't have happened. And now circumstances had freed them, which was what he'd wanted. Wasn't it?

He didn't know what he wanted. He only knew he'd lost a baby and he felt winded. Floored. He'd stared at Natasha and couldn't think of anything to say.

The intercom had sounded.

'That'll be my cab,' she'd said, and went to pick up her case.

He took it from her. He couldn't let her carry it when she looked as if she could barely stand.

She jerked her hand away from his as if he'd burned her. 'I'll get my lawyer to contact yours about a divorce,' she'd said.

And walked out.

He'd helped her into the taxi, feeling like an automaton. It was only after she'd gone that he'd regretted not doing more to stop her. He should have persuaded her to stay in bed until she was thinking straight – he should have put up a fight, at least insisted they discuss it.

But it seemed she had been thinking straight because she didn't waste any time in instigating the divorce. It had taken just days before the first of the paperwork had landed on his desk.

Their marriage had never stood a chance, and he was

surprised at how angry that made him, even now. How angry she made him. He'd thought he'd put their relationship behind him and moved on, yet now he was seething, every muscle in his body knotted. All the emotions from three years ago had come flooding back, as vivid as ever. How could he trust her when she'd left him once before?

He cursed his father for inflicting this situation on him. It was impossible. It was crazy. He needed her cooperation. He was relying on her more than he'd ever relied on anyone before, yet she was the last person he could trust.

Well, that was precisely why he had to take control. This time he couldn't risk her walking out prematurely.

He pulled a document out of his leather folder, scrawled his signature, and handed it to her. 'Here. I need you to sign this.'

Her brow furrowed. 'What is it?'

'Read it. You'll see.'

She flashed him a suspicious look, then dipped her head to read. It was short and simple, unlike the contracts he normally dealt with. She wouldn't find any problems with it, he was certain.

But when she looked up, her expression was fierce.

'I'm not signing that,' she said.

His eyes narrowed. Was she being deliberately uncooperative? Was she planning her escape already?

'Why not?'

'What's the point?' she asked. 'I'm here now. You have what you wanted.'

His lips pressed together. But for how long? When they'd married, it hadn't been in the best circumstances, but he'd believed it was for life. He'd made a commitment and he'd been shocked when she'd thrown that back in his face with a decree nisi.

'But *you* don't. This guarantees you ownership of the cottage at the end of the fortnight.'

Her blue eyes met his. 'Is there any reason why I shouldn't trust you?'

'No.'

'Then I don't need a contract.' Her words were at odds with the cold look in her eyes and her flat tone.

'I want it in writing,' he said steadily.

She might trust him, but he couldn't say the same. She'd vanished from his life once before. She might do it again. He needed to be certain she'd stay the full two weeks. For his father's sake.

She tossed the paper onto the table. It landed on the plate she'd used, a corner sticking to a blob of blackcurrant jam.

'You can't control me with contracts, Luc – or anything else.' There was a child-like innocence about her, but her eyes betrayed her fury. 'I'm a human being with feelings, and I'll thank you to respect those.'

'How am I not treating you with respect when this contract is as much about what *you* have to gain as my side of the bargain?'

Her cheeks coloured but her tone was steely. 'Because we made an agreement. If anything goes wrong, you have to take responsibility for it, Luc. You can't wave this at me and expect me to comply with the terms no matter what.'

'You're saying you don't trust me to behave? You think once you've signed this, I'll mistreat you?'

Natasha bristled at the tension that filled the cabin and reminded her of why she'd escaped their marriage. Was this a sign of things to come? That when they were alone together the air would vibrate with anger, and hostility would kill conversation? She wasn't sure she could cope with two weeks of such pressure. And she hated how he made her feel. Necessary but unwelcome. It was clear he was only doing this for his father. And that was her worst-case scenario: to be unwanted and barely tolerated.

It was too much like when they'd been married.

The temperature in the cabin was suddenly stifling. She needed fresh air and space. Away from him. But there was no way off a moving plane.

'No, I don't think that,' she said finally.

He might have caused her pain in the past, but he'd always been a man of his word. She had faith that he'd hand over the cottage at the end of the fortnight. But she already felt out of her depth: she didn't know what to expect, and she wasn't prepared to sign away the small amount of control she still had over her life.

No one, in any situation, should have to forfeit their freedom, the option to leave should they feel the need to do so.

She thought of her Aunt Thelma and how much the old woman had resented taking her in. She thought of when she'd moved in with Luc and how cold he'd been, how he'd barely tolerated her living in his penthouse. It had been one thing to say he didn't do commitment; it was quite another to treat his wife as if she'd deliberately engineered a pregnancy to win herself a permanent place in his life.

Her stomach lurched. 'I'm saying we're both adults and we have to behave as such. If things go wrong, that contract won't change anything so there's no point in my signing it.'

As he considered this, he eyed her in a way that said loud and clear he didn't trust her, but that shouldn't surprise her: he'd never trusted her.

'You said to think of this as a business agreement, but this isn't business, Luc.'

His head came up sharply. 'Of course it is. I want something, you want something. We made a deal.'

She shook her head, thinking of the guilt trip he'd laid on her that morning, the responsibility he'd placed at her feet for his father's chance of survival. 'Your father's sick and you want me to pretend to be your *wife*. That's about as personal as life gets.'

And Poppy Cottage was personal too, she thought, the only place she'd ever been loved and wanted. The only place that had really felt like home. She folded her arms and felt a secret sense of satisfaction at his visible surprise. He hadn't expected her to react like that. It was clear from the way he stared at her, then, without a word, picked up the contract, wiped it clean, folded it and slipped it back into his expensive leather case.

'You've changed,' he said eventually.

His gaze remained shuttered. She couldn't tell if his

observation was a criticism or not. What did she care either way? Her chin lifted defiantly. A man like Luc needed to be reminded that he couldn't control the world all the time. 'Yes, I've changed.'

When she'd first met him, she was twenty-four, still young for her age and finding her way around the big city. Luc was so different from anyone she'd met before. She was awed by his sophisticated looks and easy smile, by his confidence. It had bowled her over that he was so quick to make a decision and then, with a snap of his fingers, whatever he'd set his mind on was his. A business deal. A piece of land. Her.

With him the world suddenly seemed a safe place where uncertainties didn't exist and there was a solution to every problem. She'd been so in awe of him that when he'd warned her he didn't do commitment she'd simply accepted whatever was on offer.

Which had been sex, mostly.

She should have stood up to him instead of meekly agreeing to whatever conditions he laid down for their relationship. Well, she'd found her voice now. And everything was upside down. Luc wasn't a man in control. He was powerless to prevent his father's illness. Perhaps seeing this chink of vulnerability in him also made her feel bolder.

'I'm not the girl you once knew.'

'No, you're not.'

She heard the reluctant admiration in his voice, saw it in his eyes, and was ridiculously pleased. 'I've moved on. I take care of myself now, and I don't need anyone else to tell me what to do.'

She ran a successful business, she was independent, and she knew her own mind. In three years she'd come far and she was proud of that. She'd worked hard, driven by the determination to make a home for herself in Willowbrook, and one day to buy back Poppy Cottage.

But she hadn't forgotten the bleak times.

For months after she'd left Luc there had been darkness and tears. She'd thought she'd never smile again, never see anything positive in the world. A part of her had died along with her baby. When she'd moved to Willowbrook it had been a relief that no one knew about Luc or the miscarriage. She'd locked away her grief and made a new start. Rebuilt her life and put the past behind her. Yet it seemed Luc had the power to unlock all those memories and emotions.

She stared out of the window as the plane skimmed over the clouds and tried to keep her thoughts pinned on the cottage – the reason she'd agreed to do this.

'What will happen at the end of the two weeks when I go home? Will you tell your family the truth?'

'As soon as my father is out of danger, yes, I will. When he's strong enough.'

'It could take months.'

'That's my problem, not yours. I don't expect anything more of you than we've agreed. The deal is two weeks and then you'll be free to return to Willow . . .' He floundered.

'Willowbrook,' she supplied.

'*Oui.*'

She could see the coastline coming into view, and tried to dispel the mounting anxiety.

'Why did you choose to live there?' asked Luc. She turned. 'In Willowbrook, I mean.'

'Why not? It's beautiful.' She pictured the quaint little sandstone cottages and cobbled lanes, the stream that skirted the edge of the village. And the green where just last week the summer fete had been held, with pretty bunting, music and the delicious smell of a hog roast that had been served as the sun went down. There'd been cider and dancing, and the celebrations had lasted well into the night.

'It is,' he said, clearly picking his words carefully. 'But it's very small, not near the city. I just wondered why you chose to live there.'

She felt his shrewd gaze on her and knew he wouldn't let up until he'd got an answer, but she wasn't ready to tell him. 'I'd been there before and I had good memories of it.' She was deliberately vague and kept the rest to herself, just as she had done three years ago when they'd been married. She'd always harboured the dream of returning to Willowbrook, but it had been such a precious dream that she would only have shared it with someone she could completely trust. She'd come close to sharing it with Luc three years ago, very close, in fact – but when he'd laid down the no-commitment rule, she'd backed off emotionally. And then, of course, she'd become pregnant and things had deteriorated even further.

'You're happy there?' he asked.

'Very.'

He was studying her curiously. 'Don't you find it too quiet?'

She laughed. 'That's what I love. There's a different

pace of life, and everyone knows everyone else. They look out for each other. It has a real village feel.' She'd been overjoyed that some people remembered her from when she'd lived there as a child. Old Dorothy, for example, and Liberty, a friend from primary school. It had touched her profoundly to be welcomed back to Willowbrook when it held such a special place in her heart.

'It is a beautiful village with the fields and hills all around,' Luc conceded. 'You didn't like living in London, then?'

'No. No, I didn't.' She held his gaze, and resentment simmered, unspoken. 'I left as soon as I could.'

The silence between them stretched endlessly, like the sea into the distant horizon.

Luc glanced out of the window. 'We'll be landing soon. Here,' he said, opening a small velvet box. 'You'll need to wear this.'

A lump stuck in her throat as she recognised the wedding ring that had once been hers. 'You kept it? Why?' Surely he couldn't have predicted his father would be sick and that he'd need it again. Why hadn't he sold it?

He shrugged.

The simple platinum band was unassuming yet valu-able. Which was why she'd left it in his apartment. She'd refused to give him any grounds on which to justify his belief that she was after his money.

'I never got round to selling it.' A muscle ticked in his cheek.

'That was lucky.'

'Yes, it was. Take it.'

He plucked it from its velvet nest and held it out for

her, but she drew back. Every instinct warned her against taking it. Memories assailed her of the register office where he'd first produced it, the forbidding look on his face when they'd exchanged vows, the silent accusation in his eyes. Just thinking about it, she could feel nausea threatening. Yet he was right: she had to wear it if they were to convince his family they were still married.

Her cheeks burned, and she was aware of him watching her.

'I could wait until . . .' she began.

His lips pressed flat with impatience. He leaned forward and took her hand. 'There,' he said, and slid the ring onto her finger.

At his touch the hairs lifted on the back of her neck.

Their eyes locked and she had to make herself breathe. She was plunged back in time to when a look or a touch had been enough to make her mouth dry with need and he'd been prey to it too. Animal attraction. It couldn't still be there, could it?

Then Luc let go of her hand and smiled wryly. 'Now you look like my wife.'

Natasha swallowed. The band weighed heavy on her finger, an ugly lump of grey metal against the pretty blue and white daisies painted on her nails.

'About as romantic as our wedding,' she said, and watched his smile fade.

They arrived in Nice, where Luc had arranged for a flash yellow sports car to be waiting. It suited him perfectly, thought Natasha. Expensive, ostentatious and designed to make heads turn. Female heads. Though by the time they'd spotted him he would have driven off into the sunset. He wasn't a man for staying put.

'We'll go straight to the hospital,' he said, after making a brief call. 'He knows we're on the way.'

'He's awake, then?'

'Yes. Apparently, the news had a big impact. His condition has improved slightly since they called me last night.'

'Good,' Natasha said. Though this made her nervous. Could the news that she was coming really help someone get better? And, if so, what might happen if he were to learn the truth? It was a huge weight on her shoulders.

Luc reached across to put the paperwork in the glovebox. As he did so, he brushed her knee and her body reacted with a gunpowder shock. She jerked back.

'If you respond like that in front of my family you'll give everything away.'

'Comments like that aren't going to help,' she said. 'I'm just feeling tense, that's all.'

'Then relax,' he said, as if she could just press a switch and it would happen.

She flung him an angry look as he started the engine. She tried telling herself it would be his problem if they didn't pull this off, but she couldn't quell her nerves. Whatever happened, she was part of this charade now.

Chapter Four

In the hospital, Luc strode quickly through the corridors to his father's room. He pushed open the door and his mother stood up. He nodded at her and looked at his father's pale sleeping face, the tubes and wires everywhere.

'Luc,' she said, and crossed the room to him. Her movements were slow, her eyes red and swollen. She'd always been tall, slim and energetic, but now she was stooped and clearly exhausted.

'How is he?'

'Much better than he was,' she said, with a weak smile. 'He was so pleased when I told him you were both on your way.' Her gaze slid to the petite figure behind him. 'Natasha?'

Natasha stepped forward, a splash of bright colour against the clinical white walls. She smiled hesitantly.

'This is my mother, Marianne,' said Luc, switching to English for her benefit.

Marianne took Natasha's hand and squeezed it as she kissed her cheek. 'You came quickly. I'm so glad.'

'How long have you been here?' Luc asked his mother.

'They called me in the middle of the night. Your sisters too. They left a while ago to – how do you say?' Her forehead creased as she struggled to find the English word. 'Sleep.'

'You need a break.'

'I'm all right,' she said.

'We'll sit with him now. Go and get something to eat, at least. I'll call you if anything changes.'

She peered at his father's sleeping form, then reluctantly agreed and slipped out of the room.

Luc gestured for Natasha to sit, then opened the blinds a little and took a seat beside his father. He hesitated, then took his father's hand, contrasting how light it felt with how strong it had always been. Jean-Pierre had been a big man, but the weight he'd lost in the last few weeks had left him thin and apparently smaller. He remembered how his father used to pick up the soil from their vineyards and crumble it through his fingers, telling him proudly that this was what gave the wine its unique flavour. Shame ripped through him as he recalled how he had always responded with disinterest, even disdain.

'Papa, it's me. I'm back.'

He didn't expect an answer, but his father opened his eyes.

'Luc,' he murmured. A tired smile tugged at his lips. 'I thought I'd chased you away again.'

Relief flashed through Luc. This was his father: the wry humour, aware of everything around him. 'You gave us all a scare last night.'

The old man winked, though it cost him some effort. 'I like to keep them on their toes.'

'You certainly did that. Tell me what happened.'

'No idea. I felt a pain in my arm, then the lights went out – I must have slept through the rest. Lucky I was already in hospital, eh?' He paused for breath. 'But enough of me. Where have you been?'

Luc glanced up at Natasha. 'I went home.'

'To England, you mean? Your home is here.'

Luc pressed his lips together, not wanting to contradict him when his father needed to avoid stress at all costs. 'Papa, I've brought Natasha with me. She'd like to meet you.'

Across the bed, Natasha was as stiff and robotic as one of the machines Jean-Pierre was plugged into, but she smiled at him encouragingly.

His father turned to look at her and his mouth became round with surprise. Then he gave a smile so unexpected and bright, Luc knew it would stick in his mind for a long time.

'At last,' his father said. 'I thought you didn't exist. That he'd invented you to keep me happy.'

Luc expected her to clear her throat or laugh nervously. Instead, she pulled her chair closer and asked, 'To keep you happy? Why would he do that?'

Her eyes were even bluer than usual in the hospital lighting, and her hair gleamed, like white gold.

Jean-Pierre licked his lips, which were dry and cracked. 'He knows I want to see him married and settled.'

'Well, I don't know about the settled part when he travels so much with his work,' she joked. Her tone was light and cheerful, and Luc wanted to applaud her for that.

'He works too hard? This is what they always say of me. But it is a good quality, you know. Commitment, hard work.'

His father's tone was fierce and autocratic, even though he was lying on a hospital bed barely alive. Once upon a time that domineering tone had made Luc bristle. It had driven him away. He admired his father for his work ethic, for his high standards, but his demands, his unbending determination that others should follow his orders, those Luc hadn't been able to tolerate.

'Yes,' Natasha said. 'I know. It's a pleasure to meet you at last, Monsieur Duval.'

'Pff! Stop this "Monsieur Duval" nonsense. Call me Jean-Pierre. We are family, after all, aren't we?'

Luc watched as his father assessed her more closely. He looked animated, and there was a light in his eyes, which hadn't been there before. How could the old devil be at death's door one moment, then speaking a foreign language the next?

'And you work as a florist?' he asked.

She nodded. 'I have my own shop.'

They launched into a discussion about the business of preparing flowers for weddings and events, and Luc sat back a little. Natasha wasn't intimidated by Jean-Pierre – but, then, she was seeing a pale copy of the man he really was.

His father was beginning to tire, thought Luc. Just then his mother returned, a coffee in her hand. Smiling, she told Luc quietly, 'Why don't you go now? Get Natasha settled in at home.'

He and Natasha said their goodbyes.

'I'm glad you're here – finally,' Jean-Pierre said, on a sigh. 'Our home is your home, Natasha. Remember that.'

'Thank you,' she said, and they left.

They walked back to the car in silence. The sun was high in the sky and its heat contrasted with the cool of the air-conditioned hospital. Luc could see there had been a slight improvement in his father, but he was still too frail. There was no strength in him. And Luc was afraid. For his mother, his sisters – and also for himself.

He wanted more time with his father. It might be selfish, but he needed a chance to rebuild their relationship, to get to know him again. If he got that chance, this time he would do things differently. He'd be more patient, less stubborn. He'd invest more time in their relationship.

When his father had become ill, Luc's family had asked for his help and he'd given it, but he'd also rediscovered something during the last couple of weeks, and the long hours he'd spent at his father's bedside. The value of family. Of pulling together through testing times.

He'd missed his mother, and his sisters. His nephews and nieces had been like strangers at first. Now he was back, he realised he didn't want to leave. He wanted to stay in their lives, to put right what had gone wrong in the past, and he wanted his father to be a part of that.

'I thought that went well,' said Luc, as they approached the car. 'He was delighted to meet you.'

'To meet the woman he thinks is your wife,' she corrected sharply. He aimed his key fob at the car and pressed hard, as if he were firing a gun. The lights flashed as it unlocked. 'Did you hear what he said to me? "Our home is your home . . ."'

'I heard.'

'I feel bad deceiving him. Don't you?'

He didn't need the reminder that what he was doing was wrong. He was acutely conscious that if he'd been the kind of son his father wanted there wouldn't have been any need for this deception. He would have rolled up with his neat little wife, perhaps a child or four, and his father would have been proud.

His father was traditional in the extreme. Family values were of the utmost importance to him. If he knew Luc was divorced, it would confirm everything he'd always thought: that his son made bad decisions, that he didn't measure up. That Luc wasn't the man his father had hoped he would be.

They got into the car. The air was thick with heat from having been left in the midday sun. He pressed the ignition button and the engine came to life with a satisfying growl. The fans automatically powered up, but they did nothing to cool the burning sensation in Luc's chest. He turned to her.

'You're worrying too much. Leave that to me and think of your cottage,' he said, and reversed the car out of the space in one quick, jerky motion. 'You still want it, don't you?'

He glanced at her, tense as he thought of the contract she'd refused to sign. She wasn't going to bail out on him now, was she?

'Of course I do.' She took a deep, steadying breath, her eyes fixed unseeingly on the spindly pine trees in the distance as if she was picturing it, reminding herself of why she was there. That seemed to anchor her, and he was relieved, but he wondered what it was about the cottage that she wanted so badly. It was dilapidated and run-down. Perhaps she saw it as an investment. Now, he could identify with that. His business operated by buying properties or plots of land with a view to demolishing, rebuilding. And he could see the potential of that place: its situation was ideal, the walls looked solid. With some work it could eventually yield double or triple the asking price.

He pulled out of the car park and stopped at the main road where a steady stream of cars whizzed past. His indicator beat a gentle rhythm, like a healthy heartbeat, while he waited for a gap in the traffic. Eventually one came, and the car slipped out smoothly onto the tree-lined road. The air-conditioning began to kick in.

'Listen,' he said. 'If it's any consolation, I don't feel good about deceiving my father either.'

Her head swivelled and she looked up at him, eyes wide with surprise.

'But the alternative is to disillusion him. There are certain things he feels strongly about and seeing me married is one of them.'

They went through a set of traffic lights, then left the town, and sparse-looking fields stretched away from them on both sides of the road.

'Why is it so important to him to see you married?' she asked. Her big blue eyes were trained on him.

'It's what he values in life. Marriage. Family. Tradition.'

'How ironic that your father places such value on marriage when you take the opposite view.'

He kept his eyes on the road, not allowing himself to

think of how disappointed his father would be if he knew the truth. That he'd already been divorced when he had seen him at the christening last year. That he had been so shell-shocked when Jean-Pierre approached him and congratulated him on being married that he hadn't corrected him. Hadn't admitted he was divorced. He hadn't wanted to risk their tentative reconciliation by triggering another row.

Luc's silence riled Natasha, and all the old hurt and resentment from their failed relationship came bubbling back to the surface. His unwillingness to commit emotionally had been at the heart of all their problems. She flattened her skirt as if she were brushing away a crawling insect.

'What was it you told me? That settling down wasn't part of your plans. Or has that changed?'

His gaze remained fixed straight ahead, his jaw rigid. 'No change. Commitment isn't my thing.'

Didn't she know it. But then, what incentive was there for him to commit? A man like him would always have women falling at his feet. He was good-looking and owned a successful international construction business. He was intelligent enough to hold a conversation on any topic, and grounded enough to have a sense of humour. He had presence. He was sophisticated, hard-working—

She cut herself off, horrified by the list she'd drawn up in her head. What was she – his fan club? He was her ex-husband, don't forget, and she was certain he didn't appreciate how fortunate he was.

Well, at least now he seemed to appreciate his family and, judging by what she'd seen in the hospital, he and his parents seemed to have healed the rift.

'Why don't you do commitment, Luc?' she asked, genuinely curious. It was always interesting to hear someone else's reasons, even if they were plainly obvious.

'It's not my forte.'

Interesting. He almost made it sound like a failing. Though when his jaw was clenched and he cast her a hard look, he didn't look too bothered about that area of his life.

'Why not? You're committed to your work. There's no reason why you couldn't show the same commitment to a relationship.'

He'd certainly shown commitment to his father when he'd needed her cooperation. She wasn't sure he would ever have given up trying to persuade her to come here, even if she'd managed to resist his pleas in the middle of the night.

'The sticking-around part. The staying-with-one-person part.'

Yes, she thought, remembering how he'd watched her leave three years ago without saying a word, without making any effort to stop her. As if he'd been relieved, as if he'd secretly wished for the chance to be single again. Free.

Her chest squeezed, and she tried to push away the pain. Surely it should have dulled over the years. Yet being with him again seemed to bring all the emotion rushing back as vivid as ever.

'Some of us just aren't cut out for it,' he added.

She barked a laugh. 'You make it sound like it's beyond your control.' Wasn't it a personal decision? A choice? You were either committed to a relationship or not. You invested in it, or you stood back and let it happen.

She thought of Thelma and felt a sharp ruffle of anger. Her elderly aunt had taken her in so reluctantly that Natasha sometimes wondered if she'd have been better off in the hands of the state. Maybe then a loving couple would have adopted her – who knew?

'Perhaps it is.' He shrugged. 'Either way, I'm not the marrying kind.'

Luc could list the failed relationships that littered his past: he'd disappointed his father, he'd been duped by a girl he thought he was in love with, and to crown it all there had been his marriage to Natasha, which had failed so cata-strophically. Commitment, relationships – they just didn't work for him.

Even more so since the divorce. Before Natasha his relationships had always been brief – he used to get bored quickly, get itchy feet. Now they couldn't even be called relationships. In the last three years he'd dated a little, but dates were all they'd been, dinner or a show, nothing more. Losing the baby had made him realise what a dangerous game he'd been playing. A game of life and death. People could get hurt, end up in hospital. He thought of that tiny life and his chest constricted.

He was better off alone, he was happy alone, so he guarded his freedom ferociously.

'I like to be able to get up and go when I need to. My work is important to me. It always will be.'

'I thought you said your priorities had changed since your father became ill.'

'They have. But once Papa is better, I'll go back to running my company. I'll spend more time with my family, but I won't be rushing to the altar.'

He saw her watching him through narrowed eyes, her mouth pinched in disapproval.

'Anyway, you can't criticise me for my lack of commitment, Natasha. Your staying power wasn't great either.'

Her blonde head whipped round to face him. 'What the hell is that supposed to mean?'

'You didn't hang around, did you? You walked out on me at the first opportunity. Our marriage never stood a chance.'

Her cheeks fired up, and her hands curled into fists on her lap. 'I can't believe I'm hearing this! It didn't stand a chance because you didn't *want* to be married! You made that very clear.'

'Granted, the initial circumstances were not ideal, but once we'd got over the shock, we could have worked on that.'

'Worked on it? You mean I was supposed to stick around and be subjected to more of the cold treatment? More snide comments about how much I had to gain financially from having your baby? From day one our marriage was a living hell, and you have the cheek to blame me for not giving it a chance!'

'A living hell?' Well, that had told him. His jaw clamped

shut, his heart pounding furiously. The moment he'd learned she was pregnant, he'd moved her out of her cheap bedsit and into his penthouse, put a ring on her finger and made sure she wanted for nothing. 'Just *how* was our marriage a living hell?'

'You don't remember saying, "I suppose you'll want your own credit card now you're my wife," and throwing one at me? You were suspicious. You behaved as if I'd engineered the pregnancy. You made me feel like – like an impostor!'

He frowned. The thing about the credit card stirred a vague recollection.

'And all the late nights and trips away you suddenly had—'

'I've always travelled with my work,' he cut in.

'But not as much as you did then!'

Why was he feeling so defensive? She was the one who'd walked out. If she'd had a problem with his absences she should have said so at the time.

The landscape whipped past and he realised he was speeding. He eased his foot off the accelerator and took a deep breath. They were entering the wine-making region and less than an hour away from his family home. Dry shrubs were replaced with neat rows of vines and fields of sunflowers, their golden heads twisted towards the sun. Pine trees reached for the ink-blue sky, and the hills in the distance shimmered in the late-afternoon heat.

'I thought it might do us good to have some time apart while things were so difficult between us,' he said, through gritted teeth.

'Oh, yes. Feeling ill with the pregnancy and being lonely were a fantastic combination for me!'

Silence stretched while he absorbed this. He was taken aback. At the time she hadn't said anything. She'd been silent and distant, and he'd had no idea what she was feeling. Obviously their relationship had been less than ideal, but when she'd packed her belongings and left it had come as a complete shock to him. Now guilt nudged him. Uncomfortable. Unwelcome.

'You were lonely?' he asked finally.

'No, I was ecstatic. I treasure the memories to this day.' He was familiar with English sarcasm, but this cut through him. She shook her head. 'I can't believe you think I should have stayed for more.'

'We took vows,' he grated. 'They were meant to be for life.'

'Why stay in a marriage if it makes you unhappy? It would have been toxic for our child . . .' she added quietly '. . . had she lived.'

He thought her eyes dulled with pain before she turned away, but perhaps not. After all, this was the woman who had referred to the miscarriage as a *blessing*.

'Maybe things would have got better,' he said, 'given time.' If she hadn't jumped ship so soon, they could have worked at their relationship. He was abroad when he'd heard she was in hospital, but he'd had a plan for when he got home: he would make a meal, and they'd sit down to talk. Make a fresh start.

He'd never had the chance to do any of it.

Natasha shook her head. 'They wouldn't.'

Chapter Five

They spent the rest of the journey in silence, the air taut with tension. Natasha couldn't believe how just a few words from Luc had opened the floodgates to so much anger she hadn't known was locked inside her. Now she sat, arms folded, trying to calm herself before they arrived at his family's home. She reminded herself of why she was doing this: the cottage, her promise to her mum.

The road became quieter and wound through small towns with a peaceful, sleepy air. They passed cafés, busy with people eating lunch and sipping beer in the sunshine, tall stone buildings with washing strung across balconies, and the odd elderly lady sitting on her doorstep watching the world go by. Willowbrook was beautiful with its quaint church, the green and the chocolate-box cottages, but this was so different: all primary colours, vivid sunshine and intense heat. She sneaked a sideways glance at Luc: if she'd been there with anyone else she could have relaxed and enjoyed it, but she couldn't. Despite the beautiful setting, this wasn't a holiday. Far from it.

A couple of miles beyond the last village, Luc waved a hand at the fields to her left.

'This is my family's estate,' he said casually.

Natasha saw vines growing in rust-coloured soil, and made out small bunches of green grapes. They were nearly there. Two weeks, she thought. What had she let herself in for?

They drove on until they reached a set of large iron gates, propped open, a large sign announcing 'Château Duval', and Luc turned off the road. The car slowed to a crawl as it followed the track round a rocky outcrop that obscured the view of the house. It was only once they were on the tree-lined driveway that she saw it.

Natasha gasped. The place was huge. When she'd first met Luc, she'd immediately picked up that he was from a wealthy family. At some point she'd looked up Château Duval and learned that they owned land and a wine-making business that went back hundreds of years. She'd worried a little that a man as sophisticated as Luc wouldn't be interested in her, but it hadn't mattered when they were living in London and their relationship was new.

Now, though, she was intimidated by the scale and beauty of the place, and its faded grandeur. Her gaze swept over the tall stone walls and pale green shutters, the tiny windows in the roof. There were at least three floors and more windows than she could count. The plaster was crumbling in places, the paintwork was a little weathered, but the château had an indisputable elegance and a mesmerising charm.

So this was where Luc had grown up, she thought, and contrasted it with her own childhood at Thelma's modest little house. The Duvals must be the grand family of the area, like local gentry. They would see through her straight away. They would know as soon as she stepped out of the car that she couldn't possibly be a match for Luc. She glanced at him.

'I – I never imagined you living somewhere so . . . traditional.'

His brown eyes caught the light. 'Oh, yes. Everything is very traditional at Château Duval. Things haven't changed for the last two centuries.'

She turned to look at the enormous trunks of the plane trees they were passing, and again at the imposing house, which loomed ever larger. The gravelled area at the front was edged with balls of lavender in full flower, and to her right, she spotted an ancient olive tree with a gnarled trunk and silver leaves.

The car slowed. 'There's one more thing I should tell you,' Luc said.

'What's that?' she said, without taking her eyes off the house and the wide drive on which a couple of cars were already parked, dusty and battered, nothing like as glamorous as Luc's.

'My sister's getting married next week.'

Her head whipped round. '*What?*'

He swung the car round and stopped in front of the big wooden front doors.

'Luc, if this is some kind of joke, it's not funny.'

'Write it in your diary: Juliette's wedding, Saturday.'

She felt sick. 'Why didn't you tell me before?' she asked, through gritted teeth.

In the plane, in the car – he'd had all day to mention it, but he'd waited until now.

He cut the engine.

Anger changed to panic. Her lungs became tight. 'Luc, I can't . . .'

It was bad enough posing as his wife, but she couldn't take part in his family's wedding celebrations as well.

His eyes narrowed. 'Can't what?'

'I can't go to your sister's wedding.' She would be an impostor.

'Of course you can. You agreed to spend two weeks with me. The wedding is part of that.'

'Luc! Natasha!'

A young woman, dark-haired and about the same age as Luc, appeared from round the side of the house, wearing a delighted smile. Luc opened the car door to get out, and Natasha forced herself to follow suit.

'At last – we meet. I'm Caroline, Luc's sister.' As she enveloped Natasha in a hug more people appeared behind her. 'And this is my family.'

Caroline introduced her husband, Marc, and four children. Their names blended into a long list and a crowd of smiling faces who all, in turn, greeted Natasha.

She was a little startled by their warmth. But the French were known for being tactile, weren't they? Kisses and hugs – she'd have to get used to all this.

'And this is Juliette,' Luc said affectionately, as the children scattered in a noisy game of chase. 'My younger sister. The one who's the most trouble. . .'

Juliette removed her sunglasses and grinned. '. . .The one who's getting married.'

'Congratulations,' said Natasha, trying to sound as if

she meant it. As if she wasn't furious with Luc for having just sprung the news on her.

'We're keeping our fingers crossed that Papa will be allowed out of hospital for the big day. I really want him to be there.'

'He will,' Caroline said, and squeezed her shoulder. 'Don't worry. Now Natasha's here he'll get better – you'll see.'

Juliette took Natasha's hands in hers. 'I'm so glad you've come. It means so much to us to meet you. Luc has already spoken to you about the flowers?'

Natasha looked at Luc, who shook his head guiltily. 'I thought I'd leave that to you, Ju.'

'Will you do my flowers – for the wedding?'

Yet another thing Luc hadn't prepared her for. Natasha bit her lip, trying not to let her anger show.

'The florist here is about a hundred years old and her arrangements are like something from the dark ages. Luc showed me your website and I know you'll do something beautiful and modern.'

'He showed you my website?' Natasha didn't know why this surprised her so much. She hadn't heard from him in years but, clearly, he'd been thinking of her.

Only because his sister was getting married and his father was sick, she told herself.

'Well, of course. You're a florist and his wife!'

'Where will the wedding be?' she asked.

'In the village church,' said Luc. 'Then back here for the reception.'

'Is it a big wedding?'

'Oh, no. Just sixty guests or so. It was all quite last-minute – as you know, I'm sure.'

No, she didn't. She flashed Luc a hooded glance. He hadn't told her anything.

'So, will you do it? '

Natasha bit her lip.

'Please say you will,' Juliette begged. 'I'm counting on you, Natasha.'

'It will be difficult on my own without any help . . .'

Juliette's face fell.

'. . . but I can do some of the work in advance . . .'

It would be a lot of work, but she liked the thought of being useful, of doing something positive, and her work always made her feel calm and in control. Plus, it would mean time away from Luc.

'Yes,' she told Juliette, 'I'd love to.'

'Thank you!' Juliette hugged her again. 'Thank you so much!'

'Let me show Natasha to our room.' Luc was holding his case and hers. 'It's been a long day and we could do with a shower.'

'Of course,' said Juliette.

Natasha followed him into the cool of the house and her yellow ballerina shoes tapped on the tiled floor.

'Sorry about my sister,' said Luc, as they climbed the stairs. 'She's getting completely wound up over this wedding.'

'That's OK,' she said tightly. 'It's perfectly normal.'

He led her along the landing to a room on the right, and swung open the door. 'After you,' he said.

She stepped inside and took in the big bed, the chaise longue, the tiled floor. The tall window overlooked a swimming pool and the gardens at the back of the house. There was a knot in her throat because she had to share this room with Luc for two weeks. She had known this would be the case, but now she was here, confronted with the reality, the intimacy of the situation scared her. She went to the window and looked out, trying to breathe – the walls seemed to be closing in on her.

'She's not normally so dizzy,' Luc said, closing the door. 'I don't know how Philippe puts up with it.'

Natasha gripped the smooth plastic handles of her straw bag, her knuckles white. 'Well, we all know marriage and commitment aren't your thing. Perhaps you're more sensitive to her excitement than Philippe is. Or any other man.'

He carried their cases to a wooden chest at the foot of the bed. There was a long pause while he assessed her. This might be how he'd face a business rival, she thought, all calm strength with a warrior's glint in his eye.

'You're angry,' he observed.

'Of course I'm angry! Coming here – doing this fake marriage thing – is bad enough, but you deliberately hid from me that your sister was getting married.'

'What does it matter? It's just one day.'

'It's a wedding.'

He shrugged. 'A church ceremony and a meal. What's the big deal?'

Natasha's blood simmered. This was typical of him, reducing marriage to a timetable rather than recognising its significance. She remembered their own wedding:

fifteen minutes in the register office, a couple of nameless witnesses, signatures, and then it was over.

'You might see it that way, but for your sister and your family it's going to be a really special day – a huge day. And I'll be there under false pretences – an interloper!' A cuckoo in another bird's nest.

'They won't see it that way.'

'They will when they learn the truth.'

'Which they won't.'

They would eventually, she thought, but her mind was working overtime, racing on to the next problem he hadn't considered. 'What will I wear? I didn't bring anything smart enough for a wedding. What will your sisters think if I turn up looking like . . .' She stopped, as something else occurred. 'This is why it had to be me, isn't it? Why you didn't ask someone else to play the role of your wife.' His lips tightened, and she knew she was right. It all made sense now. 'You thought, good old Natasha, she'll do the flowers too while she's here.'

'I didn't.'

'And that's why you insisted on two weeks, isn't it? This is why I couldn't come for just a few days, then leave.'

There was a long pause. Then: 'We need to be at Juliette's wedding together.'

'You should have been honest with me.' Her skin prickled. She was hurt that he hadn't told her all this in advance. He was constantly one step ahead, and she was having to run to keep up. Nothing was within her control. And she didn't like it.

Until he'd turned up in her shop yesterday, her life had been ordered and just as she wanted it. Doing the job she loved, living in a place where she had friends she could rely on.

He arched a brow. 'You weren't receptive to start with. If I'd mentioned this –'

'I would have refused,' she cut in.

'– you would have been even less likely to help,' he finished.

'Too right.'

Outside, the children were calling to each other and laughing.

She hoped Luc's family couldn't hear this. How would she and Luc keep up the pretence of being happily married for two weeks when after just thirty seconds alone they were at each other's throats?

'I had to do this for my father,' he said.

'So you keep saying, but you know what, Luc? I feel manipulated.'

He didn't answer. She saw guilt in his expression and felt a small amount of satisfaction, but not enough to override her own guilt and anxieties.

'Can't you see? Getting involved in Juliette's wedding is just going to make the deception worse.' She'd be in the wedding photos, a permanent reminder. Her insides twisted.

'No. I see that you're going to fulfil your side of the bargain, which is to spend two weeks here with my family. The bargain you agreed to.'

'I agreed without knowing there would be a family

wedding. A wedding for which I would be asked to do the flowers.'

'Is that what the problem is – you don't want to do the flowers?'

'No,' she said. If anything, she was keen to keep busy and, hopefully, out of everyone's way. 'The flowers are not a problem.'

'Then what is this about, Natasha? You can complain all you like, but I don't believe you would have turned down my offer because of this wedding. You want the cottage too much.'

They fell silent. She looked away, not wanting to admit it, but knowing he was right.

'You tell me you're not materialistic,' he went on quietly, 'but we all have a price.'

She flushed. It sounded so mercenary – that she was taking part in a lie in exchange for a house. That she'd been bought. But last time she'd let slip that something mattered to her, he'd used it to his advantage: he'd bought the cottage and was holding her to ransom with it. Now she was on her guard. She'd rather let him believe that she was materialistic than reveal why Poppy Cottage meant so much to her.

'Maybe so,' she said defiantly, 'but you're being totally insensitive and not thinking about your family or your sister. Her wedding day is important to her. Just because you don't value the notion of marriage it doesn't mean you should be so flippant about other people's.'

'I'm not being flippant – or insensitive,' he ground out. 'I'm doing all this precisely because I care about my family. Because I'm determined that everything should be exactly as they want it to be – as my father wants it to be.'

'Is there anything else you haven't told me? Any other monumental pieces of information you've failed to mention?'

His eyes glittered and his jaw was like chiselled wood. 'No.'

The sound of footsteps approaching in the corridor silenced them, and they waited for them to pass.

Natasha shook her head. This was hopeless. They couldn't see eye to eye about even the most basic things.

The room became quiet and she was conscious of the intimacy of the bedroom.

When the footsteps had faded, she gestured at the double bed. 'So we're sharing a room.'

His dark eyes met hers and held them. 'We have to.' He kept his voice level. 'What would they think if we didn't?'

Luc watched as she swallowed and eyed the bed as if it were a dangerous animal. In those few moments of silence, Natasha had transformed from fierce and angry to small and vulnerable, and he battled the urge to smooth away her frown, pull her into his arms. Reassure her. Kiss her. Perhaps then she'd stop fighting him, he thought. Perhaps then he'd understand her better because, right now, she was an enigma to him. On the one hand, she admitted she was doing this for a plot of land – what did that say about her? Added to that, she was the woman who'd left him, who'd described the miscarriage as a *blessing*. Yet, on the other, she was tormented with guilt for deceiving his family.

He couldn't understand what drove her. She was a closed book – even more so now than three years ago.

'Don't look so scared,' he said. She looked up, her blue eyes deep pools of anxiety. 'You might believe I black-mailed you into this, but it isn't some sordid offer. I'll sleep on that.' He nodded at the chaise longue.

It would be hard, uncomfortable, way too small for his large frame, but there was no alternative because sharing a bed with her would never work. She was a very attractive woman, and he still responded to her on a primal level, despite everything that had happened between them.

Her face flooded with colour. 'I'm smaller. Why don't you take the bed?'

'Have the bed, Nat. This is my mess, my problem. There's no reason why you should suffer discomfort because of it.'

His nerves were strung tight. Discomfort was going to feature very strongly for him while she was so close.

He made himself focus on the fundamental reason they were there – his father.

'I need to get back to the hospital now,' he said, more abruptly than he'd intended. 'I'll meet you later – dinner will be ready at eight thirty.'

She looked surprised, but she nodded. 'Your sisters might want to go to the hospital too. Can I help cook?'

'Don't be ridiculous. Simone will make dinner – that's what she's paid for.'

'Oh – of course. Well, I'll see you later, then.'

'Yes.' He felt a moment of hesitation at leaving her alone so soon after they'd arrived. But she was a grown woman, he told himself, puzzled by a rush of protectiveness. She was also the woman who'd left him and he'd be wise to remember that. Stay detached.

His father needed him, and that was what this was all about.

Chapter Six

After Luc had left for the hospital, Natasha took her time unpacking her case. She hadn't expected him to abandon her here so soon. She hadn't known what to expect at all. She gazed around her, trying to get used to her new surroundings, but everything was unfamiliar: the streams of rapid French that drifted in from outside, which she couldn't decipher; the bedroom suffused with the smell of beeswax and old wood; the view of the hillside neatly striped with vines and lavender. What was she supposed to do until dinner tonight? There were hours to fill.

She tried to calm herself by closing her eyes and thinking of home, of Willowbrook. She pictured her shop front, its vintage wooden crates filled with marguerites and blue hydrangeas, the summery window display she'd created last week with old watering-cans of apricot roses and tangerine-orange gerberas in jam jars. She thought of her regular customers, the friendly smiles as people stopped her in the street to chat about the weather, and the friends she'd made.

Until Luc had turned up, her life had been calm and happy, fulfilling. She hadn't thought about him at all. Well, maybe she had from time to time. When she saw a sports car or heard a French accent. But that was normal, wasn't it? She had put their short marriage behind her and she was happy with her life.

Sliding her empty case under the bed, Natasha checked the time. By her calculation, Debbie would be closing the shop now. She pulled out her phone and was relieved when Debbie answered on the second ring.

'How's the shop? How are you feeling? Is everything OK?' she asked, the stream of questions pouring from her mouth.

Her friend laughed. 'It's fine. All under control. And the baby's happily kicking away so it's happy, too.'

'Good. Did Hans do all the lifting for you this morning?' Natasha pictured Debbie receiving the delivery from the enormous Dutch lorry. They knew the driver well, and usually Hans took care of stacking the boxes of flowers in the back room while they made him a cup of tea. He was always grateful for a drink and a bacon roll after his long journey from Holland.

'Of course he did. He's a true gent. Did you know his wife's expecting too?'

'No.'

'He told me this morning.'

Natasha nodded. 'Make sure you don't lift anything heavy. Did Shauna agree to help in the shop?'

'Yes. She said she'd be glad of the extra money so that's sorted.'

'Good. And feel free to use her as much as you need. Don't worry about the cost. I don't want you to overdo it.'

'Yes, boss.' She heard the smile in Debbie's voice.

'I'm serious, Debs. You need to think of your baby.'

'Stop worrying, Nat. I'm pregnant, not ill.'

'I know, but . . .' But a baby was such a fragile and precious thing. The hospital room from three years ago flashed in her mind, like a broken strip light. Hurriedly she tried to quash it, but it persisted. Memories like that stayed with you all your life. 'Be careful, that's all.'

'Nat, are you OK? You sound . . . tearful. What's wrong?'

She sniffed. 'Nothing's wrong. I'm just – just missing home a bit.'

'You're really not missing anything. It rained so much this morning that even the hardy geraniums were shivering. I brought everything in before it drowned.'

She tried to laugh and almost succeeded.

'What's it like there?' asked Debbie.

'What?' Her hand gripped the phone in panic. She couldn't tell Debbie about the deception.

'In Provence. The weather – what's it like?'

'Oh. It – it's gorgeous.' She looked out of the window. High in the sky a bird of prey circled on a warm current, peering down at the valley. 'Blue skies, gorgeously hot. There's a swimming pool, and the most beautiful garden.'

'It sounds amazing, you lucky thing.'

'Yes.'

'Your ex must be quite a catch.'

'I wouldn't say that.' She gave a nervous laugh.

There was a pause before Debbie asked, 'What's going on, exactly, Nat? I know you said his dad was very ill, but why does your ex need you there?'

Their conversation in the early hours of this morning had been brief and rushed. It was perfectly natural that Debbie had questions now. 'He – ah . . . It's complicated.'

'Right.'

She heard the disappointment in her friend's voice that she wouldn't say more, but she couldn't. Opening up didn't come naturally to her, and she'd never told anyone in Willowbrook about Luc or their shared past. Besides, if Debbie knew even half of it, she would worry, and that would not be good for the baby she was carrying.

Natasha tried again: 'It's a long story, but because Jean-Pierre is ill, Luc's sister has brought forward the date of her wedding and I'm doing the flowers.'

'Oh, I see!' said Debbie. Natasha was relieved that her friend accepted this explanation so readily. 'Have you got help?'

'Not really. Only the untrained kind.' She laughed. 'But I'll manage.'

'Oh, Nat, it's very good of you. I'm not sure I'd agree to help an ex.'

What would her friend think if she told her she was doing it in return for Poppy Cottage? 'I couldn't say no. And it'll keep me out of mischief at least.'

'That's one way of looking at it. I hope he appreciates it.'

'I think he does.' As long as Luc kept his promise, that was all that mattered.

When they'd hung up, Natasha wiled away a little more time showering and painting her nails – aware that she was hiding in her room. But she felt so intimidated by the place. Luc's family lived in a château. They had a paid cook. She looked around her, taking in the room's dimensions, the chandelier, the enormous antique wardrobe in which her dresses looked so tiny. It was intimidating. What if, during the first few hours that Luc had left her here alone, she made a gaffe and let slip the pretence?

She peered out of the window again. The gardens formed a green perimeter around the château, separating it from the vineyards beyond, and were casually elegant. White gravel paths snaked through the greenery, punctuated here and there by an iron bench or an old wine barrel spilling over with white geraniums. Her gaze ran over parasol pines and palm trees, and near the house oleander bushes waved fuchsia pink flowers in the breeze. She twisted the heavy platinum ring one way, then the other. Daunting as it was, it would look rude if she hid away any longer, and it was impossible to resist the prospect of an hour in this glorious sunshine. She put on her bikini, grabbed a towel, and went downstairs.

The house was quiet, but she'd seen the children splashing in the swimming pool from her bedroom, so she knew roughly which direction to head in. The sun felt velvety warm on her skin, and her feet crunched over the gravel as the turquoise water came into view. The children were playing in the water, and their father – Marc? – was sitting nearby, reading and keeping an eye on them. He waved as she approached.

'Natasha!' the children chorused. The two tallest ran towards her, dripping water. Another boy hauled himself out of the pool and chased after them, and a toddler in armbands scrambled up the steps. They clustered around Natasha, all chattering at the same time. She listened hard, but in the end had to tell them, 'I'm sorry. I don't understand.'

The elder girl translated this to her brothers and sister, then turned back to Natasha. 'Do you want to play?' She pointed to the pool. 'To swim with us?'

'Maybe later.' She smiled, and showed them the book she'd brought with her.

Truth was, she couldn't let herself get too involved in this family's world. It wouldn't be fair on them – or on her – if they formed bonds, only for her to disappear from their lives in two weeks. They had enough stress with Jean-Pierre in hospital, fighting for his life. Natasha knew she had to strike a careful balance between politeness and distance.

'You can't speak French, Natasha?' piped up one of the boys.

'No. I'm sorry.'

'I can teach you. I'm very good at English. I'm top in my class.'

His big sister rolled her eyes. 'He always says this.'

Natasha smiled. 'Is it true?'

'Yes,' his sister grudgingly conceded.

'I am. I'm top.' He stuck his chest out proudly.

She smiled at his confidence. 'That's wonderful. And, yes, I'd love you to teach me.' So much for keeping her distance, she thought wryly.

'I start by teaching you the important words. All the foods!' His eyes sparkled as he patted his stomach.

She laughed. 'Well, I know the word for chocolate, but I'll need to learn some others because I can't eat chocolate all the time.'

He followed her as she spread her towel on a sun-lounger, and began giving her words to repeat. The other children skipped back to the pool and resumed their games.

'Arthur,' said his father, from across the pool. She and the boy looked up. 'Is he bothering you, Natasha? Arthur, come here.'

'He's not bothering me at all,' she said. 'I've always wanted to learn French.'

Marc's phone began to ring.

Arthur went on, 'Bread is *le pain*.'

'*Le pain*,' she recited, happy to play along. 'Oh, and I know cheese – *fromage*.'

'*Oui! Très bien. Les fruits*. That is fruit.'

Eventually, Arthur was lured back into the water by a raucous game that seemed to involve jumping in backwards. Natasha watched from behind her book. The youngest child, a little girl with blonde curls, paddled around with armbands, laughing at her siblings' antics. But when the game became too rough, she hung back, and Natasha felt a tug of concern. She was so small, probably two or three. The baby Natasha had lost had been a girl. Despite Luc's hostility when they'd been married, she had been looking forward to becoming a mother. She still was. Perhaps because she'd lost her own parents so young, she felt it more acutely than most people. Living with Thelma, she'd longed to be surrounded by a real family, aching for love and warmth. Becoming a mum would be a dream come true.

When she met the right man, she told herself, and when Poppy Cottage was hers. This trip was taking her closer to that goal.

Natasha stood in the bathroom applying a little more eye-shadow, then combing her hair. Truth be told, she might have stayed there all evening, but Luc knocked on the open door.

'Ready?' he asked.

She dropped her hairbrush back into her toilet case and spun round. He leaned against the doorframe, scrutinising her carefully.

'Yes,' she said. Though she had a childish urge to lock herself into the en-suite and plead illness – anything rather than face his family. Or him, with his intense masculinity that made her so aware of him. He wasn't helping by looking her over like this. It made her feel even more nervous. She glanced down at her outfit. He was probably going to tell her she wasn't suitably dressed, that she looked out of place. All her insecurities rushed back. 'I – er – wasn't sure if this was smart enough,' she said, running one hand over her dress. Blue satin, with a pattern of green and yellow spots, it was one of her smarter outfits, but it was knee-length and this was a château. Perhaps the dress code was super-formal, with high heels and long dresses the norm.

And painting her nails in matching shades of blue,

green and yellow with white polka dots had seemed a fun idea this afternoon, but now they just looked frivolous.

Luc seemed surprised. 'You look fine.' He cleared his throat. 'Actually, you look lovely.'

Natasha's eyes widened. Her ex-husband had just paid her a compliment! And he'd sounded like he really meant it. 'Thank you,' she said quickly, and avoided looking at him.

He didn't move and she wished he would because he was blocking the doorway of the tiny bathroom. Blocking her exit. 'You have a new style,' he said. 'More colourful than before.'

'I thought you'd disapprove.'

When she'd first met Luc, she wouldn't have dared wear such brightly coloured clothes. She'd tried desperately to look as sophisticated and well-groomed as he did.

'Why?'

'Because it's unconventional. Fun.'

'I like fun.'

She thought she saw a gleam in his eyes, and her skin prickled. 'When I opened the shop, I wanted people to recognise me, and to send out the message that my flower arrangements were a bit different – modern, distinctive. Not the run-of-the-mill roses and carnations sold in the supermarkets. I hoped this would give it a point of difference, so I started wearing outfits with a vintage feel.'

She'd always liked bright colours and floral patterns but having her own shop had given her the confidence to wear them. And it seemed to have worked. Customers began recommending her, and now she had a loyal following who often briefed her with 'I want something a bit different . . .'

'From what I've seen, it was a winning formula. Your business is very successful.' His eyes were warm with admiration, which gave her a warm feeling too.

'Did you look it up?' she asked, remembering how Juliette had said he'd shown her the website.

'Yes.'

'Why?'

'I was interested.' He shrugged. 'And you didn't exactly keep in touch.'

'I had no reason to,' she snapped, automatically going on the defensive. But even as she spoke, she thought, he'd been interested – why?

'Nat, I don't want to argue.' The strain in his voice made her feel guilty. It had been a long day, and this was a difficult time for him. Really difficult. 'I'm pleased for you. You always had a passion for flowers. I'm glad things have worked out well.'

'Thank you. I guess I've been lucky.'

'Luck plays only a small part in success. You must have worked hard to achieve so much in three years.'

'I did.' She'd been determined to make a success of it, and in the initial months, working had helped take her mind off what she'd lost.

There was an awkward pause. Then Luc stepped back, freeing up the doorway. 'You might want to bring something warm with you,' he said. 'It can get chilly outside at night.'

'Oh – right,' she said. She brushed past him and grabbed a lime-green shawl from inside the wardrobe.

She didn't know why she was so pleased to have his approval, but the glowing feeling stayed with her as she followed him downstairs and into the back garden.

'Ah, Natasha, Luc, there you are!' said Caroline. 'Maman is staying at the hospital tonight but we felt we should have dinner together to keep everything as normal as possible. And to celebrate having you here.'

'Thank you,' Natasha said, as she took her seat at the table.

She was relieved that there weren't twenty-seven knives and forks or waiters hovering, and Luc's sisters weren't wearing full-length gowns but the same summer dresses they'd had on earlier.

In the moonlight it was so pretty and inviting: the long wooden table was set for six and lit by candles in glass jars and lanterns strung from branches of the trees above them. The evening air was still warm and heavily perfumed, presumably by the flowering bushes nearby, and she could hear crickets. Luc pulled out the chair next to hers and sat down. She tried to relax her shoulders, but she was tense sitting so close to him, pretending to be a couple when they were almost strangers.

Yet the awareness was still there, she thought. How ironic that it had survived when nothing else remained of their relationship. His scent drifted to her in the night air, a blend of aftershave and, well, him. It made her senses tingle.

'The children ate earlier,' Caroline told Natasha. 'They're in bed now.'

Luc had explained that Caroline's family lived half an hour away, but when Jean-Pierre had become ill they had moved into the château. The children had almost finished school for the summer so juggling childcare and hospital visits would soon be simpler. Juliette and Philippe lived in Marseille normally, but they were also planning to stay until the wedding at least.

Caroline smiled. 'I hear Arthur is teaching you French?'

'Yes. He's a good teacher, actually. I can understand the children a bit when they speak very slowly. More than I understand adults normally. I'm surprised.'

Luc nodded thoughtfully. 'They use simpler sentence structures and vocabulary.'

Just then Philippe appeared with a plate of starters and urged Natasha to serve herself first. Luc held the dish for her while she took some cold meats, roasted peppers and olives, and Juliette opened a bottle. 'Will you try the château wine, Natasha?' she asked.

Natasha smiled and held out her glass.

'Ooh, your nails! Can I see?' Juliette put down the wine to look at them more closely. 'I love it. Who did this for you? Is it expensive?'

'Not at all. I do them myself. It's not hard.'

'And they match your outfit. Could you show me how to do this while you're here?'

'I'd love to.'

'How is everything in the office?' Luc asked Caroline. 'Any problems?'

'All running like clockwork.'

'Caro's managing the vineyard in my father's absence,'

he explained to Natasha. He and his sister exchanged a look she couldn't fathom.

As they settled down to eat, Caroline raised her glass. 'Papa is looking much better tonight. Here's hoping his health improves.'

Juliette raised her glass and added, 'And Luc and Natasha – it's so good to have you both here.'

'It's good to be back, Ju,' said Luc.

'Do you mean that?' Juliette asked.

'Of course,' he said. 'How can you doubt it?' He reached to ruffle his sister's hair, dropping his usually serious demeanour to tease his little sister.

Juliette pushed away his hand and patted her hair straight. 'Because even before the argument with Papa you were desperate to get away.'

'Who wouldn't be with a sister like you?' He winked.

Juliette pretended to scowl but it was clear that she adored him. She turned to Natasha. 'Luc was always the black sheep of the family.'

'Thanks,' said Luc.

'In what way?' Natasha asked. He got on so well with his sisters that it was difficult to imagine.

'He used to go off alone, doing his own thing.'

'I had to – I was outnumbered by girls!'

'Look at him,' Caroline said quietly. 'He pretends he doesn't care, but he's as glad as we are that he's here.'

Natasha said to him, 'You should have come back sooner.' Her tone was quietly accusing. She couldn't understand why he hadn't when his family were so welcoming, so affectionate. This afternoon she'd watched his nephews and nieces splashing in the pool, chasing each other round the garden, and she knew Luc's childhood would have been the same. Full of noise and laughter and love. So different from her own. How could he have turned his back on all this?

But it didn't surprise her that a man who didn't do commitment had left, thinking only of himself, and was blind to the fact that he'd hurt his family by staying away. It made her angry because not everyone was lucky enough to have a family like his.

Everyone became quiet. Luc's jaw tightened, but he didn't respond.

Caroline put her glass down and said gently, 'As long as this is the end of it – a new beginning – that's all that matters.'

'Yes,' Juliette agreed. 'Something good has come of Papa's illness. Two good things because now we've met you, Natasha.'

Natasha smiled politely, feeling like a fraud. Just two weeks, then she would vanish from their lives, but they didn't know that. Her cheeks were so hot she thought they must be glowing in the candlelight. Luc's family would be hurt when they learned the truth, and they were suffering so much already. She had to trust him that this was the best thing to do, but it didn't feel right. Far from it.

Simone appeared with the main course: a leg of roast lamb and a potato gratin. Luc served and they passed the plates along. As they tucked in, she noticed Luc ate hungrily, and she was relieved his appetite had returned.

Though she couldn't understand why she felt concern for him. Maybe she was being sucked into the pretence of being a loving wife.

'So, how did you two meet?' Juliette asked.

Natasha swallowed and glanced at Luc. Should she tell the truth? He didn't jump in to answer in her place as she'd hoped he might, but his calm smile reassured her slightly.

'We met in a bar in London,' she began tentatively. Juliette nodded for her to go on. 'I was with a friend and when she went to get drinks Luc came over to introduce himself.'

'And what did he say?' asked Juliette.

Natasha looked at Luc and their gazes locked. His eyes creased as he smiled, and she was transported back in time to the moment when he'd walked into her life and everything had changed. She wondered if he remembered what his first words to her had been. This was a fine line she was treading: on the one hand, his family had to believe theirs was a happy romantic story; on the other, she didn't feel comfortable revealing to Luc how much that first meeting had meant to her.

'He said, "I'd like to take you out for dinner."'

'And you said yes?' Juliette asked.

Natasha reached for her wine glass. 'I said, "I don't know you." And he replied, "But—"'

'"You will by the time we get to dessert,"' Luc finished in unison with her.

She looked at him. He did remember. She was startled by the warmth in his voice, in his eyes. As if he could still feel the heat of that moment, as if he remembered it with fondness.

He was play-acting, she told herself. It was all fake, for his sisters' benefit.

'And did you know straight away that he was the man you wanted to marry?' asked Juliette. She had a starry look in her eyes, and it was clear what she hoped the answer would be. But that was only to be expected when, in a few days, she would be getting married.

Natasha took a slug of wine. 'I – erm . . . Yes. I thought he was,' she said finally. Remembering the days and weeks that had followed, how she had felt as if she was seeing sunshine for the first time, wherever she went and whatever she did. She'd been buzzing with excitement and energy, utterly besotted. He was nothing like the other men she'd dated, so confident and charming. She was swept off her feet by his exotic looks, his gorgeous accent, and those treacle eyes that darkened when he looked at her and made her tingle with desire.

That was before he'd issued his warning that he didn't do commitment.

Before she'd fallen pregnant.

She twisted the stem of the glass between her fingers and watched the light from the lanterns reflect in the dark liquid.

'How about you?' Juliette turned to Luc. 'Did you know too?'

Caroline groaned. 'Juliette, you shouldn't ask these silly questions. Men don't think like that. They think with their—'

'That's enough,' said her husband, placing a hand over her mouth and winking at Natasha.

She smiled, but she was bracing herself for Luc's response. Of course, the truthful answer was no: he'd never intended to marry her. He'd said as much right from the start. But he couldn't say that to his family – could he?

'I didn't want to marry anyone,' he said, and looked at Natasha, 'but from the moment I saw her I knew Natasha was special. I thought she was different from every other woman I had met. That's why I had to go and introduce myself. I had never done that before.'

'Really?' Natasha stared at him. She'd always assumed he'd approached countless women like that, a man as good-looking as he was, as sure of himself.

His eyes met hers steadily. 'You were the first. And the last.'

Natasha dropped her gaze, feeling the barb in his words. Of course she'd been the last. He might as well have told her he'd learned his lesson and would never repeat the mistake he'd made in getting involved with her. Well, he wasn't the only one who'd learned lessons. She might be here, she might be part of the pretence, but only in body, not spirit. Her heart was in Willowbrook, where her shop and her friends and – she hoped – her cottage were waiting for her.

'That's so romantic,' said Juliette. 'You see, Caroline? You're wrong to be cynical about men. Philippe and I knew from the start that it would last, didn't we?'

'Yes, you did, *chérie*,' Philippe said gravely, and received a playful punch to the shoulder.

'We didn't want to rush to get married,' she told Natasha. 'We were going to wait until next spring, but

Papa's illness means we've brought it forward. I just hope he can be there.'

Natasha looked to her right and saw that Luc's features were set. She could feel the family's anxiety, an undercurrent flowing beneath the delicious meal and candlelit evening in this dreamy place.

'This is why everything's so disorganised,' Juliette went on. 'It's all last-minute, you see.'

'It will still be wonderful.' Natasha smiled. 'I find that the brides who've had the longest time to prepare are the most anxious because they feel that, after all their planning, everything must be perfect.'

'Have you prepared the flowers for many weddings?'

'Dozens. Hundreds if you include those I helped with when I was training and working in London.'

'I think you're right. You can have too much time to prepare.' Juliette sat back in her chair, reassured. Then she looked at Philippe, a mischievous smile playing on her lips. 'Well, I've only had two weeks so I don't expect perfect.'

He pretended to be offended. 'Am I not perfect?'

'Of course you are.' Juliette kissed him affectionately.

Natasha smiled. Feeling Luc's eyes on her, she darted a glance at him. Had she said the wrong thing? She knew she had to try to keep quiet, but it was difficult. She was being sucked into the family's lives.

Luc watched as Natasha turned away. The unsteady candlelight flickered, making her hair gleam and lighting the smooth slope of her neck, the soft curve of her cheek. The sweet tang of lust sharpened his senses and he leaned back in his chair, trying to wash it away with red wine.

He told himself it was relief that he'd got her here, that his father had had so much more energy this afternoon. His own body must have released some of the tension he'd been holding these last few days, and the result was relief, exhaustion and a rush of hormones.

Natasha finished eating and sat back, following the conversation attentively while absently rubbing a hand over her arm. He noticed her skin was puckered with tiny goose bumps. 'You're cold,' he said, picked up her shawl and wrapped it around her shoulders.

She stiffened, as if in shock, and her gaze darted up to meet his.

She murmured, 'Thank you,' but his family would see straight through her if she looked at him like that: bashful and nervous. He draped his arm around her, telling himself this was necessary to convince the others that they were a genuine couple.

As the conversation moved on, he let his fingers explore the creamy-soft skin at the base of her neck and his body tensed. She'd had long hair when he first met her. He remembered that it used to feel like silk sliding over his face when they made love. But he liked this new haircut too, the way it left her neck exposed, and blonde strands fell over her cheek until she tucked them behind her ear. Her eyes were warm as she listened to Caroline recounting some of the antics her children had got up to.

He watched Natasha surreptitiously. *His wife*, he

repeated, trying to drill the concept into his head, anxious not to let slip the truth because he'd been alone so long this was bound to feel unfamiliar.

And yet touching her felt so natural. Her skin was like satin, glowing in the gold candlelight. She looked beautiful, and touching her was a dangerous exercise in tightrope balance. With every caress, he was winding himself tighter, but he couldn't stop.

He told himself he was silently communicating a message of togetherness to his family. Which was a deception, and he knew that was wrong – but it felt right. Look at how the mood had lifted since Natasha had arrived. Look at how she'd known just what to say to calm Juliette's wedding nerves.

Natasha was laughing at something Caroline had said, and her eyes caught the light, sparkling. Heat raced through him. It had been her dimpled smile that had grabbed him when they'd first met in that bar in London. He remembered she'd caught his eye and he'd tried to ignore it, but his gaze kept sneaking back to her. Her hair was tied in a long ponytail that flicked from side to side every time she turned her head, and when she'd caught him looking at her, her eyes had widened in surprise and her cheeks flared pink. He felt as if he'd fallen into a vortex. He was sucked down by a force that was stronger than him – and who would have resisted it anyway when it felt so good? His heart pumped hard.

'Luc,' said Caroline, snapping him out of his reverie, 'you look exhausted.'

Beside him, Natasha stifled a yawn. He remembered it had been a long day for her. Of course, when they got back to their room, the masks would come off and the space between them would reopen. The resentment, the recriminations. She was the woman who'd left him.

Yet what she'd said in the car was gnawing at him – that she'd been lonely, that he'd made her feel like an impostor. It was difficult to marry all this with the picture he'd kept of a cold-hearted woman who'd walked out on him. Whatever her reasons, she hadn't voiced them at the time. She hadn't given him – or their marriage – a fair chance.

And she looked back on the miscarriage as a *blessing*. A small shudder travelled through him just thinking about the chill in her eyes when she'd said it, and his fingers stilled on her shoulder.

'You're right,' he said, and pushed back his chair. 'I'm tired, and so is Natasha, *hein*? We've had a long day. Better call it a night.'

Caroline smiled. 'Sleep well.'

He suppressed a wry smile, certain that sleep would be far from his mind while he was sharing a room with Natasha.

Natasha lay against the cool sheets in the silvery darkness, listening to the steady rhythm of Luc's breathing, knowing he was still awake too.

They'd had a long day and she was light-headed with fatigue, but her body was as wired as if she'd drunk a flask of coffee. All because of the man just a few feet away from her.

Why had Luc put his arm around her? Yes, they had to put on a show for his family, but there'd been no need for him to run his fingers along her bare skin like that. Her neck tingled when she remembered how, in the cool night air, his warm touch had made sparks shower down her spine. Did he know how sensitised she was to his touch? Perhaps he had no idea. Perhaps he was immune to her and he'd stroked her as absently as he would have done a wooden chair.

There was a sharp rustle as he shifted position. She stared at the thin stream of moonlight that pierced the top of the shutters and tried to turn her thoughts away from him, but her muscles were tense. She was so aware of him he might as well have been in bed beside her. Memories played in her mind of when they'd first met and there had been nothing to hold them back from acting on their feelings . . .

Even when they were married and everything had deteriorated so they were barely on speaking terms, the physical connection had remained like a refrain come to haunt them from the past. She'd sometimes believed it was the only thing holding their relationship together, the wispy remains of a spider's web. When they'd made love, it had been an escape from the hostility. The bitterness was suspended for a short spell of tenderness and heat.

A flame curled deep in her stomach and she rolled onto her side with a sigh.

Why did he still have this effect on her? After all she'd

been through because of him, she was still aware of every movement he made in the dark. The sound of his breathing, the brush of his leg against the sheet as he turned over. She pictured his body, strong and lean, his bronzed skin dusted with dark hairs, which used to feel soft beneath her cheek when she laid her head on his chest at night. Sharing a room like this was so intimate that her heartbeat was frenzied. And yet there was a galaxy between them. A divorce.

Squeezing her eyes shut, she thought of that night in hospital after she'd lost the baby. The numbness, then the feeling that the bottom had dropped out of her world.

That should be all the reminder she needed of the pain Luc Duval could cause. He might not have been directly responsible for the miscarriage, but he'd made her feel she was to blame for the accidental pregnancy. Then he'd insisted on marriage and had behaved as if she'd manipulated her way into his life. She'd never know if the pregnancy might have ended differently had their marriage been happy, but certainly it would have been different if he'd been supportive. If he'd not made her so unhappy.

She felt a hard lump in her chest, like concrete. That was what she must do, she told herself, when her body lit up around Luc and she found herself drawn to his good looks and sensual charm: just remember the past. Remember the pain.

Chapter Seven

'Hey, big brother. What do you want?' Caroline looked up from the computer and grinned at him.

He glanced around the air-conditioned office where he'd spent two years working alongside his father. It was strange to see his sister sitting in the old man's chair. 'I'm here to help you. What can I do?'

'You mean you want me to update you on what's going on so you can face Papa's inquisition tomorrow?'

'He's been too tired for that. But I expect you're right. The grilling will happen as soon as he's started to get his strength back.'

She ticked off a list on her fingers. 'The deliveries are going out as scheduled. I've handled three enquiries from new customers and converted one into a sale, and I have a meeting with Luigi this afternoon to look over the vines. Everything's under control.'

He smiled. 'I thought it would be. No problems, then?'

'Why should there be any? I've worked here for ten years. I know the business inside out. If Papa wasn't so old-fashioned we could come clean and tell him the truth about who's running this place in his absence.'

'Do you think we should?'

'I don't know.' She laughed. 'On the one hand it might finish him off to think his daughter's doing it all. On the other, he might finally acknowledge that I'm capable of it.'

The phone rang, and she picked up straight away. Caroline did everything quickly and efficiently. When she'd told him she wanted this opportunity to prove herself, he'd been more than happy to go along with it. He couldn't think of anyone more suitable to take the reins of Château Duval. If only his father shared his confidence in her. Instead, he expected Luc to drop the running of his own business and take over the Château Duval vineyard until he was well enough to return.

'I'm sorry, Michel, my father is in hospital,' Caroline told the caller. A pause followed. 'I'm afraid that's not possible. He's very ill. He won't be back for a few weeks, at least.'

Luc looked around the office. It had been tidied since last week. A pile of new files, all neatly labelled, was lined up where a mess of papers had formerly been strewn. He smiled to himself. His sister had taken advantage of their father's absence to de-clutter the place.

'Yes,' Caroline continued, through gritted teeth. 'I'm running the office while he's away. If you tell me what the problem is, I can help you.' She looked at Luc and rolled her eyes. 'I'm sorry, there's no one else, no. But I can deal with that issue immediately.' Another pause. 'Yes. Leave it with me.'

She finally hung up with a sigh. 'That was Michel Gambier,' she explained.

Michel was an important customer, an elderly, portly wine buyer with a self-important attitude. 'What's the problem?'

'Just an invoice issue. It's nothing, Luc. I'll sort it.' She muttered, 'I could do it in my sleep.'

He sympathised. He could imagine how frustrating it must be to have her capability constantly questioned and doubted.

She clicked open a file on the computer and scrolled down until she found what she was looking for. Luc peered over her shoulder at the screen. 'He adopted the production software after all?' he asked incredulously.

'It's one of the only changes he's agreed to.'

He shook his head. 'Unbelievable.'

She clicked a button to print, then turned back to Luc. 'It's not just Papa who doesn't have faith in me – even our customers don't. I've no idea what it will take for all these old men to believe I can do this. Maybe they never will.'

'Don't let them get you down. You're doing a great—' began Luc. A loud knock cut him short. They both turned. A soil-engrained hand curled around the door and Luigi poked his head in. Usually he was relentlessly cheerful, but today his weather-beaten face was serious.

'Luigi?' Caroline checked her watch. 'You're early. Our meeting isn't until—'

'That's not why I'm here. There's something I need you to look at.'

'Oh. All right.' Caroline turned to Luc and winked. 'You can leave. I've got this. You're not needed here.'

It was only ten o'clock in the morning but already the sun was blazing and Natasha was wilting. She and Juliette threaded their way through the crowds and past the market stalls, Juliette's basket filled with the flowers, fruit and fresh olives they'd bought to take back to the château.

'Why don't we stop for a drink?' suggested Juliette, as they passed a café with tables in the shade of a large plane tree.

'Sounds great,' agreed Natasha, and they sank into the cushioned chairs.

Natasha placed her sunhat on the chair beside her, glad that she'd brought it and that she'd chosen to wear a halter-neck dress of white and mint-green cotton. Once they'd ordered drinks she sat back and enjoyed the bustling scene. The air was filled with the scent of ripe fruit and cooked food, and the square was busy with shoppers inspecting the stalls.

'I'm glad you brought me here,' she said. 'I've never seen a market like it. It's an amazing place.' The sunshine, the heat and the delicious smells were quite different from the markets she'd been to in London.

Juliette smiled and pushed her sunglasses up onto her head. 'I knew you'd like it. Plus, you've seen which flowers are in season here. And Luc won't mind. He's going to visit Papa anyway.'

Truth be told, Natasha had been relieved to get away from Luc – she was constantly on edge around him and she didn't like the way her skin broke out in goose bumps whenever he came near. But she was also worried about spending time alone with Juliette in case she said the wrong thing and blew her cover.

She pulled out her notebook. As long as they were

discussing the wedding flowers she felt on safe territory, and they still had a lot to get through. 'So, you'd like sunflowers,' she said, recapping what Juliette had told her as they'd woven in and out of the flower stalls.

'Yes, but I want something modern and simple. Elegant. Perhaps sunflowers aren't the right choice for that.'

Natasha took in Juliette's long brown plait and her navy dress, which accentuated her slim figure. She'd told her in the car on the way there that she worked as a photographer and Natasha could see that she was effortlessly stylish. Yes, her wedding flowers needed to be as modern and as casually elegant as she was.

'Actually,' said Natasha, 'I've done something before that would work with sunflowers.' She drew a quick sketch, then showed it to her. 'Here, what do you think of this?'

Juliette's lips curved in a wide smile. 'A ball of sunflower heads – genius! Can you really do that?'

She nodded. 'They would work for the garden and I can do something similar on stands for the church. And then, for your bouquets, would you like a few daisies in there too? They would break up the yellow a little and tie in with the white of your dress, but still keep the look very simple and fresh.'

'Yes! That sounds perfect. Luc said you would have good ideas. He's always right.'

Natasha cocked a brow. She guessed that Juliette was roughly the same age as her, but when it came to Luc she was clearly the adoring younger sister. 'Not always, surely?'

Juliette laughed and tipped her head to the side. 'OK, maybe not always.' Her expression became pensive. 'But

I'm so glad he's here. I don't know what we would have done without him the last few weeks.'

Natasha shot her a look of sympathy, and a waiter appeared with their coffees. He placed the tiny cups in front of them.

When he'd gone, Juliette continued, 'I knew we could count on Luc when it mattered.'

'What do you mean?'

'He came back as soon as Maman called him. It can't have been easy for him.'

Natasha found it hard to share Juliette's admiration for him. As far as she could see, Luc had brought on his own problems by staying away so long. 'I'm glad he did. Family is important.' Nothing could be more important.

Juliette poured sugar into her coffee. 'Tell me about your family. Do you have many brothers and sisters?'

Natasha watched as she stirred her drink. 'No. I'm an only child and my parents died young. I don't have any family.'

'Oh.' Juliette's face fell. Her chocolate-coloured eyes, so much like Luc's, filled with sympathy.

Natasha had seen this reaction so many times that she was almost unaffected by it. She didn't ask for the pity other people want to pour on her when they learned the facts. But now anxiety swirled through her. Would it seem strange that Luc hadn't mentioned this before? Would Juliette realise she was a fraud?

'I'm sorry.' Juliette reached across the metal table and placed her hand over Natasha's. 'We consider you part of our family now. You know that, don't you?'

Natasha swallowed, more than a little taken aback, and Jean-Pierre's words echoed through her mind: *Our home is your home* ... 'I – it's very kind of you to say that. Thank you.'

The trouble was, all this kindness just made her feel even worse. Château Duval felt as much like home as an art gallery – full of beautiful objects, but a world apart from where she belonged.

'It's not kind, it's true.' Juliette beamed at her.

The anxiety deepened and she reached for her coffee, avoiding Juliette's gaze. Then she changed the subject. 'Now, what about table decorations – have you got any ideas?'

Luc settled himself near the pool, but not so near that the children's splashes would reach his phone and his laptop.

He'd had a busy morning, first visiting his father, then checking on Caroline at the vineyard. Guilt rippled through him that he was part of yet another deception his father didn't know about. But Caro desperately wanted this chance to prove herself. How could he deny her that when she was clearly so competent? Plus, Luc couldn't neglect his own work.

He made a few calls to the people in charge of his various offices around the world, checked his emails, fired off a few replies, and satisfied himself that everything was in hand. Then he took off his reading glasses, sat back and watched the children run and jump into the water.

He was missing the buzz of work. Whereas other people pledged commitment to a partner, his loyalty was to Solo

Construction. Nothing else gave him the same satisfaction, the same sense of reward and achievement. His forte was for spotting opportunities, and each new venture was a gamble, but most of the time his judgement was accurate and the risk paid off. He'd built holiday resorts, converted warehouses into apartments, and helped to lay down infrastructure in developing countries that would transform people's lives, making a real difference. He ran his gaze over the hillside behind the house, striped with vines. Could he give all that up to be tied to a place like this, small and hemmed in by the constraints of a centuries-old business? It was what his father wanted . . .

Glancing up, he saw Natasha had arrived back from her trip with Juliette. She wore a cheerful dress patterned with large green spots, but her expression was far from cheerful. As she made her way through the garden towards him, she looked anxious, unhappy. He got up to greet her and glanced about him: the children were playing nearby, Simone was in the kitchen, and his mother was around somewhere. He needed Natasha to relax or his family would begin to ask questions. They'd wonder why his wife looked so ill at ease with him, why her brows were permanently furrowed.

He dropped a quick kiss on her lips and she blushed, then turned away quickly and put her straw bag down.

'How was your father this morning?' she asked.

'He was looking very bright,' said Luc. 'He's eating again. And giving his opinion on just about everything – all signs that he's improving.'

'I'm glad.' She nodded at his laptop. 'Are you working?'

'I was. Now I'm trying to write a speech for the wedding – Juliette has asked me to say a few words. But I'm – ah – struggling to find anything to say.' He glanced at the blank document on his laptop, trying not to dwell on the irony of it. If his sister knew the truth, she'd realise he was the last person qualified to give this speech. 'Apart from good luck.'

Natasha stiffened. She narrowed her eyes. 'I can see that writing a wedding speech can't be easy for a man who doesn't do long-term relationships.'

There was a pause while he absorbed her acidic tone. Then he said carefully, 'I meant that my track record – a marriage that lasted less than three months – is hardly exemplary.'

'No, it's not. But, then, you get out what you put in.' Her blue eyes burned with resentment. 'You might have put a ring on my finger, but you didn't commit emotionally.'

His shoulders went back at the injustice of that. *She*'d left *him*.

But then he remembered what she'd said about feeling lonely and realised it wasn't so black and white. He'd had good reason but he had entered marriage as others might start a prison sentence.

The rusty squeak of an old hinge made him turn, and he saw his mother lean out of an upstairs window to pull the shutters closed against the heat of the midday sun.

Conscious that they had to keep up the pretence of being a happy couple, he took a deep breath. 'This isn't about us,' he said. 'It's about Juliette and her wedding.'

Natasha followed his gaze. When he sat down, she did

so too, perching on the sun-lounger beside his. He saw her glance at his bare chest. The midday sun bounced off her white dress, and she ran a finger under the ties at her neck to loosen them. Her cheeks were flushed the colour of rose petals. She wasn't used to this heat, he thought with concern.

'You have to find something positive to say, for Juliette's sake,' she said quietly. 'She'll be devastated if she feels you're not completely supportive. She did nothing but rave about you all morning and tell me how delighted she is that you've come back here.'

He glanced at his laptop and the blank page, knowing Natasha was right. 'How was your trip to the market?'

'Very successful. I've ordered the flowers, and I'll be able to prepare quite a lot beforehand, which will reduce the workload on the day.'

She twisted the ring on her finger and glanced about her. 'Luc,' she said, 'we need to talk.'

He noted that her blonde brows were knotted. 'Go ahead.'

'I'm worried I might give the game away. That your family will see through me.'

He pulled his lounger closer so their legs were almost touching and her face was just inches away. 'You're feeling guilty again,' he said, keeping his voice low. 'I told you – leave that to me.'

'It's not just that.' Her fingers were still twisting the ring back and forth, and when she looked up at him her eyes were murky puddles of anxiety. 'I'm worried I don't fit in here. I don't belong in a place like this.'

'What do you mean, you don't belong?'

She waved a hand at the château behind him. 'The

house that's so big I need a map, with staff who prepare the food – it's intimidating, so different from what I grew up with.'

He wasn't prepared for another rush of protectiveness, this time provoked by her confession. 'You're intimidated by the cook, Simone?' he asked incredulously. 'She's practically part of the family.'

'By the whole set-up,' she admitted. 'I'm not the kind of woman you would have chosen to marry, Luc, and I'm worried that, as they get to know me, your family will realise that.'

He studied her long and hard, then said, 'Natasha, you fit in here as much as any of us. And I *did* marry you.'

'Only because I was pregnant. Before that you'd had no intention of staying with me. You told me that. I'm not a match for you—'

'I told you I didn't do long-term – with anyone.' He dragged a hand through his hair and glanced at the children splashing noisily in the water. 'Marriage isn't my thing, but if it was, you'd be as good a candidate as any other.'

She looked so anxious that Luc felt a sharp tug. But her worries were totally unfounded. She had no reason to feel intimidated or out of place. Why on earth wouldn't he marry a woman like her? She was bright and successful and talented. She was being ridiculous.

But while she was in his home, far from her own, he felt a duty to set her mind at rest.

She stared at him in surprise, then shook her head and gave a wry laugh. ' "As good a candidate as any other" – that was meant to be a compliment, wasn't it?'

He was conscious of his mother crossing the garden, casting them a curious look as she approached. He saw the deep frown cutting through Natasha's brow.

'It was meant to reassure you. Now stop worrying,' he commanded softly.

His niece and nephew got out of the pool and came towards them. He knew why. He'd promised them earlier that he would come back into the pool and play with them some more.

'You can't order someone to stop worrying,' said Natasha.

'No?' He wanted to fold her into his arms, draw her against him and shelter her. He also wanted her to stop glaring at him, like an angry kitten. 'Then how can I persuade you to relax?'

He said it with a smile, half joking, and he leaned in, touched her chin. Their eyes locked. Then the mood changed and the air became charged.

The smile slipped from his lips and he bent his head and kissed her.

A moment later, they drew apart. Her eyes were huge and had turned a deep shade of indigo.

'Why did you do that?' she breathed.

He could have asked himself the same question. 'Because we have an audience.' He could hear his mother's voice getting closer, speaking to the children.

'That's no excuse!'

Natasha's shocked expression should have warned him off. So should past experience. He knew better than to get involved with his ex-wife. The arrangement they had would only work if there was no emotional attachment.

Yet he drew her closer. Tenderly, he slipped his hand behind her head. 'Play along,' he murmured, and brushed his lips over hers again.

His intention had been to touch his lips to hers. It should have been a quick, calculated show of affection for the benefit of his family. Instead, it became something else entirely.

He found himself seeking her heat, tasting her sweetness, and something took hold of him. It held him in its grip so he wasn't aware of anything but her response. Her lips answered his and he felt her breathing quicken, her pulse fire up, and adrenalin shot through him. For a moment he fell into a place where nothing mattered but Natasha, this and him. A place of now, of sensation so intense it pierced his centre. It felt . . . right.

Then he came up for air. And remembered where he was, who she was.

His ex-wife.

The pretence.

He wanted to shake off the feeling that something had taken him over and snatched away his control. His chest tightened. A kiss, a touch, was fine – but it mustn't progress beyond that. They had to stay focused on the task in hand, on convincing his father and the rest of his family that they were a happy couple. And for that to happen, control was essential.

Yet when he'd kissed her, control had eluded him completely.

Chapter Eight

Natasha woke first. She sensed she was in a strange place before she'd opened her eyes, and it took her brain a little while to catch up: Luc, France, a room together.

Even after two days, she couldn't get used to sharing a room with him – it was just too close, too intimate.

Sunlight filtered in through the slats in the shutters, casting light across the room and hinting at the cornflower-blue sky outside. She lifted her head and saw Luc was fast asleep, his large body sprawling from the chaise longue, one foot on the floor, his mouth open. Her gaze drifted to his bare legs, tanned, covered with dark hair, and she remembered how they used to entwine with hers while they slept, how he used to wrap his arms around her and pull her tight against his chest. She had loved that closeness, the quiet intimacy of sleeping together. It had made her feel treasured and grounded, as if nothing could ever prise them apart.

She closed her eyes and took a calming breath. He was a very attractive man, but she had to stop responding to him like this, being so . . . aware of him. It annoyed her that he'd been blessed with such good looks. Perhaps if he hadn't, he might not have had such a self-centred attitude to relationships. She might not have responded to him like a light show when he'd kissed her by the pool yesterday, her body singing and shimmering. Far from pushing him away, she'd wanted more, and her response had appalled her. That kiss had been nothing more than a piece of play-acting for the benefit of his family, Luc had said so, then proven it when he'd casually left her and dived into the pool, much to the children's delight.

So why hadn't she been as indifferent and detached?

She wrapped her fist around the sheet in frustration and tried to work out how to get out of the room without waking him. Grabbing a flowery sundress, she tiptoed across to the bathroom and closed the door. Ten minutes later she emerged, having showered, brushed her hair and made herself presentable for breakfast. Luc was still sound asleep so she slipped out and made her way downstairs.

In the kitchen his mother, Marianne, greeted her with a warm smile and a kiss on both cheeks. 'Help yourself to breakfast. We have bread and jam and fruit – but no croissants today. I've not had time to go to the village because I was at the hospital and it's Simone's – er, how do you say? She's not here.'

'Her day off?'

'Yes.'

'Don't worry about me,' Natasha said, grabbing the coffee pot and pouring herself a cup. 'How is Jean-Pierre?'

'He's very well today.' Marianne smiled, though the lines around her eyes betrayed the strain she felt. 'He looks better and he's not so tired. The doctors are very pleased. He's getting better, thanks to you.'

Natasha's stomach flipped. What would Marianne think if she knew that, since their divorce, she and Luc had become strangers?

'I haven't done anything,' she said weakly.

'You have – by coming here. He's more peaceful because all his family is united and close by him. And it means so much to him to see that you and Luc are happy together. So you see, Natasha, you are helping him – and us – just by being here. I'm very grateful.'

Guilt laced through her. Even if their history hadn't come between them, she and Luc wanted such different things from life. He was determined to stay single and commitment-free, whereas she wanted the opposite.

'Being happy in your relationship is the most important thing,' Marianne went on. 'More important than a job or financial success.'

Natasha was in full agreement: she might have found good friends and built up a successful business, but what she really wanted was a loving relationship and a family of her own. She longed for it, probably more than most people, because she'd grown up without one. But she was no closer to finding it, and Luc was a painful reminder of her failure in that department.

'Jean-Pierre enjoyed meeting you and he's hoping you'll visit again – maybe later this morning.'

'Yes,' she said. She had no idea what Luc's plans were, but she was certain they would revolve around visiting Jean-Pierre. For all his faults, she couldn't help admiring his dedication to his father. If only his family knew just how dedicated he was.

'Good,' said Marianne. 'Well, I'd better get on. I'm looking after the children this morning. Enjoy your breakfast.'

Feeling more relaxed now that she was alone, Natasha glanced around at the rustic wooden table spread with pots of jam and the everyday clutter of breakfast, the chunky blue crockery faded with use, and the oven, not dissimilar to the stove Thelma had used. It was homely, and there was nothing intimidating about it. No polished silver or fine china or staff standing on ceremony. As Luc had said, the cook, Simone, was more like one of the family than staff.

Perhaps he was right, and she shouldn't feel intimidated by this house or his family. If she'd been there under different circumstances, she might have been able to relax.

'Tell me more about you and Luc.'

Natasha looked at Jean-Pierre and tried to hide the spike of panic she felt. 'Erm – what do you want to know?'

When they'd arrived, he'd already been sitting up in bed and his cheeks had more colour today, she noticed. But with that, it seemed, came sharp-eyed questioning.

'You said he travels a lot with his work. How much time does he spend with you?'

'Oh – er – well, he's away a lot,' she said carefully, her gaze flickering to Luc. His expression remained shuttered. 'So maybe . . . not as much time as he'd like.'

Was that the right answer? What else could she say? Anyone who knew Luc must be aware of how much time he spent at the office.

'You don't like it when he works long hours?' Jean-Pierre persisted.

His questions made her uncomfortable. She was nervous that, if he carried on digging around, she might unwittingly expose the cracks in their so-called marriage. 'I don't mind . . . too much.'

She had hated it – she'd felt so alone in his empty glass-walled flat. She used to stand at the window staring at the river Thames below, thinking that if he loved her, he would surely choose to spend more time with her. He would miss her just as she missed him.

She blinked and realised Jean-Pierre was watching her closely. She mustered a smile. Across the room, Luc stood, his hands in his pockets, and scowled at his father.

'Do you ever travel with him?'

'No, never.' Again, she dug into her memories. Luc had never suggested it, and when she'd offered to take time off work and accompany him on a particularly long trip to Australia, he'd looked horrified. She'd never suggested it again, and when she'd become pregnant she'd felt too ill and tired to travel anyway.

'How long have you been married now?' Jean-Pierre looked from her to Luc. 'Three years? You're not getting any younger. When are you two going to have children?'

Natasha flushed, shocked by such a forward question. Luc was equally appalled: 'Papa, behave yourself!' he scolded. 'That's none of your business.'

'Of course it's my business. I need to think about the future of the vineyard, and your mother wants more grandchildren.'

'You have grandchildren already – plenty, in fact.'

'You haven't answered my question.' Jean-Pierre turned to Natasha.

She felt herself go pale. 'I – I don't know,' she said quietly, and stared at the pale blue waffle-weave blanket, squirming, struggling to fight back the choking emotions that had surfaced. She hadn't expected this inquisition. Why was he asking so many questions? Had they already given themselves away? Was it obvious that there was no love lost between them?

'Papa, this is enough,' Luc warned.

That didn't stop the old man. 'Then I'll ask you something you *can* answer, I hope. I would like a photo of the two of you.'

She lifted her gaze. 'I – er – I don't have one with me.' She looked at Luc.

Luc's eyes narrowed. 'Why do you want a photo of us?'

'Because I'm your father. I want one to put here.' He pointed to the table beside his bed, and the little framed shots of Marianne, his children and grandchildren. 'With the others. Surely this is not too much to ask. Perhaps,' he looked at Luc, 'you have one in your wallet?'

Natasha froze. There seemed to be an interminable pause before Luc shook his head. 'No,' he said.

'What about from your wedding day? That would be a nice one to have. To fill in what I've missed,' Jean-Pierre said pointedly.

The corners of Luc's lips curved in a humourless smile. 'I see what you're doing, Papa. Trying to make us feel guilty. Well, it's not going to work.'

'I just want a photo.' Jean-Pierre threw his hands into the air. 'Can an old man not ask for this? Is it not a reasonable thing to wish for?'

'Fine. I'll get you a photo,' said Luc, and nodded to Natasha. 'Come on. It's time to go. Papa needs to rest and to stop asking so many questions.'

She said goodbye hurriedly before Luc ushered her out of the room, but as she glanced over her shoulder, she thought she saw Jean-Pierre smiling to himself.

'Did you always know you wanted to be a flower – er, how do you say *fleuriste*?' asked Juliette.

Natasha smiled. 'Florist.'

'*Oui. Voilà.*'

They were sitting in the shade at the table outside. Lunch had been eaten and the dishes cleared away, the children had gone upstairs to nap, and Natasha was painting Juliette's nails with tiny yellow sunflowers. They'd had a quick flick through some pictures online and Juliette had seized upon this design to match her wedding flowers.

'No, I didn't know. I loved plants, though, and I was thinking of studying horticulture at college. I went to an open day and, by chance, I walked into a talk about floristry. I was hooked straight away. And it suited me better than a college course in the end because I was able to work while I trained.' It had solved a lot of her money worries because, after parting company with Thelma, she'd had no choice but to be financially independent.

The floristry apprenticeship meant she was paid to train in the job she loved.

'How lucky. You were in the right place at the right time, *hein*?' Juliette's eyes gleamed. She was so expressive, she was having trouble keeping her hands still for Natasha to paint them.

'It's strange to think how your life can change direction on a chance event like that, isn't it?'

Juliette nodded.

'But I like to think I would have found floristry in the end, even if I'd taken a longer route to get there. It's something I really love.'

'Did you train in London?'

'Yes.' Natasha put her brush down and searched through her box for a brown varnish. She added a tiny spot to the centre of every flower.

'Is that when you met Luc?'

Natasha glanced at a nearby window of the château. Luc had set up his laptop on a polished walnut desk, and when she'd passed earlier, he'd been frowning with concentration as he took a call. 'No, I'd finished my apprenticeship when we met. I was working in a busy shop in the city centre.' She paused to look at her work. Satisfied, she put her colours away and pulled out the top coat. 'What about you? How did you get into photography?'

'I did it at school as part of our art classes. I wanted to do an apprenticeship, like you, but my father insisted I get a degree first.'

'What did you study?'

'Biochemistry.' Juliette pulled a face.

Natasha giggled. 'Why biochemistry?' It seemed a strange choice if she was artistic, and it had nothing to do with photography, as far as she could tell.

Juliette shrugged, which made her hand move. '*Oh, pardon!* Biochemistry was what my father pushed me to study because he finds it interesting. And it was what Caroline had studied. But I hated it. I failed every exam and gave up after a year.'

'Oh dear.'

'My father was very disappointed.' She smiled ruefully. 'He's not an easy character, you know.'

'No?' She thought of all the questions he'd asked her that morning. He'd already looked much stronger than yesterday, and she tried to imagine the man he'd been before he'd fallen ill. Luc had never spoken about him in the past and hadn't said much during the last couple of days either, so she had gleaned only tiny snippets of information about him. It was like collecting jigsaw pieces and trying to build a picture.

'Papa thinks his way is the right way,' Juliette went on, 'the only way. And he's angry if people don't follow his wishes.'

Natasha paused to consider this. Choosing a career was such a personal thing. 'No one else can know what will make you happy. Only you.'

'*Exactement.*'

She went back to painting on the clear top coat. 'How does he feel about your work now?'

'He's not very interested. I don't win awards or make lots of money. I just do portraits of families and couples.'

'Do you do weddings?'

Juliette grinned and rolled her eyes. 'Lots. You and me – we have this in common. Look.' Careful not to smudge the varnish, she tapped the screen of her phone to show a collage of pictures.

Natasha screwed the lid onto the little bottle and took a closer look, magnifying the images. They weren't the standard studio shots she had been expecting. They were very artistic and unusual. A couple in an olive grove. 'This was an engagement,' explained Juliette. Then Caroline's children were ducking behind the vines. Another family was climbing over the father and swinging from the branches of a tree. 'These are my friends,' said Juliette. 'They love sports and being outdoors – skiing, windsurfing, you know, this kind of thing. They have a lot of energy, and I wanted to show this.'

'You've captured it perfectly. Juliette, these are amazing.'

'Thank you.'

Natasha handed back the phone. She was amazed that Jean-Pierre didn't recognise his daughter's talent, and it made her wonder again what he and Luc had argued about.

Of course, she couldn't ask because his 'wife' would surely know.

'What are you two looking so pleased about?' Luc's deep voice made her turn. He had his hands in his shorts pockets as he strode towards them, and his feet were bare, which explained why she hadn't heard him approaching. For some reason, Natasha found this impossibly sexy – or was it just his legs? She made herself look away.

'My beautiful nails,' answered Juliette. 'Look. Natasha painted them. She's so clever.'

'She is,' agreed Luc, and briefly placed his hands on her shoulders. She tried not to tense at his touch and did her best to ignore the tiny shower of fireworks that burst through her. 'Wherever she goes, there are flowers. On her dress, her nails, in every room of the house.' He circled around the table to face her, and his gaze connected with hers as he spoke those last words.

There was something intense in his expression that made her still. She wondered if he remembered how she used to decorate his flat with flowers. Even before she'd moved in with him, she used to bring them home from work to brighten it. He'd once laughed and asked, 'Are you planning to fill the whole place with flowers? They're everywhere I turn – and I don't even own a vase.' It didn't matter. She'd used empty jam jars, washed-out tins – anything she could lay her hands on – in an attempt to bring colour and life to the sparse, empty rooms.

'Be careful, Ju,' he went on, 'they'll appear in your bedroom before long. They're in ours already.'

Natasha straightened the skirt of her dress. It was patterned with tiny tea roses, and it was true that she'd filled a glass jug with flowers from the garden after checking with Marianne that she could pick some. '*Bien sûr, bien sûr!*' she had cried, and looked so delighted that Natasha had filled one for her bedroom too.

The sudden clatter of footsteps and excited chatter made them turn towards the French windows.

'Uh-oh,' said Luc. 'Sounds like the *sieste* is over.'

Natasha grinned as the children spotted them and bounded across the terrace, their sandals slapping against the tiles.

'Natasha! Natasha!' called Arthur. 'Are you ready for our French lesson? Today I teach you insects!'

'Insects?' She chuckled.

'He loves insects,' said his big sister, Mathilde.

His brother Xavier also confirmed it with an exaggerated roll of his eyes. 'Spiders, worms, beetles – he adores them.'

'Is that right?'

Arthur produced a picture book. He slapped it down on the table and climbed onto the chair beside her.

Juliette glanced at her watch and got up. 'I must go and find Philippe. We are collecting the men's wedding suits this afternoon.'

As she disappeared into the house, Arthur opened the big book and pointed to a ladybird. 'This is *une coccinelle*,' he said, tugging her arm for her to look.

'Cossinelle?'

'No no no. Cok-si-nel.'

'Coccinelle,' she repeated.

'Oh dear, this could be a long afternoon,' said Luc, drawing up a chair.

'I don't mind,' she mouthed, before repeating after Arthur, '*Un cafard*. Ew! That's a cockroach, isn't it?'

This triggered fits of delighted laughter from Arthur. 'Yes!' He picked up the book and waved the picture of a cockroach at his siblings.

They squealed, and Élodie ran to Luc. She held out her arms to him, and he lifted her onto his knee. She was so small, and he held her protectively, his muscles bunching as she buried her face in his T-shirt. Natasha felt a sharp tug in her chest.

'*Un scarabée*, Natasha!' said Arthur. '*Scarabée.*'

'*Un scarabée*,' she murmured obediently, but it was difficult to concentrate on the picture of a beetle because her gaze was drawn to Luc, who was bouncing Élodie up and down on his knee. It roused painful memories of her own pregnancy, but it also brought back the hope she'd felt – still felt – that one day she'd be a mother. She shifted in her seat and, not for the first time, wondered what she'd got herself into, coming here. Everything about this trip was unsettling, but watching Luc with little Élodie especially so. Natasha hadn't expected him to be so good with children, so tender, so focused, so patient. She would never have guessed he'd be like this from his reaction a few years ago when she'd told him she was pregnant.

Her mind spun back to the busy London flower shop where she'd been working. Her day began early, often before dawn, and she cycled to work, but over the last few weeks she'd been finding it hard to get up in the morning, and she'd been sick once or twice on the way to work. She'd taken a few days off, thinking she had a stomach bug. Resting had helped, so she'd gone back to work but wondered if she'd done the right thing because she still felt grey and washed out. Perhaps it was anxiety. She'd been worried about her relationship with Luc ever since he'd warned her he didn't do long-term. It had thrown her. When they were together it felt so good, so right. She knew she loved him, but how could she tell him that now? She couldn't. Yet she couldn't switch off her feelings, either. Working took her mind off it, so she'd carried on.

Then one day a customer came in asking for flowers for a friend who'd just had a baby boy. She wanted a blue bouquet.

'All blue?' In the back room, Natasha racked her brains trying to think of blue flowers. 'Forget-me-nots? Borage?' she said, thinking aloud.

'They're weeds, not cultivated flowers.' Her boss was horrified. 'Anyway, it's too late in the year.'

Natasha blushed. 'How about sea holly or delphiniums, then?'

Her boss nodded. 'Agapanthus and iris, too. Maybe a globe thistle if you can get one. And use lots of white as a backdrop to bring out the blue.'

The customer was thrilled when she came to collect the finished bouquet, but as Natasha watched her leave the shop, the pale blue ribbon flapping in the wind, she had a nagging sense that something was wrong, that she'd missed something . . .

Then it dawned. What if the nausea wasn't a bug?

Not possible. She was on the pill. She tried to think back. But she'd had food poisoning a few weeks ago, hadn't she?

In her lunch hour she raced to the chemist, and that night she did the test. There it was, in blue and white. She was pregnant.

Luc was away or working late, she couldn't remember which, and she knew better than to call and disturb him, so she left a message instead asking to see him. He replied that he'd stop by her place on his way home.

She'd curled up in bed, feeling scared. She could have done with someone to talk to, confide in. She knew a few people in London from work, but she'd found it hard to make close friends: the city was an impersonal place, everyone always in a hurry, minding their own business. She could imagine how Aunt Thelma would react if she called her: she'd disapprove. Not that Natasha would have gone to her in a million years.

She hugged her knees. Luc would support her. He'd said all those things about not doing long-term, but when he realised what had happened, he'd come good, she was certain of it. The doorbell made her start.

'You're still awake? Everything all right?'

She shook her head. And told him.

'*How* did it happen?' His features had become frozen. Bizarrely, he didn't look surprised. 'You're on the pill.'

'That's what I can't understand. It must have been when I had food poisoning last month. I can't think what else it could be. . .'

Her heart pounded like gunfire in her chest because he looked so angry.

'Luc, this is a shock for me too,' she went on. 'We're going to have to make the best of it. After all, this is a life we're talking about.' Her hand moved to her stomach. 'A baby, a little person.' She smiled bravely, a seedling of hope fluttering at the idea. They could adjust, couldn't they? They could be good parents if they tried. This had just taken them by surprise, but once they got over that . . .

'I told you I don't do long-term,' he'd said. 'I thought

I made it clear from the beginning.' She'd watched him pace the length of her tiny bedsit, stunned by how cold his tone was. Fury had darkened his eyes. 'How did you engineer this – and why – when I've made it so clear that I don't want it?'

Her chin went up. 'I didn't engineer it!' She couldn't believe he'd accuse her of that. They'd only been together a few months, but didn't he know her at all? 'How can you—'

'You have proof?' he cut in. 'That you're pregnant?'

A wave of queasiness made her stomach twist. She nodded forlornly at the sticks beside her bed. She'd done three to be sure. He came over to examine them, then stepped away. The yellow roses on the bedside table hung their heads as if the hostile air had poisoned them. She'd never seen this side of him before. He was so angry and intimidating. She was certain he was going to end it then.

Her spine stiffened. She was scared, but she'd have this baby alone if it came to that. She certainly wouldn't get rid of it, if that was what he was hoping.

'Then we'll have to get married,' he said.

'What?' She turned. 'But you just said—'

'The sooner the better.'

Silence resonated around the room.

'I don't understand. You say you don't want commitment or long-term, but you want to get married. That doesn't make sense.'

'It's the right thing to do – for the child.'

Was it? She stared at him, her head swimming.

'And you can't stay here.' He waved his hand to indicate

the room around him. 'This is no place for a baby. You'll have to move in with me.'

It was true that her basement room was cramped and dark. But his anger, his accusations and now this pledge – they confused her. She wrapped her arms around herself. Would it be better for the baby if she moved in with him? He was angry now, but it seemed like he was proposing they make a go of it for the baby's sake. Her heart was full of love for her child already – she had to put it first. And Luc was shocked now, but he would calm down, wouldn't he? Two weeks ago, they'd been at the seaside, laughing, having fun.

And she loved him.

That was the game-changer. She loved Luc. And he was the father of her baby. Hope immediately took seed. They both wanted the best for their baby. They could work through this and build something more stable, more solid. Even if he didn't love her, surely he would grow to love his child.

So she decided to stay.

Within the fortnight they were married, but as they took their vows, he still looked angry. And it was clear he didn't believe that the pregnancy had been accidental, that he didn't want the baby, and he laid the blame for it squarely at her feet. And now, looking back, she saw how naive her hopes for their relationship had been.

Chapter Nine

'Sleep well?' Luc asked.

'Yes. Fine.' Natasha's head was bent as she concentrated on making the bed.

He noticed that whenever they were alone together she avoided his gaze and liked to keep herself busy. She pulled the sheet hard and flicked him a glance.

'What plans do you have for today? Are we visiting your father?'

'Later, yes, but first I thought we could drive to Cannes.'

She cast him a querying look.

He explained: 'You said you didn't have anything to wear for the wedding. I thought we'd go shopping.'

For a moment she seemed about to argue, and he could have kicked himself for phrasing it as a statement, rather than as a question. Then her face cleared. 'That's a good idea. I'm ready when you are.'

A little later they were in his sports car, steaming down the country lanes towards the coast. She looked pretty in a poppy-red dress with a fitted bodice and a flared skirt that emphasised her neat waist and feminine curves. Her legs were bare and slender, and there was a hint of the 1950s about her outfit. His hands gripped the steering wheel and he made himself concentrate on the road as it wound down the hill through the village.

'It's a relief to get away,' she confessed quietly. 'It can be hard to keep up the pretence at times.'

'But my father's improved so much the doctors can scarcely believe it. He'll almost definitely be able to attend Juliette's wedding.'

It was a relief to see his father's health picking up, and Luc was grateful to Natasha. Jean-Pierre had been so pleased to meet her. She'd charmed him, and his mother and sisters too.

'That's good news,' said Natasha. 'I still don't understand why you didn't tell them about the divorce. They all seem very understanding.'

All except one, he thought. His father. 'It just – never came up.'

'Not even in telephone conversations?'

'No.'

He didn't tell her that every time Natasha had come up, he'd hastily changed the subject or cut short the call. He hadn't wanted to discuss his marriage then, and he didn't want to discuss this now. He wasn't proud of what he'd done. He wasn't proud that his relationship with his father had been so strained.

He released a slow breath. He hoped it would be different from now on. He hoped his father would pull through and they might start again.

'It's a shame it took a crisis for you to appreciate what you have,' she said. 'You're lucky to have such a loving family.'

'You think I don't appreciate them?'

'If you did, you wouldn't have left and stayed away for eight years.' She was staring out of the window at the coast. The Mediterranean Sea was just visible in the distance, its turquoise waters shimmering in the sunlight.

There was truth in what she'd said. He should have tried sooner to patch things up.

But there was no point in raking over the past. Instead, he turned the subject back on her: 'You never spoke about your family.'

'Because I don't have any.'

'I know your parents died when you were young,' he said gently, 'but you never told me what happened.'

She sat back in her seat, looking straight ahead, and said flatly, 'My father was killed in an accident on the building site where he was working. Then my mother became ill and she died within a year.'

As if they were mere facts, indifferent and irrelevant. Luc glanced at her cautiously, but her expression gave nothing away. She'd closed up, like a clam.

Still, he persisted. It was important that they talked. They hadn't done enough of that in the past, he realised.

'How old were you?'

'Seven – when Mum died.'

'So you went to live with your aunt?'

'Great-aunt,' she corrected, her words clipped, 'on my mother's side.'

'In Willowbrook?'

'No.' Her mouth clamped shut. He waited for her to say more, but she didn't.

'Where, then?'

She shrugged. 'Near London. Just a dull suburban town.'

'Tell me more. I know nothing about your past – where you grew up.'

When they'd been married it had been the same. Neither of them had wanted to speak about their family or their past. But now he was curious to understand her better. He'd been considering what she'd said about their marriage. *You mean I was supposed to hang around and be subjected to more of the cold treatment? More snide comments about how much I had to gain financially from having your baby?* Guilt had been niggling at him. For the last three years he'd regarded himself as the victim because she had left him and divorced him. Until two days ago he hadn't known that she'd been so unhappy. That he'd made her feel so because he was suspicious of her. Now it was preying on his mind.

'There's nothing to tell.'

'Natasha, you're not making this easy for me. If you opened up more . . .' He took a deep breath, biting back his frustration–

'What?' she asked. 'We'd still be happily married? Don't kid yourself.'

There was a pause. 'I was going to say we might get along better.'

'Oh.' She blushed and he wanted to touch the fuchsia-coloured spots on her cheeks. 'Yeah – well, we're not here to get along, are we? We're here to put up a front for your family, and that's all that matters.'

Her phone rang. She reached into her bag and pulled it out quickly. 'Hi, Debs,' she said. 'Is everything all right?'

Luc concentrated on the road ahead while she explained to her colleague where to find the file she was looking for, but his muscles were locked with frustration and he couldn't understand why.

She was right: this was only about convincing his family they were a happy couple. Nothing more. So why was he so infuriated by her refusal to talk to him? He usually spent his time trying to keep his distance in relationships, and there was no reason why things should be different with her. In fact, she being his ex-wife, he should keep her at arm's length.

Instead, he was digging to understand her better, and he was aware of her physically. He told himself it was because this was the first time they'd been alone and able to speak freely since they'd arrived, but then he thought back to that kiss yesterday. Something had changed then. It had affected him more than it should. All night he'd replayed it in his mind. He gripped the wheel and pushed the thought out of his head.

Natasha found an outfit in the second boutique they visited. She had walked out of the first as soon as she'd read the price labels, saying it was too expensive. But now they were done, Luc was surprised at how quick she'd been. He had the feeling she wasn't enjoying the experience, and was disappointed. He'd hoped the trip would help her to relax a little but she'd hardly smiled at all since he'd told her he'd bought the cottage.

When she went to pay, he produced his wallet and said quickly, 'I'll get this. It's only fair when it's my sister's wedding.'

Her blue eyes narrowed. 'No,' she said. 'I've got it.'

'You can't have planned for this – I want to buy it for you.'

'It's my dress. I'll pay for it,' she said, and thrust her card at the shop assistant. 'Unless you're planning on wearing it too,' she added.

The shop assistant smiled, but Luc didn't.

Natasha was proud, he thought, as he watched her turn away and punch her PIN into the machine. And he felt another needle of guilt because three years ago he'd been convinced that she'd deliberately got pregnant to gain access to his wealth. Time had proven him wrong. When they'd divorced, she'd refused to take a penny from him in settlement.

'I insist on paying for that dress,' he snapped, as they stepped out into the sunshine.

'Why? Will it ease your conscience? You're deceiving your family, but it's OK because you bought me a dress?'

He glared at her. 'My conscience is fine,' he said, though he wasn't sure that was true. 'Let me buy the shoes, then,' he offered, as they stepped out into the sunny street.

She dropped her shades down to mask her eyes. 'I brought some new heels with me. They'll be fine.'

'There's nothing else you need?' he asked, thinking of the lengthy discussions his sisters had been holding about handbags and hair accessories and goodness knew what else.

'No. I don't need you to buy me anything, Luc. I earn my own money and buy my own clothes. I'm not out to make a profit from this.'

He raised a brow. 'Apart from the cottage.'

Instantly, her features closed. 'That's different. It's not about the money.'

'What is it about, then?'

He wanted to believe her, but what else could it be about?

'It doesn't matter.' She marched away from him.

He caught up with her in two quick strides. 'You're being stubborn, Natasha.'

'Yes, I am. And I won't back down.'

Guilt stabbed at him again, hot and uncomfortable, but they were standing in the middle of a busy street in Cannes. It wasn't the place to discuss this.

'Come,' he said, steering her by the arm. A dart of electricity shot through him. She shook his hand off. 'Let's go and get lunch. There's a place I know down this way.'

He took her to an expensive rooftop restaurant where the food was guaranteed to be of excellent quality and the sea view was spectacular. However, Luc quickly discovered he'd made a mistake.

They settled at one of the best tables in the shade. But the waiters were overly attentive, and when Natasha tried to pour herself a glass of water one rushed over and insisted on doing it for her. She blushed furiously, as if she'd done something wrong, snatched away her hand and knocked her fork off the table, prompting yet another waiter to scuttle across and pick it up.

'I'm so sorry,' she said.

The waiter waved away her apology, saying, '*Mais c'est rien du tout, Madame*,' but she was clearly mortified. While the other diners looked relaxed and happy, she sat straight-backed and tense.

Luc remembered what she'd said at the château about feeling intimidated, out of her depth, and wondered if she would have preferred to eat somewhere more modest.

'Do you like the *amuse-bouches*?' he asked, as they helped themselves to four tiny circles of toast topped with crab paté.

She finished chewing and ran her tongue over her lips. His muscles flexed, male instincts on alert.

'I prefer food I recognise,' she said, with a small smile.

Which confirmed to him that his instinct about her was right. Some people would have been delighted to be entertained in a place like this, but she found the attention unsettling. Luc cast his eye around the numerous waiters hovering watchfully and saw this from Natasha's point of view. How could anyone feel comfortable with six people ready to refill their wine glass the moment they'd taken a sip?

When their salads arrived, he waved away the staff, telling the waiter, 'My wife and I would like privacy while we eat.'

'You don't like it here, do you?' he asked, when they were alone.

She pushed her sunglasses up on to her head and wrinkled her nose. 'It's pretentious.'

'It is,' he agreed. She looked up at him in surprise and he smiled apologetically. 'I'm sorry. I made a poor choice. You've been tense. I know you've been finding this difficult, and I wanted to give you some time away from my family. The chance to relax.' He shook his head. 'I should have chosen somewhere more casual.'

She was stylish, and turned heads with her blonde hair and petite figure, but she was also fun. Today her nails were painted like ladybirds to match her red dress. She was anything but pretentious.

There was a pause. 'I appreciate the intention,' she said. 'It was . . . thoughtful of you.'

'Actually, it was partly selfish too. You see, the keys came through for the cottage.' He reached into his pocket and pulled them out. They jingled and glinted in the light.

A look of hunger darkened her blue eyes before she had time to hide it.

'Natasha, why do you want that house so much?' he asked softly.

Instantly, predictably, she became stony-faced. 'You don't need to know why. The deal is I'm here for two weeks, not that I have to talk to you.'

'The deal is we look like a married couple,' he said carefully, determined not to add to the hostility, determined that they should make this work. Otherwise his family would see through the act, and then what? 'We can't do that if we're barely on speaking terms. Besides, it would be more pleasant for us both if we can at least be civil to each other.'

There was a long silence. He heard the cry of seagulls behind him, the hum of cars in the street below.

She remained obstinately silent. He remembered how soft her mouth had felt when he'd kissed her, how sweet she'd tasted, and the honeyed lick of desire stirred in him.

'If you'd accepted the divorce settlement I offered, you would have had enough money to buy the cottage.'

Her cheeks flushed as dark as the terracotta roof tiles on the buildings around them and her eyes narrowed to glittering blue slits. 'I didn't want your money. Despite what you thought, that wasn't why I was with you and I didn't plan to become pregnant. You were as instrumental in making that happen as I was.'

'You must admit, it looked suspicious. You were on the pill yet you became pregnant.' He broke off a piece of bread, his gaze never leaving her.

'Accidents happen,' she said. 'I told you the truth. I didn't ask for anything from you. I didn't even want to get married. You were the one who insisted on it.'

He put the bread down. 'You didn't want to get married?'

She shook her head firmly, and her neat blonde hair became ruffled. 'No.'

'You didn't say that at the time.'

'You didn't ask me my opinion. You presented it as a *fait accompli*. "We'll have to get married," you said. "The sooner the better."'

He pursed his lips. He'd believed he was doing the

right thing. For her. For their child. 'You should have spoken up if you objected.'

'I didn't dare.' She hesitated, as if unsure whether to continue or not. Then: 'You were very intimidating, Luc. I'd never met anyone like you before.'

'You married me because you were scared of me?' He stabbed a piece of chicken, and flicked her a glance from beneath his lashes. 'That doesn't sound like you, Natasha. You're not some trembling little pushover.'

She'd been fighting him since he'd walked into her shop and he liked her new-found courage. She was his equal now – which hadn't been the case three years ago.

She tilted her head to one side. 'I agreed to marry you because I wanted our child to have a home. A real home.' Her voice softened. 'It was important to me.'

Something about the way she said this made him put his fork down and study her more closely. Her blue eyes were steely with determination, yet he saw wistfulness in them too.

'Why?' he asked, hungry to understand the woman opposite who was such an enigma to him.

'Because every child deserves to be raised in a loving environment.'

Why did her eyes cloud as she said that? She'd been raised by her great-aunt, by family.

But she was right, and he agreed with her. 'I didn't appreciate at the time that that was how you felt,' he said gently.

And if that was how she'd felt, why had she described losing their child as a *blessing*?

Confusion flickered across her face, then her expression hardened. 'No,' she said. 'You thought I wanted your credit card and to move into that horror of a flat. Do you still have it, by the way?'

That horror of a flat? He wanted to laugh. His penthouse was in one of the most sought-after areas of London. Architect-designed, it had every luxury imaginable, glass walls, and stunning views over the river. 'Yes, I do. Why didn't you like it?'

'It was ostentatious and ugly and . . .' she searched for the word, '. . . lonely.'

He picked up his glass of water, lost for words. *Lonely?*

The word, so reluctantly spoken, tugged at him. Made the guilt rise inside him again, even stronger than before. He hadn't known she'd felt like that because they'd barely known each other. Their relationship had been short, founded on lust, and he'd kept her at arm's length. He'd been determined not to commit – just as he still was. Yet after she'd left, his flat had felt empty. The flowers she'd filled it with wilted and died, scattering shrivelled petals on the floor.

'You're changing the subject, Natasha.'

'Am I?' She pushed her empty plate away and leaned back in her seat.

'Yes. My penthouse isn't the issue here.'

'You really want to talk about our marriage? I don't see the point in dwelling on the past.' She stuck her chin into the air and looked out to sea, as if enjoying the view. But the little crease in her forehead betrayed her.

'Actually, yes – I do want to talk about it.' He knew he had to get this off his chest. 'I want to apologise.'

Her head swivelled and she stared at him. 'What for?'

While they were forced together in these circumstances, it was impossible to ignore the past. Which was why he wanted to get this ironed out.

'For the way I treated you. I'm sorry I was so suspicious of you at the time.' He took a breath. 'Nat, after you refused the divorce settlement it made me realise that I'd treated you unfairly.'

She studied him closely. 'I told you then I didn't want your money.'

'I know that now.'

Their gazes held and he hoped she saw sincerity in his eyes. He saw simmering resentment in hers and wondered if any number of apologies would ever be enough.

'I didn't give you any reason to suspect it then. I never asked for anything.'

'No, you didn't. But I'd grown up used to so-called "friends" sniffing around after my family's money. Plus I'd had a bad experience with a past girlfriend – a very similar experience – so when you became pregnant I couldn't shake off the suspicion that maybe you'd also engineered it for personal gain.'

He'd misjudged her, but he'd only realised that after the divorce had gone through. When it was too late.

'A similar experience?' she asked tentatively.

He nodded. 'Why don't we get away from here?' he said, tossing a bundle of notes onto the table. 'We could take a walk along the beach and I'll explain.'

When they reached the sand, they took off their shoes and wove their way through sunbathers to the water's edge.

'Before I met you, I had dated a model,' he began. 'She was beautiful, successful, and our relationship was straightforward at first, just as I liked it. But she was nearing thirty and her luck changed. She lost a big contract, she was dropped by her agency, and suddenly the work dried up. She became clingy, wanted us to get a place together. I refused at first, but then she lost her apartment so I let her move in with me as a short-term measure.'

'In the penthouse?'

He nodded. 'She assured me she was looking for work and a new place to live, but that nothing had come up. Then one day I came home and overheard her telling her friend that I was her "retirement plan". She was planning to get pregnant, marry me, and then she'd never have to worry about money again. Those were her exact words.'

The realisation that he'd been taken for a ride had hit him like a demolition ball.

Natasha looked up at him. With each step she took, her toenails flashed scarlet against the sand. 'What happened then?'

Luc's spine stiffened. 'I told her to leave.' It had been dealt with quickly and efficiently. She was dismissed from his life and he never saw her again.

But he couldn't dismiss her from his thoughts quite as easily. Her duplicity wouldn't have mattered if he hadn't begun to have feelings for her, and he'd believed – stupidly

– she felt the same. He'd been aware of gold-diggers all his life – that was what came of growing up in a wealthy family – so to discover it had all been a sham, a calculated ploy . . . Well, it had destroyed his faith in his own judgement.

He hadn't made a conscious decision not to trust women, but from then on he had kept them at arm's length. He played the game, flirting, seducing – but it was all physical and he never got involved. And that way he stayed in control.

Until Natasha. Until their baby.

He glanced at her, her hair shimmering in the sun, her expression thoughtful as she absorbed his words. He realised he'd been a fool, allowing one manipulative woman to warp him so badly. There had been ghosts in their marriage and Natasha had been their victim. But she didn't have a manipulative bone in her body: she was straightforward and honest.

Natasha stopped suddenly, and turned to face him. 'Why didn't you tell me about this then?'

He raked a hand through his hair. 'It was still fresh.'

And it had marked him – badly.

'I couldn't understand why you were so suspicious of me,' she said. 'Why you suddenly turned on me.'

'We hardly knew each other.'

'So why did you insist on marriage when you so clearly didn't want it?'

'Call me old-fashioned. When you said you were expecting my baby, I felt I had to.'

Her slim shoulders lifted as she gave a humourless

laugh. 'You looked like a man walking to the gallows when we went into the register office. I should have followed my instinct and run.'

'Why didn't you? I know you think it was a "mistake" to marry me,' he said, quoting what she'd said in the plane.

'I told you, I wanted us to be a family. And although things had been difficult between us, I believed – I hoped – you'd relax over time and go back to being the man I'd first met, the man I'd fallen in love with.'

Immediately she bit her lip, as if that had slipped out unplanned and she regretted saying it.

Something shifted in his chest. 'You loved me?'

There was a pause. Their footsteps were in unison as they walked.

'Yes, I did,' she said quietly. Her shoulders went back. She stared out to sea, her eyes following the path of an approaching yacht. 'Then.'

He heard the emphasis she placed on that last word. Past tense. He also heard the brittle edge.

'If I could turn back time I would have walked away. Told you I was pregnant, then left.'

His eyes narrowed. And what would she have done? If she'd seen the miscarriage as a blessing, would she have ended the pregnancy? 'We made mistakes, Nat, but there's no point in having regrets.'

'You don't have any?'

'I wish I'd behaved differently, been less suspicious, but I have no regrets about having married you. It was the right thing to do for the baby.'

Chapter Ten

Natasha kept her eyes down, watching her feet sink into the sand with each step. She hadn't been prepared for this apology and it had completely thrown her. How could you go on regarding someone as Public Enemy Number One when they started admitting their mistakes, looking genuinely remorseful, being approachable and human? And winning her respect. Because it couldn't have been easy for a proud man like Luc to apologise.

She hadn't known about the ex-girlfriend, but it all made sense now: his over-the-top reaction when he'd learned she was pregnant, his suspicion. He'd felt betrayed by that woman so when Natasha had told him she was pregnant he must have believed he'd been betrayed a second time. She couldn't prevent the wave of sympathy that washed over her, but it wasn't welcome. She didn't feel comfortable bringing up the past like this, stirring buried emotions.

'Yeah, well,' she said, 'it's all in the past now. Water under the bridge. Things have moved on. You have your life and I have mine.'

That made her think of the cottage, of the promise

she'd made to her mother. And she tried to use that thought to refocus and remind herself of why she was there. Because it was easy to forget. In the restaurant Luc had referred to her as his wife. Now, as they walked along the beach, sunbathers glanced up at them and saw a couple. Women watched Luc admiringly, and shot her envious looks. Natasha remembered how, when she'd first met Luc, she used to love being out with him, loved the way he was protective and attentive. He'd made her feel like a princess, the centre of his world.

A smile tugged at her lips. She'd forgotten about those early days. The good times. Before she'd fallen pregnant. She'd often wondered what would have happened to that happy couple if she hadn't. How long it would have been before Luc called time on their relationship. Because he undoubtedly would have. Even now, he didn't do commitment. The man would never change. She cast him a surreptitious glance. He'd rolled up his trouser legs and her eyes kept drifting to his bare legs and feet. As much as she tried to fight it, she couldn't shake off her awareness of him.

'Do you remember when we went to Brighton beach?' she asked.

His eyes creased as he smiled. 'Where you won the giant panda?'

'*You* won it. On that stall where you had to shoot moving ducks. You were a good aim. Worryingly so.' He'd presented the cuddly toy to her, and they'd laughed all the way home because it barely fitted into the back of his tiny sports car.

'Worryingly? Why?'

'Because most people have never touched a gun in their lives.'

'I still have the panda,' he admitted.

Her head whipped round. 'Really? Why did you keep it?'

'I don't know.'

She wasn't sure what to make of this revelation. But she knew better than to read too much into it. 'I searched your apartment when we got home because I was sure you must have a gun hidden somewhere.'

He laughed. 'Were you disappointed you didn't find one?'

'I was relieved.'

A couple of children ran across their path into the sea, splashing and shrieking as they entered the water.

'You really were scared of me, weren't you?' Luc said.

She considered this a while. 'Not *that* scared. Mostly I just . . . I felt I didn't really know you. The real you.'

How ironic that now, with his family, she was seeing a side of him she'd never known existed: Luc the son, brother, uncle.

He didn't speak for a long moment, but stared at the water, looking thoughtful. The tangy smell of the sea carried in the air. It felt surprisingly good to get these things out in the open, all the memories and unresolved emotions from the past. Not that it would change anything. They could never repair what had been so fragile to start with, and so brutally cleaved apart in the end.

'We used to go hunting for wild boar,' said Luc. 'That's how I learned to shoot.'

'Who took you hunting?'

'My father. I never shot any, though,' he added.

'No?'

He smiled fondly at the memory. 'I let him think I was a terrible aim and missed each time because I didn't want to kill them. They were just pigs with tusks. Hairy, clumsy and ugly, but pigs all the same.'

'Why didn't you tell him the truth? Or just not go?'

His eyes glinted in the sun. 'He would have been furious. He would have lectured me on the damage they did to the vines and told me not to be so soft. He was a hard man.'

She pictured the pale, frail man she'd seen lying in a hospital bed, wired up to drips and machines. She said cautiously, 'He doesn't seem hard now.'

'No . . . He's changed.' He threw her a crooked smile. 'And I'm not a little boy any more.'

No, she thought. He was all man. And everything that was feminine in her was acutely aware of that.

'You want an ice cream?' she asked, spotting a small hut selling cool drinks and snacks at the end of the beach. 'My treat.'

Luc grinned. 'You mean that expensive salad from a Michelin-starred restaurant didn't do it for you?'

She tipped her head to one side. 'It was OK, but an ice cream would be good too.'

They bought cones and began to walk back. The sun was warm on her shoulders, and the ice cream deliciously cold and sweet. They were silent, but it was a comfortable silence and she realised this was the first time since he'd burst into her shop that they'd found some kind of calm.

'Poppy Cottage was where I was born,' she said, after a while, 'where I lived with my parents. Until they died.'

She wasn't sure why she told him – perhaps by way of concession to his apology earlier. Perhaps because, the more time they spent in each other's company, the more she felt she could trust him. And because she wanted him to understand why she was there.

Luc stopped and studied her. Understanding dawned, brightening his features. 'That's why you were willing to go to such lengths to get the cottage back,' he said.

She nodded and carried on walking. 'It's not about the money. It's about the place. Its meaning. When the estate agent said they were going to bulldoze it . . . Well, imagine if they did that to Château Duval.'

'Yes, I see,' he said.

'I made a promise to my mum that I'd look after the cottage. After Aunt Thelma sold it, I told myself I'd buy it back one day. It just came up for sale too soon – before I had enough money put by.'

He stared at her, the revelation sinking in. She ducked her gaze away and finished her ice cream, feeling as if she'd bared a little of her soul.

'Why didn't you tell me this before?' he asked.

She wrapped her arms around herself, trying to raise emotional barriers. But it was difficult. They were getting weaker with each passing day and didn't reach quite as high. 'You didn't need to know.'

'It would have helped, though. It would have . . .' He sighed. 'You always held back with me.'

'What do you mean?' She shaded her eyes from the sun to look at him.

'You were so self-contained. As if you didn't need anyone.'

'That's not true!' Was that how he had seen her? She had needed him. Especially when she was pregnant. She'd been so scared, so overwhelmed by responsibility for a new life. She'd felt so alone. 'Anyway, you hardly encouraged me to open up, with all your talk of not doing long-term relationships.'

He didn't respond, and she couldn't tell if he thought that was true or was holding back from entering into another argument. A lock of hair had fallen over his brow and he pushed it back impatiently. Then he turned and began to walk again. 'Do you remember much of those early years?' he asked.

'Yes – quite a lot.' She pictured herself at five years old, running through the long grass at the back, climbing on to the fence and looking out at the fields beyond. She remembered the freedom, the carefree happiness. 'My parents grew their own food and I remember helping in the garden, baking with my mum. Dad used to play the guitar, and the three of us would sit outside watching the stars until late.' She smiled and confessed, 'They were hippies, really. More relaxed with me than most parents.'

'I see.'

'My great-aunt Thelma was horrified when I ran barefoot into her garden, but that was what I'd always done at Poppy Cottage.'

Luc's phone rang, interrupting her. She realised her

mouth had been running away with her and her smile faded.

He reached into his pocket, looked at the screen, and told her, 'It's Caro,' before answering.

Natasha understood from the urgency of his tone that something had happened, and her heart skipped a beat for Jean-Pierre. She hoped he was all right.

'We're needed at home,' Luc told her, when he'd finished the call. Slipping his phone into his pocket, he headed back towards the road. Natasha almost had to run to keep up with his long strides. 'There's a crisis at the vineyard – a disease has infected the vines – and we need to get back to help.'

'Help – how?'

'Babysitting,' he said, with a wry smile. 'My sister needs us to look after the children while she goes to the laboratory.'

They brushed the sand off their feet and slipped on their shoes.

'Where is everyone else?' Natasha asked, as they rushed to the car.

'Marc is working, Juliette and Philippe are out some-where organising their wedding, Maman is at the hospital, and it's Simone's day off.'

When they reached the car and got in, she asked, 'Have you done this before? Babysitting?' She enjoyed playing with the children, but until now their parents or Marianne had always been around.

'No. But the kids are good fun. How hard can it be?' He winked at her, and her heart jumped.

'It's a responsibility,' she said gravely. Fighting down the murky feelings at the back of her mind.

'It is,' he said, and his gaze locked with hers. 'But there are two of us. We'll manage.'

Something shifted inside her. She watched him as he put the car into gear and concentrated on snaking his way out of the city.

There are two of us. We'll manage.

As if they were a team. As if they were together.

Don't be ridiculous, she told herself. Of course they weren't together – well, only as part of the pretence. She was just ruffled by his apology. It had unnerved her. Forced her to reassess everything, ask questions of herself, wonder what might have been.

What if she'd stayed and given their marriage more time? What if they'd got to know each other, understand each other better? He'd accused her of not giving their relationship a chance, and she'd scoffed at him, but perhaps he was right. Perhaps she had to share the blame.

Stop it, Natasha. Don't go there.

What was the point? The past was the past, and she had ten days left of her stay. So she'd enjoyed their time alone together today. So it had made her feel strange when he'd apologised and looked at her with warmth. None of that mattered. He'd only cleared the air to make the time pass more smoothly. Not because he cared. Not because he'd ever loved her. He hadn't. He didn't do love or long-term.

And that was just one of a dozen reasons why she

needed to keep her distance from him and remember why she was there.

Poppy Cottage. Her future. Her plans.

'The sea monster's back – and he's hungry!' Luc shouted. Or, at least, that was what Natasha thought he'd said. Her French was improving fast, but she mostly understood odd words and used guesswork to fill in the gaps.

The children squealed with delight as he chased them around the pool and they scattered in every direction. Natasha smiled and ducked as Luc splashed them.

They'd been in the pool for two hours now, playing games, having races – at this rate she and Luc were going to collapse in an exhausted heap, but the children weren't showing any signs of tiring.

The youngest, Élodie, paddled clumsily over to Natasha and threw her arms around her neck.

'Don't be scared,' Natasha told her. 'He's only being silly.'

Élodie was tiny, around two at a guess, and as the little girl clung to her, Natasha felt a jolt, sweet and painful at the same time. She thought of the baby she'd lost, and she thought of the children she still hoped to have. Yearned to have. And she had to swallow hard before she could smile down at the little girl.

After a while, Natasha needed a rest so she dried herself in the sun and watched the four children pile on top of Luc and try to push him under. She was surprised at how good he was with them. She'd have thought he would be bored by now, but he was fun and endlessly patient. She pulled up a lounger and sat down. The sun was fiercely hot, and when the odd splash of water rained down on her it was refreshing and welcome. She leaned back, admiring the scarlet geraniums that tumbled from ancient urns and the wild rosemary that had seeded itself in the dry-stone wall. This place was captivating. It was steeped in history, and she wondered how many generations of Luc's family had played in the gardens, shrieking and having fun, as the children were doing now. Their laughter was like music that carried through the air.

Xavier was learning to dive, and Luc went to help him. As he pulled himself out of the pool, the muscles in his arms knotted, his swimming trunks clung to his thighs, and Natasha knew she should look away but couldn't. He showed Xavier how to bend his knees, hold his arms straight up, hands sandwiched together. He spoke encouragingly, and when the boy belly-flopped into the water Luc glanced at Natasha and smiled in a way that made her heart flip.

'Better, Xavier,' Luc said, when he resurfaced. 'Remember to roll into the water. You've nearly got it.'

'You're a good teacher,' she said, when Luc came over. 'Very encouraging.'

He scooped up his towel and shrugged. 'He'll get it sooner or later. Children need lots of encouragement. Tell a child he's a disappointment and he'll believe that's all he can be.'

She wondered why he'd looked so fierce as he said that.

'Thank you for helping me do this. I'm not sure I could have managed four of them by myself,' he added.

'I don't mind at all.' She grinned. 'They're lovely children. It's been fun.'

He sat down beside her. 'Does that mean you've changed your mind about wanting a family of your own?'

'Changed my mind?' She wanted a family more than anything.

He lowered his voice so only she could hear him. 'You said the miscarriage was a blessing. I deduced from that that you don't plan to have children.'

All the sparkle in his eyes had gone and he looked deadly serious. Angry, even.

He was referring to their conversation on the plane, Natasha realised, and she flushed, embarrassed at what she'd said. 'You're wrong. I do want children. Just in the right circumstances and with the right person. Our marriage was neither of those.'

She didn't expect him to understand, but she still hoped that one day she'd meet someone who would be solid, dependable and would love her. A man who would make a loving father. She visualised Poppy Cottage filled with chatter and laughter. Noisy meals at the dinner table, a living room cluttered with toys, happy chaos, warmth and love. Her heart squeezed.

Luc turned away to look at the children. Natasha followed his gaze and watched little Élodie as she pulled herself out of the pool and copied her brothers and sister, who were all jumping in now. Despite her small size, she was trying desperately to keep up with the others, her little blonde curls bobbing up and down.

'Our baby would have been about the same age as Élodie,' Luc said quietly.

Unexpectedly.

Natasha heard the emotion in his voice and blinked at him. She felt a stab of grief. 'Don't say that.' Every muscle became stiff and tight.

'Why not? It's true.'

She shook her head. The splashing, the children's shouts – it was all suddenly too loud, the sounds jarring. 'I don't want to talk about it – about her.'

'Our daughter?' he asked, his features pinched with anger. 'Why don't you want to talk about her?'

'Because she's not here.' Her throat had become so tight it was difficult for her to swallow.

'So?' A muscle pulsed in his jaw. 'Why should that stop me remembering her? Don't you?'

'Don't I what?' The emotions were so strong, they were threatening to suffocate her. She was shaking and her head spun, thoughts flying, like snowflakes in a blizzard. She wrapped her arms around herself, feeling cold despite the sun.

'Think about her?'

Of course she thought about her. But she never talked about her. There was no reason to since no one in Willowbrook knew about her. Not even Debbie or Suzie.

She turned to Luc with a stony look. 'I don't want to discuss it.'

'Why not, Natasha? Because our baby was a "mistake"? Because she "should never have happened" and you think the miscarriage was a "blessing"?'

She knew he was quoting her words back at her, and she was horrified at how they sounded: heartless and cold, so very far from her true feelings for their baby. The look on his face made it clear he shared that horror.

'No . . .' she said, trying to get her brain to react, to respond, when her heart was making it so difficult to think.

'Isn't that what you said?' he insisted, and his voice was like iced water.

She swallowed and glanced at the children again. 'We can't have this conversation now. Here.'

She got up to go inside. She could feel tears at the backs of her eyes, and she didn't want the children to see her cry.

His eyes narrowed. 'You might refuse to talk about our daughter, but you can't pretend she never existed. She was my baby girl, too, and I won't let her be forgotten, buried in a vow of silence.'

He tossed his towel down and stalked back towards the pool, where he was greeted by noisy shouts.

Natasha seized the opportunity to go inside and went to the kitchen. At one end of the wooden table were the remnants of the snack the children had eaten earlier. Breadcrumbs and the empty wrapper of a chocolate bar, a bottle of grenadine syrup and a jug of water. At the other end of the rustic table there was a bowl of jewel-coloured peppers, aubergines and courgettes. Marianne had been planning to make ratatouille later. Natasha poured herself a glass of cold water and went over to the window. She watched Luc and the children. Her hand shook so much she had to put the glass down.

How had they got to the point where Luc believed she'd never wanted their baby? It was madness. He was so far from the truth. What she'd said in the plane had been stupid – she'd blurted it out on the spur of the moment because she'd felt vulnerable, felt the need to protect herself from him. She should have been honest. She'd had no idea that he'd grieved for their baby, or that he'd felt anything at all. After all, he was the one who hadn't wanted a family, who, even now, didn't do commitment.

Yet he hadn't forgotten their daughter. He'd calculated how old she would have been and matched this to Élodie's age. She watched the little girl as she bent over to peer at something on the ground and reached out a chubby little hand. Sunlight bounced off her red plastic armbands.

If her baby had lived, the past three years would have been so different, Natasha thought. Especially if Luc had turned out to be as good with their daughter as he was with his sister's children.

But those were two very big what-ifs. The reality had been bleak, and it was still fresh in her mind. How she'd loved him. How he'd hurt her. How she'd lost her baby.

Natasha gripped the stone sink as pain and grief resurfaced, jagged, like broken glass, making it hard to breathe.

Coming here had revived all the old emotions she'd battled to overcome. It was unsettling, challenging. Luc was constantly surprising her, making her re-evaluate her memories, contradicting the role she'd cast him in of cold-hearted businessman who cared about no one but himself and his construction business.

He did care about his father and his family and, apparently, he'd cared about their baby. So who was he after all?

She shivered, unsure of the answer to that question. Unsure of anything any more.

Marianne, Marc, Juliette and Philippe were back by early evening and everyone pitched in to prepare dinner and put the children to bed while Caroline worked late.

The adults sat around the table as they had done every night, but tonight there was tension in the air, and not just between Natasha and Luc. She couldn't follow the urgent stream of French that was spoken, but then Luc glanced at her and reminded them, '*En anglais.*' They apologised to Natasha and switched language.

'Jean-Pierre will be worried sick if he finds out about the vines,' said Marianne. 'You mustn't tell him anything.'

'Maman, eat something, please,' said Juliette, pointing to the ratatouille and ham untouched on her plate.

'Yes, yes.' Marianne picked up her fork and pushed the food around distractedly.

'It's under control,' said Luc. 'Caro's got the test results back and she's having them sprayed tomorrow.'

'He'll be furious,' said Marianne.

'Why?' Luc wondered. 'This would have happened whoever was in charge – me, Papa . . .'

'Of course, but you know what he's like.' Marianne scrunched up her cotton napkin and squeezed it. 'What if we lose the vines? What will happen then?'

'It won't come to that. You must trust Caro. And Luigi. He spotted the problem early. He knows what he's doing.'

'Yes. You're right.'

There was a long silence. Natasha tore off a piece of bread, feeling for the family. It didn't seem fair that they were being bombarded with so many problems all at once. She wondered if Juliette's wedding would go ahead as planned. Perhaps they'd have to postpone it while they dealt with this crisis.

Luc put down his wine glass. 'I think we should tell him.'

Everyone stared at him. Marc and Philippe exchanged a look.

'What?' said Marianne.

'Tomorrow. I think we should tell him everything.'

Natasha's heart was thumping. Everything? Surely not . . .

Luc went on: 'About the vines and, more importantly, that Caro's dealt with it. Not me. How well she's managed.'

Relief washed through her that he wasn't talking about their sham marriage, and she relaxed back into her chair. But her curiosity was piqued. Did Jean-Pierre think Luc was running the vineyard in his absence?

'*C'est de la folie!*' cried Marianne. 'That's madness! Of course we must not. Why would you do that? You know how ill he is!'

'Because it's the only way he'll see how well she's managing the place. We need to tell him so Caro gets the credit she deserves.'

Silence stretched. A gentle rustling nearby made Natasha turn, but she couldn't see anything. The bushes were mere shadows in the darkness.

'You're right,' said Marc, eventually.

Juliette and Philippe murmured their agreement too. Marianne looked from one to the next. 'Perhaps we should.'

Luc nodded.

Natasha watched him. His expression was one of resolve. Now, as in the past, she couldn't help but admire his strength, his certainty. He was a rock for his family.

After dinner Luc went to visit his father in hospital. He waved away her offer to go with him, so Natasha went up to their room alone.

But their conversation about the baby went round in her mind. He'd misunderstood her completely. He'd quoted her word for word, and it was clear he'd been stewing over it since they'd arrived. She got into bed and stared at the empty chaise longue, its grey velvet covering and gilded frame, feeling bad that he had so much to deal with right now. Remembering how fiercely determined he'd been to keep the memory of his – their – daughter alive.

When Luc came in late, she was still awake, reading. They exchanged a few polite words, and then he got ready for bed.

She switched off the light, but sleep wouldn't come. Her mind played over and over all they'd talked about today. At the beach in Cannes they'd shared so much – but at the pool it had all been spoiled by a misunderstanding. Luc had looked so angry, talking about their baby. She couldn't let this lie. It was playing on her conscience.

'Luc?' she whispered. From his restless movements she was fairly sure he wasn't asleep either. She leaned up on one elbow, trying to see him, but it was so dark she could only make out the vague outline of the chaise longue.

'*Oui*.' His tone was gruff.

She swallowed but told herself some things had to be said.

'I didn't mean what I said about the miscarriage.' Her heart thumped heavily against the silence of the room. When he didn't respond, she went on, 'I didn't think it was a blessing that I lost her. I wanted our baby.'

In the distance, a fox's cry pierced the night.

Luc was silent. She pictured him in the darkness, all hard angles and eyes narrowed in that sceptical look he wore when he wasn't pleased. What he thought of her didn't matter, but he deserved to know the truth. For their daughter's sake.

'Did you?' he said eventually. Softly. 'You said the miscarriage solved all our problems.'

'I said that – but I didn't mean it. Truth is, I was heartbroken.'

She caught her lip between her teeth. It was so painful talking about this, so hard to find the words. But she couldn't let him go on believing she was heartless, or that he'd been alone in grieving for their baby.

'I wanted our baby more than anything – even though it would have bound us together and you didn't want to be with me.'

'I never said that . . .' he began half-heartedly. But they both knew the truth. He might have apologised for treating

176

her with suspicion, but he wouldn't have treated her like that if he'd loved her.

'You didn't need to.'

She sat up, hugging her knees to her chest and feeling small in the vast oak bed. The scent of lavender drifted from the dried posy she'd hung on their window after her trip to the market with Juliette.

'On the surface, losing her did solve all our problems.' Her throat burned. 'Beneath the surface, it felt like my world had ended.'

But she hadn't been able to admit that to him at the time.

She'd fled, needing to be alone to lick her wounds. It had been instinct back then. She was used to suffering in silence, on her own.

There was a long silence and she wished she could see his face because she had no idea what he was thinking. She wished she could reach out into the darkness and touch him. But that wasn't the kind of relationship they had any more. She tugged the sheet against her chest.

Then his voice reached through the darkness to her; 'Most women would have wept, would have talked it over, but you lay in that hospital bed and said nothing.' She heard him draw breath, and she pictured his broad chest expanding. 'You were so closed up. So quiet and difficult to reach.'

She asked quietly, 'Can you blame me?'

Had she been closed up?

Perhaps she had.

'I was grieving too. We might have helped each other.'

'No.' She sat up taller. Her heart was banging and the sudden rush of anger came out of nowhere. She looked for him in the darkness, but saw only the grey outline of his large frame. 'Don't pretend our marriage broke down because our baby died. It was broken long before then. In fact, I've often wondered what would have happened to our baby if our marriage had been different. Maybe things wouldn't have turned out the way they did.'

There was a stunned silence. His silhouette didn't move.

'You blame me for the miscarriage?' He sounded incredulous. Disbelieving.

She didn't reply because, yes, she did. At least, a part of her did. It wasn't logical: rationally, she knew it had probably been no one's fault – after all, miscarriages happened – but in her head there had been so many questions. Perhaps if she'd rested rather than struggling to work each day . . . If she'd been to the doctor about the terrible sickness she'd felt . . . And if she and Luc had been happy: what if she'd felt safe and loved?

That was the big one. If she'd been relaxed, if she hadn't been tiptoeing about, hurt by his hostility, if she hadn't been tense, miserable, anxious about the future, would that have changed their baby's chances? Could any of those factors have had a bearing on what happened?

'And myself,' she said eventually.

It was difficult to speak, like swimming against a strong tide. 'Maybe I should have just left. Maybe I didn't do the right thing for her . . .' Her voice broke. She closed her eyes but a tear still slipped out.

'The miscarriage was no one's fault, Natasha,' he said, his accent suddenly thick, his voice fiery with emotion.

As it always was when he spoke about their baby, she realised, and that made her heart fold over.

'It happened. There was no reason for it, no one is to blame.'

He was so sure, yet she'd spent the last few years tormented by doubt. It was tempting to accept his certainty, to lap it up and cling to it. She'd loved that about Luc: how safe it had made her feel to be with a man who was so sure of himself and of how the world should be.

Tears filled her eyes. She blinked them back. 'I know,' she said weakly.

'But you blame yourself – and me. It was nobody's fault. Understand?'

Chapter Eleven

She said, 'I know', but in the darkness, she sounded unsure, as if she was holding back tears. And he realised this was why she hadn't wanted to speak about their baby every time he'd brought it up – because she'd been fighting the pain and the loss.

The same emotions he had felt.

Truth is, I was heartbroken.

She wasn't cold or heartless. Why had he believed her when she'd pretended she was?

Because she put on a good front. She withdrew into herself, making it impossible for him to know what she was thinking or feeling. It had been the same when they were married.

He heard the rustle of fabric. A faint sliver of light slanted in through the shutter on to the bed and he saw her make a jerky movement, as if she was wiping away tears. That small gesture of vulnerability tugged at him. It made him want to reach out to her in the darkness, climb into bed with her and draw her into his arms. He put one foot on the floor to go to her – then stopped himself.

He couldn't.

He'd promised her this wouldn't be a sordid arrangement, and even if he hadn't made that promise, they'd already made their mistakes: they weren't going to be foolish enough to repeat them. He didn't do relationships. He'd only brought her here because his father had made it necessary for him to do so. He and Natasha must not become emotionally involved.

And yet he felt involved.

Emotions were piling up inside him, creating pressure, straining to find an outlet. Speaking about their baby, she'd sounded so lost. Her voice had cracked with pain, and he felt her grief. He was aching to hold her, to console and comfort her.

She sniffed, and that was the last straw.

He crossed the room so fast his feet hardly touched the cold tiles. He sank on to the bed behind her and put his arms around her, leaned his head against hers. Her hair was like satin against his cheek and when she gripped his arms he felt a jolt. She clung to him, and he held her like that for a long moment. Warm. Safe. Close.

Then he whispered, 'It wasn't your fault, it wasn't mine. Losing our baby was just one of those terrible things life can throw at you . . .' His voice became hoarse. 'Like my father's illness.'

He turned his head away, battling against fear, because his father wasn't out of the woods yet. Far from it.

'Oh, Luc.' Natasha twisted round and reached out. Cupping his chin, she brought his head back to face her. The whites of her eyes were grey ovals in the darkness. Her breath was a warm whisper on his face.

'Your father will be OK,' she said, her voice husky.

Her fingers stroked his jaw and lust shot through him, sharp and fierce. The air became thick with emotion. With need.

The moment hung, suspended. Time became heartbeats, quick breaths, a look that he couldn't see in the dark. He'd never felt closer to her. To anyone.

Their heads leaned in and their mouths found each other. It was a hungry kiss, a desperate one, weighted with grief and pain and anxiety from the past, for the future. She smelt sweet, of sunlight and peaches, and he buried his fingers in her hair, pulling her to him, needing to feel her closer, pressed harder against him. And she kissed him back just as hungrily.

Her breathing became shallow and urgent and she moaned against his mouth, her hands grasping at him frantically. He felt the softness of her breasts against his chest, the dip of her spine as she arched against him, and he cursed as his body kicked in response.

He tore his mouth away from hers and pressed her head to his chest.

'Natasha,' he murmured into her hair, his voice loaded with frustration.

Because this couldn't happen.

It was just lust, heat-of-the-moment stuff – the kind of thing they would regret in the morning. The kind of thing that had led to her pregnancy.

'We can't – we shouldn't,' he said, and drew away.

Though it was the hardest thing to let go of her.

She didn't say anything. She didn't have to. After all,

she'd told him she wanted a family but with the right person, in the right circumstances. Not with him. Of course not with him.

He was her ex, and she'd only agreed to come here because she wanted the cottage, because it meant so much to her. He understood that now. He understood her.

He got up and went back to the chaise longue, pulled the sheet up around him, and lay back, breathing deeply to try to dispel the tension that gripped him.

It didn't work.

Across the room, he heard her lie down and then become still.

He sighed, cursing himself because he'd gone to her wanting to comfort her, but all he'd done was make things worse.

Sleep slowly released her and Natasha's eyes drifted open. She had a sinking feeling even before the memory of last night properly hit her. Then she buried her head in the pillow and bit back a groan.

'Good morning,' Luc said, when she sat up a few moments later.

Damn. She'd hoped to get up before he woke. But, no, his eyes were definitely open, though he was carefully avoiding looking at her.

'Morning,' she muttered. Her toes curled beneath the sheets.

She was at a loss for what to say, and apparently Luc was too. It rapidly became clear that he regretted what had happened as much as she did. The room fell silent, as if even the elegant antique furniture, which had borne witness to their fumble in the dark, shared their embarrassment.

She glanced at the en-suite bathroom. 'Erm – do you want to shower first?'

'No,' he said quickly. 'You go ahead.'

She nodded, and pattered across the cold tiles, then shut the door and leaned her head against it. Oh, God, things couldn't be more awkward than they were now.

When she'd finished in the shower, she waited until he'd gone into the en-suite, then dressed hurriedly, hoping she would have left their room before he emerged.

She tugged on her underwear and glared at the spot on the bed where last night he'd joined her. How had she got so carried away? She'd been so enchanted by his touch that she'd forgotten who he was, and how dangerous was that? How far would she have gone?

Her skin tingled as she remembered the hunger of his touch, urgent yet tender, the feverish sound of his breathing. She'd wanted to pull him down over her, to wrap herself around him.

She'd wanted to make love.

She zipped up her skirt, appalled at herself. Thank goodness he'd had the sense to pull away.

Even if she'd felt bereft.

Even if the bed had felt empty, the sheets cold without him.

She smoothed her camisole top, slipped his ring onto her finger and tried to be more positive. At least she'd cleared the air and explained how she'd really felt about their baby. It was a weight off her chest, as if she'd released something that had been bottled up for years. Feelings of guilt, of blame.

It was nobody's fault. Luc's words had laid to rest some of her worry. They'd comforted her. Only he could understand what she'd been through. Only he had been there too.

She got up and retrieved her wedge sandals from beneath the bed.

But he hadn't comforted her at the time, had he? He'd caused her only pain, and though he'd apologised, she would be a fool to open herself up to that kind of hurt again. Which was why, when he was close and her blood tingled and her pulse jumped, she had to fight it. She had to.

He came out of the bathroom, a towel wrapped around his waist, before she'd finished fastening her shoes. Water glistened on his torso, his wet hair gleaming in the morning light. She ran a brush through her hair, then crossed the room. But before she could reach the door, he put out his arm and stopped her.

'Natasha,' he said, his voice gruff. Her stomach tightened at the touch of his hand on her waist and she wanted to roll her eyes at her reaction to him. So much for her ability to fight it. 'About last night—'

'There's no need,' she said. 'It's fine. Totally fine.'

Their gazes met briefly, but she had to turn away. It was completely irrational, but she was certain that if he looked into her eyes, he would see how she felt, how she was barely in control of herself. Silence stretched and she twisted his ring back and forth.

'You were upset. I wanted to comfort you –' He pushed back a strand of wet hair. 'I didn't mean things to . . . develop from there.'

Of course he didn't. She could tell he regretted it even more than she did.

If only her body would tune in to that regret, instead of being so aroused by the sight of his naked chest, his skin still damp from the shower. She ran her tongue across her lips.

'I know. It's all right,' she said, unable to meet his eye. 'Let's just pretend it never happened.'

Easier said than done when it was imprinted on her mind.

He studied her a moment longer. Then he nodded.

Natasha slipped out of their room into the corridor, releasing a long slow breath.

Downstairs, she found Marianne and Simone busy in the kitchen. Simone was dicing vegetables, and Marianne was rolling out a disc of pastry. Simone was humming as she worked. They both greeted her with a cheery '*Bonjour.*'

'What are you making?' asked Natasha, as she poured herself a strong coffee.

'Simone is making *soupe au pistou*,' said Marianne. 'Do you know what this is?'

Natasha shook her head.

'It's typically Provençal. A bit like the Italian minestrone but with courgettes and lots of . . . What is this?' She reached across and picked up a head of garlic.

'Garlic.' Natasha smiled. Everything she ate here seemed to be cooked with lots of garlic. She wasn't complaining. Simone's food was delicious, with flavours as robust as the fierce sunshine.

'Yes, garlic. And I am making *une tarte aux abricots.*'

Natasha followed her gaze to a bowl of fruit by the sink. 'Apricot tart,' she translated. 'Can I help?'

'*Ah, oui.*' Marianne beamed. She folded the circle of pastry back over the rolling pin and transferred it to a ceramic flan dish. Once she'd tucked the edges into place and slid it into the fridge, she dusted off her hands and said, 'You can help me slice the *abricots*, if you like? I hate this job,' she added, with a wink.

'Of course,' said Natasha.

Marianne passed her a plate and a knife, and they sat down together with the bowl of fruit between them. As she sliced them open and removed the stones, the apricots' sweet perfume tickled her senses. She marvelled at how temptingly soft and ripe they were, the flesh darker than any she'd ever seen in England. Her stomach gave a loud growl.

Marianne laughed. 'You're hungry? You must try one.'

'Oh, no, it's fine, honestly. These are for the tart.'

Marianne tutted. 'We have plenty. Eat. You should always taste the food before you feed it to others, my *grandmère* used to say.'

Natasha gave in and popped a half into her mouth. It

was delicious, and her eyes must have widened because Marianne smiled her approval. '*C'est bon, hein?*'

At the other end of the kitchen, Simone placed a tall pan on the hob and lit the gas flame. She tipped in the vegetables and began to hum as she pushed them around the pan.

'I hope you will come back and visit us another time,' Marianne said.

Natasha smiled politely, not knowing how to answer that. She concentrated hard on slicing the next apricot and adding it to the growing pile of halved fruit.

'I mean it,' Marianne went on. 'When Jean-Pierre is better and things are normal, not so . . . *frénétique*. I feel I've been such a bad hostess. I'd like the chance to show you this is not how it is normally here.'

'It's completely fine. You have so much going on, and you don't need to worry about me . . .' She looked out of the window at the garden. The plane trees cast dappled shade over the mosaic tiles of the terrace, and the vivid pink flowers of the oleander bushes glowed in the morning sun. The soft crooning of doves carried on the air. '. . . I really love it here.'

She was surprised how heartfelt her words were. But how could she not love this enchanting place? Anyone would.

'Do you? I'm glad.' Marianne looked delighted for a moment. Then her expression changed. 'You know, when I first came here as Jean-Pierre's wife – I was young, I was just a girl from the village – I found it, how do you say? Too much . . .' She waved her hand in the air, trying to summon the word.

'Overwhelming?'

'*Oui!* The big house, the old furniture, the enormous estate . . .'

Natasha smiled, remembering how intimidated and anxious she'd felt when she'd arrived. 'I know what you mean.'

Marianne wagged a finger at her. 'But that is not how you must think. You must see beyond all this *extérieur*. It is a home like any other and we are a family like all families.'

Natasha made herself ignore the pinch of guilt that she was not part of this family, despite what they believed. Despite how much she'd like to be.

That thought stopped her. She shook it off hurriedly. She was an outsider: she didn't belong.

'We argue,' Marianne went on, 'we're noisy, we talk and cry and laugh together. That is what makes this big château a home, not the Louis XV furniture or the wine in the cellar which is two hundred years old.'

'Yes.' Longing welled up inside her as she contrasted this beautiful welcoming place with Thelma's austere home. Meals eaten in silence, the lack of interest, the frosty, unspoken resentment. 'This is what I'd love to have one day,' she said, so quietly her words were little more than a hoarse whisper.

'But, *chérie*, you have it now. With Luc, you can come here any time you want. You can come home.' Marianne put her knife down and placed her hand on Natasha's.

Her touch was warm. The look in her eyes was earnest. Loving.

Natasha swallowed. 'Yes,' she managed. But she couldn't meet Marianne's eye.

'What's happening with my vines?' It was the first thing Jean-Pierre asked when they arrived at the hospital.

He was sitting up and, other than looking anxious, he seemed livelier. Natasha put her bag down but didn't sit. Luc had been tense all the way there. She knew he dreaded telling his father the truth about the vineyard, but he was also determined that his sister should have the credit for all she'd done.

'Your vines are fine. Caroline has sorted it,' said Luc, as he dropped his car key on the table and sat down beside his father. 'They've been sprayed today.'

'You helped her?'

'Indirectly.'

'What do you mean?'

'I babysat her children.'

Natasha watched Jean-Pierre closely. He was worried about his business, probably frustrated that he wasn't well enough to deal with it himself. She understood completely. She would be climbing the walls if there was even the smallest problem with her shop. Fortunately, she knew from their daily calls that Debbie had everything in hand.

His father snorted. 'Babysitting? This is all?'

'That's what she asked me to do. It was no trouble, was it, Nat?' He glanced at her and they shared a smile.

Jean-Pierre looked furious. 'Why didn't you help her?

You should be in the office taking care of this. It's a crisis – this disease could destroy the entire crop, the whole vineyard!'

'Caroline can manage perfectly well on her own.' Luc added quietly, 'You can trust her, Papa.'

The old man pulled a face and waved his hand as if to dismiss his words. 'She's conscientious, all right, but she's not as bright as you.'

Natasha frowned. How could Jean-Pierre speak about Caroline like that? She had the feeling that a whole lot of stuff was going on here that she hadn't fully understood. Her gaze darted from one man to the other.

'You're wrong,' Luc said, and held his father's gaze defiantly.

Natasha felt a wave of admiration for the way he defended his sister.

Jean-Pierre glared at him. 'That vineyard has been passed from father to son for eight generations. Eight! It should have been yours.'

Luc's chin lifted and he shook his head. 'Don't.'

'If you'd lived up to my expectations . . .'

'Papa, this is what caused us to argue in the first place,' Luc warned, a muscle ticking in his temple.

Natasha stared at him. Was this what the rift had been about – the vineyard?

'No, *you* are what caused us to argue.' Jean-Pierre pointed a crooked finger at him. 'You and your stubborn refusal to take on any responsibility.'

'To take on the roles you imposed on me, you mean.' He turned to Natasha and explained, 'He wanted me to work for him, to manage the vineyard and take over when he retires.'

'Is it too much to ask, that you should take over the running of a business that has been in the family two hundred and fifty years?'

'But you didn't ask – that was the problem. You always decreed, and I had to fall into line.' Metal scraped as Luc pushed back his chair then marched to the window, arms folded, muscles bunched, barely controlling his anger.

Jean-Pierre sank back, suddenly looking too weak to argue. He looked at Natasha. 'Don't you think this husband of yours should put his duty to his family first? He is my son. The vineyard is his right, his legacy.'

She glanced from one man to the other and it all became clear. They were both strong personalities, determined men, each battling for what they wanted.

But she could also see that what Jean-Pierre wanted was impossible.

'I don't think Luc would have been happy to stay here and be second in command or even run a business that is already so well-established and successful,' she said carefully. 'He needs to be challenged, and he probably gets great satisfaction from being free to do his own thing.'

Luc swung round and stared at her.

She twisted the ring on her finger, feeling guilty that she'd sided against Jean-Pierre, but he couldn't see that to try to force Luc to take over such a traditional business would be like caging a tiger. Luc was so full of energy and drive. A man like him needed challenge, new opportunities. He would never have realised his full potential if he'd simply stepped into his father's shoes.

For a long moment Jean-Pierre said nothing. Then he turned to Luc. 'Your wife is diplomatic. And astute.'

'She is.'

'Hmph.'

Silence echoed around the hospital room, bouncing off the polished white floor tiles. Luc's relief was clearly visible as he exchanged a look with her. His smile reached his eyes, and her heart beat a little faster.

Jean-Pierre looked at them each in turn. 'I like the photograph you gave me.'

'Photograph?' she said.

Luc pointed to the bedside table. There, in a small oval frame, was a picture of them both with the giant panda, Brighton beach behind them. She picked it up. They were laughing at the camera. It was a murky day – she'd forgotten that detail – and clouds bruised the sky, but they looked so happy, with such uninhibited joy in their eyes that Natasha's lips curved.

'Where did this come from?' She realised too late how astonished she'd sounded and cleared her throat. 'I mean, I haven't seen it for years.'

'It was on my phone,' Luc said casually. 'I printed it.'

'Right . . .' She absently rubbed her thumb over the moulded frame. They looked like any other couple in love, she thought. And it made her feel sorry for the young girl in the photo because it was obvious that she'd adored Luc – and she'd had no idea how badly her heart would be broken.

Finally, Jean-Pierre said, 'I'm tired now. Go – I'll see you both in the morning.'

Luc crossed back to his father's bedside. 'Papa, I don't want to argue with you. Not now . . .'

'Not when I'm weak, you mean? When I might die and leave you with this on your conscience?' Jean-Pierre smiled wryly. 'Don't worry, son. I'm not going anywhere tonight. I will live to finish this discussion.'

'Good. You'd better. But it was important that you know the truth.'

'The truth? Was it indeed?' Jean-Pierre's eyes danced with amusement.

Natasha looked to Luc for an explanation, but he seemed as puzzled as her.

'You're right. I prefer to know the truth than have you all conspire to hide it from me. I expect your mother didn't want you to tell me, but you decided to do it anyway.'

Natasha couldn't tell if his tone was disapproving or admiring. She knew it had taken courage for Luc to admit the truth.

'I did it for my sister.'

Jean-Pierre pointed a crooked finger at his son. 'Make sure you offer your help to Caro so that if she needs you . . .'

'I have. She knows I'll always be there. But she doesn't want my help. She can do this by herself. She wants the chance to prove herself.'

The old man gave the merest hint of a nod in response.

Then Luc turned, and Natasha followed him.

Outside in the corridor, he held the swing door open for her. 'Thank you,' he said quietly, as she passed through it.

'What for? I just spoke the truth.'

They walked to the car in thoughtful silence. As they got in, Luc turned to her. 'Juliette said you need to buy supplies for the wedding.'

'Is it still going ahead? I thought with the vines and everything . . .'

'It's still going ahead,' he confirmed, and his mouth set with grim determination.

She had to hand it to him: no matter what life threw at him, it seemed he would stand by his family and the promises he'd made, come what may.

They drove to the nearest town and the big department store Juliette had assured her would stock everything she needed for the table decorations. 'We'll need a trolley,' she told Luc. 'I've got a lot to buy.'

They reached for the nearest one at the same time and their arms brushed. She pulled her hand back. Luc steered the trolley into the shop and she began to search for vases.

All morning she'd been careful to avoid speaking to him or even looking at him, worried that her gaze might lock on his beautiful lips or strong cheekbones. But the events of last night had been somewhat overshadowed by what she'd just witnessed, and when she allowed herself a surreptitious glance at Luc, his brow was furrowed, his expression preoccupied.

'Your father must be getting stronger,' she said. 'I've never seen him so fired up.'

Luc shook his head. 'I'm sorry you had to become involved. Unfortunately, this is the way things are with my father. Tempestuous.'

'Were things always difficult between the two of you?' she asked, as they threaded their way along aisles of furniture and bed linen. She was curious to know more about his relationship with Jean-Pierre. Added to that, talking about his father meant she didn't have to think about her relationship with Luc.

'Oh, yes. What you saw was nothing. There was one row when he threw a bottle of wine at the wall, he was so angry with me.' She gasped. He smiled wryly. 'It was red wine, too.'

'Why?'

'I can't even remember. I just know I was a constant source of disappointment to him. And I felt he was always trying to control my life.'

His words came back to her – *Children need lots of encouragement. Tell a child he's a disappointment and he'll believe that's all he can be*. Was that how Jean-Pierre had made him feel?

Her heart went out to him. It was hard to believe this strong man, so brimming with confidence, felt he'd been a disappointment to his father, but she'd glimpsed how formidable Jean-Pierre must have been before he was ill.

'He always put pressure on me to take over the family business. I tried it, stuck it out for a couple of years, but I hated it. Nothing I did was good enough. Everything had to be done the way it had been done for centuries . . . And the day came when I just had to leave.'

She spotted some cobalt-blue vases and picked one up for closer inspection. They'd look fabulous filled with sunflowers. The contrast in colours would be stunning, and they would mirror the landscape around the château; the golden fields of sunflowers and the deep blue sky. She began to load the trolley.

'Did you leave to do your own thing?' she asked.

He nodded and took the vases from her, stacking them carefully side by side. 'I loved every minute of starting up my own company, making my own decisions, taking risks – and the satisfaction when those risks paid off. No one to answer to but myself.'

She stopped. 'Solo Construction . . .' she said, the significance of the name dawning on her only now.

And it was a breakthrough in her understanding of him. He'd gone it alone, and perhaps it had been an extreme reaction to the pressure his father had imposed on him, but she sympathised. She'd also been shaped by the events of her childhood: losing her parents, then living with Thelma had killed the exuberance she saw in Caroline's children. She'd withdrawn into herself, become a very private person, and she couldn't change that any more than Luc could stop being a free spirit dedicated only to his work. She understood now why he needed his independence, why he was determined not to be constrained by anyone. He needed to be in control of his own destiny. He'd be as unhappy working for the traditional family business as he would being tied to one person. Anyone who loved him must see that.

Not that she loved him.

She'd just loved him in the past, and she understood him better than most as a result. That was all. She reached for more vases.

He smiled. 'Yes. I wanted to strike out on my own. Prove I could do my own thing and do it well.'

'And then? Once you'd made your point and established your business, why didn't you go back? Try to patch things up with him.'

'I couldn't . . .' he faltered.

Hurt pride, Natasha supposed. What a clash of egos he and his father must have been.

Luc manoeuvred the trolley round another shopper. 'He disowned me and told me never to set foot in his home again.'

Natasha stopped and blinked. 'Your father disowned you?'

He nodded.

'What about your mother, your sisters? Couldn't they make him see sense?'

'When my father's decided something, no one can make him change his mind.'

She believed him. Though Jean-Pierre was still frail, she'd seen a different side of him that afternoon. In fact, she saw everything in a new light now.

When they were married, she'd thought he hadn't told his family about their shotgun wedding because he was ashamed of her. How wrong she'd been. He hadn't been able to tell them because his father had cut all ties with him. And she'd been wrong, too, to think he'd stayed away because he didn't appreciate the family he was blessed with. She'd seen for herself how much he loved his mother and sisters. He must have missed them terribly.

Knowing what she knew now, she realised just how much commitment he'd shown his father by coming here despite their past conflict and persuading her to come with him. He'd done it all to please Jean-Pierre.

'I can see that he has a strong personality.' She counted the vases and, satisfied that she had enough, pulled out her list again. Luc took back the trolley.

'Why didn't you tell me about your dad before? Three years ago, I mean. I had no clue what had happened, that he'd banned you from your home. You would never speak about it or explain.'

There was a long pause. Then he admitted, 'I was ashamed.'

'Ashamed? Why?'

He barely met her gaze. 'Not many people become estranged from their family. I didn't tell anyone about it.'

Understanding came to her as she thought of her own experience and the difficult years with Thelma. The rational part of her knew Thelma had been lacking all maternal instinct. Yet Natasha had always wondered if she was unlovable. If she'd been a different child would her great-aunt have loved her?

She touched his hand. 'You shouldn't feel ashamed.'

Chapter Twelve

Luc's jaw clenched as he tried to fight off the familiar guilt and anger. The row with his father at the hospital earlier was a reminder of what he'd run away from – the sense of inadequacy, of suffocation. It might have been his destiny to take over running the family business, but he couldn't live with his father breathing down his neck, making sure he followed the traditions and didn't deviate. He needed excitement and possibilities. It was in his nature – the need to take risks, to act alone and make bold decisions, whatever the consequences. But his father hadn't been able to accept that, and the clash of wills had led to their angry showdown eight years ago.

'Why are you doing it that way?' Luc had asked, irritated by his father's approach.

'This is how my father did it. And his father before him.'

Luc had picked up a sheet of paper he'd printed out and shown it to him. 'This software would do the same thing as your handwritten notebooks, but it would make the calculations a hundred times faster, and—'

'No. This is how it's done. It's always been like this.'

His father glared at him. It was the same look he'd given him as a boy. It said, *Do as you're told.*

Luc scowled. 'That doesn't mean we can't develop or evolve. This is simple to use and more efficient, more cost-effective.'

'Our wine is one of the best in the region!' his father had shouted. His face was red, his eyes bulging with fury. 'Do you think that's happened because we skimp on cost? The Duval name is about quality and heritage and – and tradition!'

'I know that!' Luc was shouting, too, now. 'But this is the twenty-first century. We use computers, not scribbled notebooks that can be mislaid. We drive cars instead of horses and carts. Things have moved on. *You* need to move on. But, no, you never want anything to change, you're so – so stuck in your ways!'

He slapped the sheet of paper onto the desk and marched towards the door.

'Where do you think you're going?' Jean-Pierre roared after him.

'Out.'

'Don't you dare walk out! It's three o'clock. You're paid to stay until—'

'I quit!' Luc yelled. The blood rushed to his face, and he felt beads of sweat spring up on his forehead. 'I quit because I'm wasting my time here. You never listen to anything I suggest, anything! You're too bloody stubborn and you think you know everything!'

His footsteps echoed around the office as he stamped away.

His father's voice was a low growl. 'If you walk out of that door you will never be welcome here again. Not in this office, not in my house.'

Luc stopped. His gaze fixed on the stone archway in front of him as the threat sank in. His hands had become tight fists at his sides. He turned. His father's face was creased with anger. Luc said quietly, 'Fine. If that's how you want it, so be it.'

And he had walked out.

Now Luc gripped the handle of the shopping trolley with both hands. If he had known then how much it would cost him – breaking contact with his mother, his sisters and Caro's children – would he still have walked out of that door? He glowered at the fire-exit sign ahead, unsure. Solo Construction was his life. It had brought him so much challenge, recognition and satisfaction. But striking out on his own and starting up his business had come at such cost.

Could there be a way of having both in his life: his business and his family? If there was, he couldn't see it. But at least his father's illness had given him the opportunity to come home. It was the one good thing that had come of all this. He glanced at Natasha. Okay, one of two good things, perhaps.

'He can't take all the blame, though. I was a pig-headed young man. Rebellious by nature. Determined to be my own person.'

'You *are* pig-headed,' Natasha said, eyes gleaming, 'but he could have shown more understanding. It sounds like he heaped a lot of pressure on you. And he didn't listen to what you wanted or needed.'

'Perhaps.'

'After he cut you off, did you still see your mother and sisters?' Natasha asked.

He shook his head. 'For a long time I was angry with my mother for not standing up to him. And my sisters – it was easier not to see them. He forbade it and I didn't want them to get into trouble. But we spoke on the phone and met from time to time. I bought a villa not far from here so I could see them.' The house had sea views and he'd had it renovated to his specifications: in theory it should have been perfect. But in his mind it served a purpose, nothing more. Only Château Duval, where he'd grown up, could ever feel like home.

She stopped and faced him. 'I think it's wonderful that you were able to put aside your differences and be here when he needed you,' she said softly, with a look in her eyes that made him think back to last night when he'd held her, when his mouth had hunted for hers in the dark.

His gaze was drawn to the fullness of her lips, the soft slope of her cheek. Tiny details that shouldn't matter, but his body was homing in on them, aching to touch. 'He's my father. Anyone would have done the same.'

'I'm not sure that's true. Especially not after he'd disowned you.'

'If I'd been the son he'd hoped for, that wouldn't have happened.'

She placed her hand on his and her expression was one of understanding. The unexpected contact sent a dart of heat through him, reminding him again of last night in the dark when they'd kissed. 'Just because you're family doesn't automatically mean you'll get on. Sometimes personalities clash. He made you feel bad for leaving, but I think you did the right thing. You would never have been happy here.'

He wasn't sure why her approval meant so much to him, but it felt like the sun had come out when she looked at him with such warmth in her eyes.

'If he hadn't become ill, do you think you'd have settled your differences eventually?'

He thought about this. 'I don't know. In this respect we're both the same: too proud to back down.' Anyway, they hadn't completely resolved things, he thought. 'He wants me to take over the business, but he's foolish. Caroline will do a fantastic job. She *is* doing a fantastic job.'

'Maybe when he sees that, he'll rethink.'

'Maybe,' he said half-heartedly. Because his father didn't often rethink anything.

She ticked the last item off her list and put it away. 'I've got everything. We'd better go back. There's so much to do for the wedding.'

'Of course,' he said, though he felt a heaviness at the thought of going home.

'I'll need a lot of help. Juliette said she'd lend a hand but I don't want to rely on her too much. I mean, she's the bride, she needs to . . .'

He frowned, zoning out as he realised he'd begun to covet these moments alone with Natasha.

It was because they could relax, he told himself. Because keeping up the charade was a strain.

Except it wasn't, really, was it? It was reminding himself that they weren't a real couple, that she wasn't his to touch or hold or confide in, that was becoming the real strain. Like last night when he'd held her.

She headed towards the lift, and when she realised he hadn't followed, she stopped and turned back to him. Her blue eyes caught the light and gleamed. Desire fizzed through him.

They'd agreed to pretend last night hadn't happened, but the scene, the sounds, the heat were embedded in his memory and he couldn't delete them. He didn't want to be attracted to her – his rational mind could cite a dozen reasons why he shouldn't go there – but his body wasn't listening.

He wanted her. And with each passing day, passing hour, the connection was growing stronger.

'He took the news better than I'd expected,' Luc told his mother, thinking back to his visit that morning with Natasha.

They stood by the window. A slight breeze ruffled the palm trees in the car park.

Marianne looked over her shoulder at his father, who was snoring. 'Good. I'm glad. And you're right – it's better to be honest with him. Caroline is desperate to be given more responsibility.'

The door opened quietly and a nurse came in. She checked the readings on the machines, told them she'd be back later when Jean-Pierre was awake, then slipped away again.

'Do you think being ill has mellowed him a little?' asked Luc.

Marianne laughed. 'Perhaps. It wouldn't be a bad thing, would it?'

'Definitely not.'

Marianne patted his cheek. 'He's so happy that you're back, and that the rift is over. He won't tell you that, of course, but he is.'

'How do you know if he doesn't say it?' Luc was glad she was pleased. He wasn't convinced his father was. Satisfied, perhaps, that his son carried out his wishes and come when he was summoned, with his wife, as instructed. Where his father was concerned it was all about orders being given and obeyed. Luc had never been very good at obeying.

'I know him well. We've been married a long time. Thirty-five years.'

He nodded. 'He doesn't argue with you the way he does with me.'

'True. But he's still difficult and bossy.'

In the car park below, a car horn sounded. Two drivers were arguing over a space. One wound down his window and shook his fist.

Marianne continued, 'Don't take it personally, Luc.'

He laughed sharply. 'How can I not? I'm the only one who disappoints him constantly, who doesn't toe the line and live up to his expectations.' He strode across the room and back again. 'I don't know why he has those expectations of me. Why not of Juliette or Caroline? With them he's a hundred times more accepting.'

She tutted her disagreement. 'They argue with him too. Anyway, your father is old-fashioned. You know this. He grew up in a time when the son of the family was expected to follow in his father's footsteps. Just like his father had, and his father before that.'

'Oh, please. The world has moved on.'

'It has. But Jean-Pierre is slow to keep up with progress. Think of how Caroline suffers for this, too. She battles with him constantly to modernise the vineyard.'

'I know.' His sister must have the patience of a saint.

'I tell him he's lucky she has such a passion for the place. But he doesn't see it.' She touched Luc's cheek again affectionately, and the gesture reminded him of when he was a small boy and she used to do the same. 'So don't go feeling sorry for yourself. He's a grumpy old man, but we love him in spite of it.'

'Hm. Thirty-five years,' he said, with a low whistle, and winked. 'I don't know how you've stuck it out that long.'

She laughed and gazed fondly at her husband. 'Oh, they've been happy years, all of them.'

'Really?'

'Really. He has many good qualities, too, you know.'

'Remind me of what they are.'

She smiled and pretended to grapple for things to say. 'He's persistent. He's fiercely protective of his family.' Her smile faded and she became serious. 'He would do anything to help you and your sisters.'

Luc shook his head. 'Ju and Caro, perhaps, but not me. I didn't see him for seven years.' And even then, at Élodie's christening, his father had approached him warily, not with open arms. They had exchanged a few stiff words. It hadn't been an emotional reunion.

'And that broke his heart,' she said softly. 'He thought of you every day.'

'Then why didn't he say something?'

'He's too proud. And so are you. He hoped you would make the first move.'

The room fell silent. Luc watched the red line on the monitor by the bed; it beat in time with his father's heart, spiking and dipping, like waves at sea. He'd thought about making that first move so many times . . . but he hadn't. His mother was right.

She turned to him. 'And another thing about your father. He's hard-working. He's given his all to the estate, to the vines, to making the Duval wine the best it can be.'

Luc frowned at his father's sleeping form. Why dedicate your life to a wine? Was it more important than the relationships you forged? He sighed. Who was he to judge? He had an international business – but no partner, no family of his own to share it with. Who was he doing it for? Perhaps he and his father were not so different, after all.

'He never expected to, of course,' Marianne murmured, staring pensively at her husband.

'What?'

Her eyes clouded with a guilty look. 'I probably shouldn't tell you . . . He would never speak of it.'

'Of what?' His curiosity was aroused now.

'You knew his younger brother – before he moved away.'

'Uncle Armand? I remember him vaguely.' He'd emigrated to Canada when Luc was small.

'But you never knew Claude. Your father's big brother.'

Luc had heard the name mentioned occasionally, by other people, villagers mostly. 'Papa never talked about him.'

Marianne pressed her lips together. 'This is how your father deals with sadness and pain. He locks them away and refuses to admit that they affect him.' Her shoulders lifted in a shrug. 'Claude died when Jean-Pierre had just got his first promotion in the army.'

'Promotion?' He remembered his father talking about a brief spell in the army. 'I thought he'd done a year's military service, that's all.'

She shook her head. 'Five years, and he planned to stay. He loved it, and was tipped to go far. His first posting was in the Far East, and he hoped to see the world . . .'

Yes, Luc could well imagine he had loved the military. The discipline, the rules, its regimented nature would all have appealed to his father.

Marianne went on: '. . . and Claude was the eldest, already helping with the family business. He was supposed to take over from their father. But he died suddenly. He was taken ill and within a week he was gone. So your father came home.'

'And took over the vineyard?'

She nodded. 'His parents were devastated to lose their son so young. If Jean-Pierre hadn't stepped up to the plate, who knows what would have happened to the vineyard and the wine? They leaned on him. And they never got over losing Claude. Your grandparents died a few years later.'

Luc blinked. His father had sacrificed his preferred career to carry out his family's wishes. 'He's never said a word. How did he feel about taking it on?' Had he resented the role he was thrust into? Had he felt stifled coming back to the château?

'I don't know. He wouldn't discuss it. He just got on with it.'

Without complaint, presumably. Was that why he'd been so angry when Luc had refused to do the same? 'What about his hope for a career in the military?'

'He never spoke of it again.'

Luc stared down at the car park. The tarmac shimmered in the afternoon sun, but the air-conditioning in the hospital room lent the air a pleasant chill. He tried to imagine what it must have been like for his father to be left holding the fort and coping with the aftermath of his brother's death, his parents' grief, their failing health, and his own sadness.

'How long are you two going to talk about me as if I'm not here?'

Luc and Marianne spun round. Jean-Pierre was watching them through narrowed eyes.

'Jean-Pierre!' cried his mother. She rushed over to his side. 'We thought you were asleep! How long have you been awake, you sly devil?'

Luc hung back near the window.

'I'm not a sly anything. I'm innocently resting while you discuss me as if I were a cadaver.'

She and Luc exchanged a look. 'Of course we weren't. We were discussing you as if you were a cantankerous old fool who drives us all up the wall.' She stroked the white hair back from his brow until he batted away her hand.

'Well, that's nothing new.'

'How are you feeling? Can I get you anything?'

'A new heart. One that works.'

Marianne laughed. 'How about some water? Or something to eat? And don't ask for chocolate because you know you're not allowed . . .'

Luc cleared his throat and made for the door. 'I'll go and tell the nurse you're awake – she said it was time for you to take your medication.'

He ducked out of the room and into the corridor. He needed a little space to process all he'd just learned about his father.

Chapter Thirteen

'Natasha, I love your flower arrangements,' said Marianne. She reached across the remnants of their lunch to touch the roses and sprigs of greenery Natasha had tucked into an empty bottle. 'They're beautiful. Did you really find all these in the garden?'

'All of them . . .' She enjoyed exploring the gardens early each morning, taking different paths each time, getting to know the grounds and seeing which plants were growing. There were lots of flowers she couldn't identify but they seemed to thrive in the arid conditions. 'Though some might be weeds,' she added. 'The flowers that grow wild here are so beautiful.'

Marianne dismissed this with a wave of her hand. 'Weeds, wildflowers – they can be beautiful too. All flowers were wild once. We've just decided to cultivate some and not others.' She picked up her fan and flicked it open. Over the last few days the temperature had soared.

'I love wildflowers,' said Juliette, as she stacked the children's empty plates and moved them aside to make room for their colouring books. 'Daisies, violets and . . . how do you say? *Myosotis?*'

'Forget-me-nots.' Natasha smiled. 'Yes, I like them too.

Their blue is so intense. They look small and delicate, but they're tough as old boots and they seed themselves everywhere. Once they're introduced into a garden, you can never get rid of them.' They used to grow at Poppy Cottage, clouds of blue with tiny yellow eyes that brushed against her legs as she ran up the garden path. She felt a spark of resolve. When Poppy Cottage was hers again, she'd fill the garden with forget-me-nots, lupins and rambling roses. It would be packed with colour and scent, just like her shop.

'When are the flowers arriving for the wedding?' asked Luc.

'Tomorrow morning,' said Juliette. 'I'll need to borrow the van to collect them.'

Natasha knew they'd have an early start because it was a two-hour round trip. Fortunately, she had everything else ready – wire, pins, ribbon – so she planned to make a start on the big arrangements as soon as they got back, then deliver them to the church on Friday. There was a lot for one person to do alone, but she was well organised and confident that she had it all in hand.

'I can pick them up with Natasha,' said Luc. 'You'll be busy enough tomorrow.'

Juliette beamed. 'That would be great. Thanks, Luc.'

He turned to Natasha. 'Where will we store the flowers?'

'I need somewhere as cool as possible. Juliette mentioned the wine cellar.'

'*La cave?*' asked Marianne.

Luc nodded. 'Good idea.'

'It would be great to get it all set up this afternoon, actually. I'm going to have a lot to do tomorrow.'

'Why don't I show you now?' Luc offered. 'I can help you.'

Natasha's sandals tapped on the stone steps as she followed Luc. When he reached the bottom, she heard the click of a switch and lights illuminated a vaulted room with a large solid table in the centre. Wine racks lined one wall from floor to ceiling, and ancient barrels were stacked on their sides along another. The smell of old wood and cool stone was inviting. Natasha looked around. It was dusty and shrouded in cobwebs, but the temperature was much lower than it was outside: perfect for storing the flowers.

'Is this all wine for the house?' she asked. There must have been dozens, if not hundreds, of bottles, and at the far end of the room an archway seemed to lead to more rooms.

'Yes, though some of it is very old and valuable so we probably wouldn't drink it ourselves. This is where the wine from the vineyard was stored before my grandfather had the new cellar built down the road.'

They'd passed the new building in the car: it was much bigger and also housed the office.

Luc continued, 'This place isn't really used any more. Shall I show you round?'

He ducked his head as he led her through a series of rooms and passageways. Old wooden barrels were lined up everywhere.

'Wow,' said Natasha, when they finally reached the end

and stopped. 'It's enormous. You could fit a whole village in here.'

Luc raised a brow. 'Funny you should say that. Historically it was occasionally used to hide objects – and people.'

She stopped. 'When? In the war?' He nodded. 'What kind of things? Who?'

'I don't know, to be honest. People are still tight-lipped about it, even now.'

It wasn't difficult to imagine the place a hundred years ago. Even the electric lights were ancient, and everything else looked as if it hadn't changed in centuries. She wondered how many feet had walked over the smooth flagstones she was standing on now.

'I think the entrance is the best place for the flowers, don't you?' asked Luc, as they headed back.

'Yes. That table will be perfect to work on. I might need your help carrying the big vases up and down, though.'

'I'll do that. There's water here,' he said, pausing to show her the tap.

'Fantastic. I'll go and get my equipment and set it up ready for tomorrow.' Thursday was going to be a long day.

Outside, the afternoon heat hit hard. It was like a weight pushing down as she stepped into the bright sun.

'The flowers will be happy down there in the cool,' she said, while Luc shut the doors to the cellar and turned the key. 'So will I.'

He laughed. 'Yes. No need for air-conditioning.'

'The house doesn't have it either. How does it stay so

cool?' Even during the last few days of intense heat, their bedroom had been comfortable.

'These old buildings were built with the heat in mind.' He pressed his palm flat against the wall of the house. 'The walls are almost a metre thick, and the windows are deliberately small. As long as you keep the shutters closed in the day, the heat can't penetrate and the air inside stays cool.'

'Right.'

They walked slowly back towards the rest of the family. 'It's cold in winter, though,' said Luc. 'The heating bills are huge. Papa always moans about them, and Maman complains that he's too stingy and doesn't heat the place enough. She once wore her coat on Christmas Day in protest.'

Natasha laughed. That fitted so well with what she knew of Marianne and Jean-Pierre that she could easily picture it. 'The drawbacks of living in such a beautiful old house, I suppose.'

Luc glanced at her. 'You like it here, then?' He seemed pleased.

'I didn't say that,' she said quickly. 'I – I meant it's a historic place, that's all.'

'Oh. Right.' His smile faded and she felt bad.

But she was trying not to get attached. She wasn't staying: this wasn't her home, despite what they all thought. She hung back while Luc went ahead. At the table Marianne was listening to Arthur read and cradling a sleepy Élodie on her lap, while the two older children had started a game of *boules*.

You are getting attached, though, aren't you? Natasha stilled. She hadn't intended to, but she'd got sucked in. The big, noisy family and the château had cast a spell over her. She yearned to belong in a place like this. Luc's family had been so welcoming – how could she have resisted when she'd spent the last fifteen years desperately wishing for one of her own?

But it wasn't hers to have. She had to resist. Her fingers pinched the skirt of her dress. Preparing for the wedding would keep her busy for the next couple of days, and then it wouldn't be long before she flew home.

'This can't be right,' said Natasha, opening one of the boxes and peering at the sunflowers inside. There were only half a dozen stems in each. She did a quick count of the boxes: twenty.

'What's wrong?' asked Luc.

'All the daisies and the greenery are here, but we're short of sunflowers. I ordered way more than this.'

The supplier came over and said something in French. She couldn't understand the words, but his half-apologetic expression told her he knew about the problem. Her stomach twisted with panic. How was she supposed to create the look Juliette had asked for without all the flowers she'd ordered?

'He says there's been a problem,' Luc translated.

That much was obvious. Natasha cut to the chase. 'We need over three hundred flowers. Can he get them?'

While Luc and the guy spoke in increasingly heated

French, she went through the boxes, checking the quality of the flowers. At home she knew which suppliers she could rely on, but here it had been more of a gamble. Juliette had called someone she knew who'd called someone else, and so on.

Luc came over to her. 'He's offering us the same number of lilies for a discounted price. That's all he can do.'

'Juliette won't want lilies. She told me they remind her of funerals. Is there another supplier we can go to?'

They loaded up the van with what flowers they had, then Luc dialled Caroline's number. 'If Juliette finds out about this,' he explained, as his sister picked up, 'she'll be beside herself with worry. We'll say nothing and hopefully we'll find a solution before she notices.'

After a quick internet search, Caro called them back with the names of three suppliers in the area. 'It's last-minute but I'm sure you'll find sunflowers without any problem,' she said. 'After all, it's the right time of year and they grow everywhere round here.'

But at midday Luc and Natasha arrived back at the château having called or visited everyone on the list with no success.

'We need to think creatively,' said Luc, as they carried the boxes down to the cellar. 'Can you make do with what we have?'

They had daisies, greenery and a third of the sunflowers she'd ordered. It wasn't much to work with. Natasha racked her brain, trying to work out how she could modify the design. 'I could use more daisies for the table decorations, but Juliette wanted the garden to be filled with sunflowers. That's what she asked for.' She checked her watch, thinking she really needed to get started soon. Doing the flowers for this wedding by herself was always going to be a challenge, but she'd counted on getting as much as possible prepared in advance. Now the clock was ticking down.

'Let's try the local farmers,' said Luc. 'Caro's right. There are fields of sunflowers all around. If we pay the right price I'm sure they'll let us cut some.'

Natasha bit her lip. 'They're very big,' she said. She opened the nearest box. 'See how slender these stems are? And the flower heads are the size of my hand. The ones I've seen round here are like dinner plates or bigger.' She added gently, 'I'm sorry, Luc. I don't think that'll work.'

His expression hardened. 'I'm not giving up that easily,' he said. A muscle pulsed in his jaw. 'This is my sister's wedding. If she asked for sunflowers, I'll find them one way or another. I can't let her down.'

Her heart did a little flip. The steely determination and loyalty were Luc through and through. How would it be to have someone like him in your corner? She envied his sister.

'Come with me,' he said. 'Please, Nat. We'll drive around and maybe you can help me find some smaller ones.'

Two hours later, Luc pulled onto the main road and headed home. The van rattled over every bump in the tarmac, like a reproachful reminder that it was empty, and they hadn't found any sunflowers. They'd visited half a dozen fields, hopping out of the van each time to inspect the flowers. But Natasha was right: the sunflowers growing locally were far too big and woody for flower-arranging.

Beside him, she didn't say anything, but when he glanced at her, he saw the deep grooves where her blonde brows pulled together in a frown and he knew she was worried too. The wedding was creeping closer, and she had hours of preparation to do. His hands gripped the steering wheel as he navigated a roundabout. He'd told Juliette he had this in hand, but what if he couldn't pull it off? Imagine how disappointed his sister would be to have a wedding with no flowers.

'Could you use the flowers that grow in the garden?' he asked. All week Natasha had been creating new displays, which his mother and sisters had been oohing and aahing over.

'I could,' she said carefully, 'but I'd have to run it past Juliette first. It would be much more understated. It wouldn't have the impact sunflowers have.'

'What about plastic flowers?' he asked. 'I'm sure I saw some for sale in the place where we bought the vases.'

'Don't ever say that to a trained florist,' she said, through gritted teeth. 'And your sister definitely wouldn't be happy with plastic.'

At any other time, he would have laughed at the way she wrinkled her nose. 'We're running out of options.' Juliette would be devastated. His sister had agreed to bring forward her wedding for Jean-Pierre's sake, but he knew she'd been worried about the lack of time for preparation.

Luc had promised she'd still have the wedding she'd dreamed of. He had to keep that promise.

Natasha chewed her lip and stared out of the window. Suddenly she sat up straight. 'Stop!'

He braked. She pointed to a field on the right. 'Over there. They look different from the others we've seen. They're smaller.'

He followed her gaze, but his hopes deflated when he saw where she was pointing.

He turned the van round and they parked on the edge of the field. Natasha crouched to look more closely at the flowers.

'I reckon these are a dwarf variety,' she told Luc. 'There are several flower heads on each plant. See?' She touched one and let the silky petals run through her fingers.

Luc remained tight-lipped.

She got up and dusted off her hands. 'These are perfect. They're exactly what we've been looking for.' Her smile faded when she looked at him. 'What's wrong?'

'We can't take these.'

'Of course not. That would be stealing. But we can speak to the owner and ask to buy them, surely?'

'No.' He peered into the distance at the farmhouse set back from the next field. Only the rooftop was visible.

'Why not? I don't understa—'

'That's the Roger's farm. Madame Roger had a big argument with my father twenty years ago. They've never spoken since.'

Chapter Fourteen

Luc steered carefully along the farm track. It was riddled with potholes deep enough to swallow his car but it was impossible to avoid them and he wished he'd brought the van. He'd left it at the château where Natasha was preparing the vases. Apparently they had to be washed and bleached before she filled them with the flower arrangements.

The farmhouse came into view. The dusty ground in front of it was littered with rusty wheels and discarded tractor parts, and goats were grazing on straw-coloured weeds. The farmhouse was more run-down than he remembered, with a roughly patched roof and a couple of shutters hanging loose, but the Rogers must be getting on now. He made a quick calculation – in their eighties, he guessed. They didn't have children and they'd always been careful with their money, so he couldn't imagine they employed anyone to help around the place. He made a mental note to speak to Caroline about it. Maybe they could send one of the vineyard workers round every now and then, see if there were any jobs they wanted help with.

He parked near the goats, tucked the box he'd brought

under his arm, and knocked on the front door. It was open but he waited. Victor took a long time, but eventually he shuffled to the entrance.

His eyes became sharp slits when he saw Luc. 'Well, well, well,' he said.

'I wondered if I could speak to you both?'

'My wife is at her sister's. There's just me. But that may be a good thing. She would almost certainly have chased you off the property with a broom.' His eyes danced with humour.

Luc smiled politely, unsure if that was a joke or not. 'I brought you a gift.'

The old man inspected the box of finest Duval wine that Luc held out to him, but didn't take it. Instead he gestured for Luc to come in. 'Put it on the kitchen table.'

Luc did as he was told. It was a heavy box, and the old man was probably too frail to carry it himself.

'A Duval bringing us a gift?' said Victor, and leaned on a chair. 'What's going on?'

'I'm hoping you can help me – us – my sister, that is.' The old man peered at him. 'I know there's been . . . animosity between you and my father for a long time now. I know he argued with Laurette—'

'Madame Roger to you, young man.'

Luc tried to hide a smile. 'Sorry. Yes – Madame Roger.' He cleared his throat. 'The thing is, Juliette is getting married in two days, and the sunflowers she ordered for her wedding didn't arrive. We're running out of time.' The old man remained stubbornly silent. 'But you're growing them in the front field and they're perfect because they're not too big, they're beautiful, so I – ah . . . Can we buy some from you? Please? We would pay you well, and it might be an opportunity to make peace between the two families.'

His words hung in the air for a long moment before the old man finally said, 'I've heard about Jean-Pierre. He's in hospital, isn't he? His heart.'

Luc nodded. 'That's why the wedding is so last-minute. It's my father's wish to see us all married.' He couldn't tell if the news had sparked sympathy or not. Victor's face was difficult to read. The kitchen clock ticked slowly.

'So, you want to make peace, hm?'

Luc nodded.

'Does your father know you're here?'

'No.'

'Then how would that be making peace?'

'Well – I – ah . . . I'm just trying to help my sister,' he admitted. 'I don't even know what caused the disagreement between you and my father, but wouldn't it be nice to put it behind us now?'

Victor's eyes glinted. 'Now you need our sunflowers, you mean?'

Luc's teeth clenched. There was no way round this, and the old guy was right. It would have been far better if he'd tried to settle the feud before he'd come begging for their help. 'I'm willing to pay any price. It means so much to my sister . . .'

A long silence followed. Luc's shoulders sagged in

defeat. He should have known better than to come. He'd have to go home and break the news to Juliette. She'd be so disappointed.

'How many do you need?'

Hope flared in Luc. The other man's expression didn't reveal anything. 'Two hundred flowers or thereabouts. I don't know how many plants that is. We could take whole plants or just cut single stems from each – whichever you prefer.'

'Take them.'

Relief washed through Luc. Surprise, too. 'Thank you! That's very good of you.'

The old man glanced behind him, as if his wife might have crept up on them. 'But make sure she doesn't see you. She'll be home any time so you'll have to wait until it's dark.' He slid open a drawer, pulled out a torch and handed it to Luc. 'Take them from the far end of the field so she doesn't see you.'

Luc frowned. He wasn't comfortable with sneaking around in the dark, like a thief. But, then, what option did he have? He needed those flowers. 'Thank you. How much do you want for them?'

A silver tooth winked as Victor smiled. 'You can pay us in wine.'

'In wine? Not cash?' He glanced around him at the dark, ancient kitchen. Their home was so dilapidated, he'd have thought they would welcome the money.

The old man nodded at the box on the table. 'At least ten more of those.'

'Ten bottles?'

He shook his head. 'Ten boxes.'

Luc added up the value in his head. It was huge. Judging by the look of challenge in the other man's eye, he knew this too. But Luc would have paid any price to make his sister's wish come true. 'No problem. I'll send Luigi round.' He'd tell him to take the tractor and fill in the potholes first, or they'd have a hundred broken wine bottles on their hands.

'Make sure it's a good year, too. Not too young.' The silver tooth flashed again. 'At our time of life we can't afford to wait for it to age.'

Luc smiled. 'Yes, Monsieur.'

'Laurette will appreciate that.'

'I thought you weren't going to tell her. How will you explain the wine?'

Victor considered this. Then: 'I'll tell her it's an olive branch. What do you think?'

Luc smiled. 'That's a very good idea.' He hesitated. 'And perhaps you'd both like to come to the wedding – or the reception afterwards. If Madame Roger feels ready, it would be good to clear the air once and for all.'

'We'll see. You know yourself your father doesn't rush to smooth things over,' the old man said sharply. Luc shuffled his feet because, where arguments and estrangements were concerned, that was true. 'He's good at picking arguments, but apologising, backing down . . .'

'Yes.' Luc gave him a rueful smile. 'But you might find he's mellowed a little. These last few weeks have been a shock – for all of us.'

Victor nodded. 'There's nothing like a crisis to remind us of what's important in life, is there?'

Natasha finished rinsing the last of the vases and set it upside down to drip on the terrace. The sound of footsteps made her turn. 'Luc! Did you have any luck?'

'Kind of.' His voice was low. Juliette still had no idea about the sunflowers. Only Caroline and Marc were in on the secret.

'What do you mean? Did they say you could—'

'If they arrive tonight, after dark, can you work with that? It's not too late?'

'After dark? Why?'

'You don't need to worry about the detail.' He winked. But his brow was furrowed with worry and she had to resist the urge to reach up and smooth away the lines.

She made a mental calculation of all she needed to do, 'I'll manage, yes. I'll work through the night.'

'Through the night?' He looked horrified.

'There's a lot to do, and I have to deliver the church flowers tomorrow morning. They were very strict about when it would be open.' He still looked appalled so she added, 'Don't worry. It sometimes happens with weddings, and I don't mind. Really. I'll catch up on sleep tomorrow so I won't be exhausted for the wedding day.'

They paused while the children traipsed back from the pool, their father close behind. Natasha checked her watch. It would be dinner before long. When the children were all inside, she whispered, 'What's going on? How are you planning to . . .'

He raised a finger to her lips. 'You don't need to worry about that.'

His conspiratorial smile made her heart spin. He withdrew his finger, but her lips still tingled where it had been.

Luc leaned against the bonnet of the van and checked his watch. It was almost ten o'clock. The sun had set, darkness had finally fallen, and although it was a clear night, the moon was a thin crescent, its light subdued. Perfect.

He was ready to go. He had torches, empty boxes and secateurs. He'd checked the lengths of the stems Natasha wanted, the size of the flower heads, and the quantity. He was just waiting for Marc.

A fox's cry made him turn. He couldn't see anything in the darkness, but the urgent, haunting sound echoed across the valley, setting an ominous tone for the night. He couldn't believe he was going to have yet another misdemeanour on his conscience. Until three weeks ago he'd been a law-abiding citizen, who paid his tax bills on time, regularly donated to charity and prided himself on being upfront and honest. But since his father had become ill, he'd amazed himself with what he was willing to do when pushed into a corner. He was learning fast that life was not black and white. Right and wrong were not always clear-cut.

'There you are,' he said, straightening up when he spotted his brother-in-law.

Marc threw him a regretful look. Only then did Luc notice Caroline following him.

'I want to come too,' she said.

'Caro, there's no need. We've got this.' There was no point in involving and incriminating her too.

His sister stood firm. 'I know what you're planning. You're going to poach from our neighbours.'

'It's not poaching. I have Victor's permission.'

'In writing?'

'No, but—'

'If you get caught, you can't be sure he'll stand by his word. Especially if his wife finds out he's done a deal behind her back.'

She was right. 'That's why I want to protect you, Caro. If we get caught, I'll take full responsibility. You can say you didn't know anything about it.'

'I live and work here. Whatever happens tonight, I'll be the one who has to deal with the Rogers tomorrow. I want to be part of this.'

Luc and Marc exchanged a look. They both knew how stubborn Caroline was: it would be pointless to argue. And he should have foreseen this, anyway. You could rely on his sister to want to be at the centre of the action. Luc's lips curved. 'You mean you don't want to miss out on the fun?'

She pushed her hair back and grinned. 'Too right. Now, are we going or what? Natasha needed these flowers twelve hours ago.'

'What about the children?' asked Marc. 'What if one of them wakes while we're gone?'

'They won't. And if they do Maman is there, and Natasha. They'll hear.'

'It will be quicker with three of us,' Luc decided. 'Come on. You two will have to squash up in the front seat.'

Why don't you go to bed, get a few hours' sleep, and I'll wake you when I have the flowers? Luc's words rang in her ears as Natasha restlessly turned this way and that. She couldn't sleep. Every time she closed her eyes she remembered something else to add to her list of jobs, and her mind simply wouldn't slow down.

Sighing, she got up and crept downstairs. The house was quiet and the tiles felt deliciously cool beneath her bare feet. She padded along the hall to the kitchen and reached for the light switch. A nice cold drink would—

The noise of a kitchen chair being scraped back made her jump. At the same time Juliette shrieked with fright.

Then they both laughed.

'I thought you were a thief,' said Juliette. She looked at Natasha's short white pyjamas and added, 'Or a ghost.'

Natasha smiled. Unlike her, Juliette was still fully dressed. 'I just came down for a glass of water. Why were you sitting in the dark?'

'Oh – I needed to be alone. To think.' She flashed Natasha a watery smile, but her eyes looked haunted, and she was twisting the belt of her dress.

'Is everything OK?'

Juliette shook her head. 'Not really. I wanted to speak to Luc or Caro, but no one is around. They've all gone to bed so early tonight.'

Natasha bit her lip. Luc had been adamant that she must not breathe a word about the sunflowers to his sister. He'd said she had enough to worry about. It seemed like he'd been spot on. 'I – er – it must be the heat. Making everyone tired.'

'I – I don't know what to do. I need your advice, Natasha.'

'Me?'

Juliette began to pace up and down the room, her sandals tapping with each step. 'I'm getting married tomorrow.'

Natasha frowned. 'You mean on Saturday?'

'*Non*. In France we are legally married at the town hall,' she explained. 'This is tomorrow. Then on Saturday we have the ceremony at the church but it's more of a formality.'

'Oh. I didn't realise . . .' She'd been so preoccupied with the flowers, and Juliette and Philippe had been so busy that this had passed her by.

Juliette went on, 'Tomorrow will be just us with the witnesses and Maman.' Her brow furrowed. 'But I'm scared, Nat. I don't know if I can do it.'

'Do what?'

'Marry Philippe. It – it's such an enormous thing!' Her voice was high-pitched with fear, and Natasha's heart went out to her. But inwardly she was panicking. How could she offer reassurance when she was only pretending to be married? 'I'm not sure I'm the best person to speak to. Have you spoken to Marianne? She's been married a long time.'

Juliette waved away this suggestion. 'She's too worried about Papa, I don't want to add to her problems.'

Natasha wished she could comfort her, but what could she say? Marriage *was* a big commitment, and marrying the wrong person could end in heartbreak.

'It's a lifetime we're talking about,' Juliette continued. 'For ever!'

'That's true. But try to put that out of your mind for a moment. Do you love Philippe?'

'Yes,' she said, without hesitation. 'Yes, I do. I love him *énormément* – but that is now. Today. What if in five years' time my feelings have changed?' She threw her hands into the air.

'You're having last-minute doubts,' Natasha said gently. 'It's completely normal. Everyone gets them.'

'Do they?'

'Yes. I've seen it a lot.' That wasn't quite true, but she'd *heard* of it happening, and brides always looked nervous when she delivered bouquets on the morning of weddings. Fortunately, the nature of her job meant she didn't hang around to talk to them.

'Perhaps Philippe and I don't need to get married at all,' said Juliette, as if the thought had suddenly occurred to her. 'We could just go on as we are, living together. We're happy. Why change things?' She began pacing again, and almost tripped over a basket Simone had left out.

Natasha steered her to a chair and sat down facing her.

'Why did you decide to get married?' she asked. She took Juliette's hands in hers. 'Are you doing it simply to please your father?'

Juliette shook her head. 'Of course not.' She thought about the question. 'I suppose we wanted to make it formal, a public commitment that the world can see. This is – it's . . . reassuring for us, too.'

'And do you still want that?'

She nodded. 'Yes. Yes, I do. But I'm scared, too.'

'But that's good. Can't you see? It means you've thought about what you're going to do. You're not sleepwalking into it without any consideration.'

'I suppose.' She looked at Natasha. 'Did you ever have doubts? Before you married Luc?'

The house was silent. 'Yes.'

She'd had doubts before *and* after her wedding. She wondered what she would advise her past self if she could go back in time. *Don't do it.*

And yet. Sitting here, having got to know him, having seen Luc as she'd seen him this week, she wasn't so sure any more.

'Were there ever moments when you thought it wouldn't last? When you wanted to give up and walk away?'

She swallowed. She didn't know what to say. Finally, she admitted quietly, 'Yes.'

Juliette's eyes widened. 'How did you get through it? What's the secret?'

'There is no secret. No magic solution . . .'

Juliette's shoulders dropped. Seeing her disappointment, Natasha tried to put out of her mind her failed relationship with Luc. Instead she thought of Poppy Cottage and the future she hoped to make for herself with a man who loved her and a family of her own. 'There's no magic,' she went on, 'but there is hope. And faith. Have faith in Philippe and in yourself that you'll always try your hardest to make it work.'

Why did Luc's face still flash up in her mind? Why was she thinking of the lengths he'd gone to to meet his father's wishes and Juliette's for the wedding? Of how tenacious, loyal and reliable he'd proven himself to be.

Juliette nodded.

'How long have you known Philippe?'

'Four years.'

'Then I'd imagine you've already been through difficult times together, haven't you? The last two weeks, for example, your father being ill, it can't have been easy.'

'Yes. You're right.'

'So you've done it before. And you'll do it again. Marriage *is* a big step. There will be difficult times. But the important thing is to stick at it. Stay with him. Give it everything you have, and your marriage will have the best possible chance of success.'

She felt a shiver of guilt and was glad Luc wasn't there, because she'd given up on their marriage at the first hurdle. She'd run away rather than facing their problems head-on. Rather than standing up to Luc and asking questions and making clear how she felt. Juliette wasn't like that. She and Philippe had a great relationship: they were equals, they talked, they laughed, they shared.

Juliette seemed to relax a little.

Natasha went on, 'Take it one day at a time, like you do in your job. You focus on one customer at a time, don't you? Not a month or a year. You go to one place and take photographs. Then the next day you start another assignment.'

'Yes. One day at a time,' Juliette repeated. Then beamed. 'That's not so frightening any more.'

Natasha looked at the open boxes, all filled with sunflowers, which lit up the wine cellar, like gold lanterns.

'What do you think?' asked Luc, as she crouched to look more closely. 'Will they do?'

She touched the thin stem of one, the soft petals of another. 'They're fantastic,' she said. It wasn't quite true – they were all different shapes and sizes – but she could work with that. And where the stems were too thick or too thin, she could discard them and use only the heads for the flower balls, which would be suspended from the trees around the terrace.

He looked relieved. It was after midnight. He'd been gone ages: it had taken longer than he'd expected but there'd been an awful lot of flowers to cut.

She reached for the apron she'd borrowed from Simone. 'Thank you. I'll get started now.'

She reached to lift a box onto the table. When she looked up, he hadn't moved. 'You can go. You must be tired.'

'I'm staying to help,' he said. 'What can I do?'

'You've done enough. Honestly, I can manage now. Go and sleep.'

He shook his head. 'I'm staying with you.'

'Luc, you're not a florist,' she said, as kindly as possible. 'You've never done this before.'

'I can bring you cups of coffee, fetch water. And I'm sure there must be other jobs an unskilled idiot like me can do.' He slanted her a lopsided smile. 'I feel too guilty to go to bed while you're working through the night. On top of everything you've done already.'

She relented, touched by the gesture. 'You don't need to feel guilty. I like your sister. I'm happy to do this for her.'

She liked his whole family, she thought, with a tiny spike of anxiety. But there wasn't time to dwell on that when she had so much to do.

'Give me a job,' repeated Luc.

She paused to think. 'You could strip the leaves off the stalks and cut the stems so they're all this length.' She showed him what to do and he set to work.

Meanwhile she returned to her side of the table, and began with the pew ends, wiring solitary sunflowers so they'd hang straight and the heavy flower heads wouldn't droop. She'd swept and dusted the cellar, and every surface was spotless. It was a really nice place to work, deliciously cool but cosy with the haunting scent of aged wood. Simone had brought chairs down from the garden, which made her smile because she had no intention of sitting down, but she appreciated the gesture. The church flowers were her priority. Then she'd move on to the

236

decorations for the reception in the château gardens. Despite the late hour, she was excited, her mind buzzing with ideas. This was what she was good at. She loved working with flowers, creating beautiful modern displays to make someone's day feel really special.

As she worked, she glanced at Luc. He was frowning with concentration, and a lock of dark hair flopped over his eyes. Every now and then he pushed it back impatiently, but it fell forward again. They worked in silence. There was no sound but the whisper of leaves falling on leaves, or the quiet snip of her wire-cutters. It was comfortable. Intimate. Her senses were alert, as they always were when he was close by. But after almost a week in each other's company things had become relaxed between them.

'Did it go smoothly, your adventure picking sunflowers in the dark?' she asked.

'Yes. It was good fun, actually.' He chuckled. 'Marc spent the whole time complaining that the stems were too prickly to touch.'

'They can be. These aren't too bad, though.'

'He didn't get any sympathy. Caro told him he was being a softy.'

She laughed. 'Are you planning to tell Juliette?'

He snipped off the end of a stem and laid it to one side. 'After the wedding, yes. When things are less . . . intense.'

She thought of her conversation with Juliette in the kitchen earlier. 'It has been pretty full-on, hasn't it?' she said softly. 'What with your dad and the crisis at the vineyard and now the wedding . . .'

'It has. It's been a week I won't forget for a long time.' His gaze met hers and held.

The air became charged. In that moment she felt a deep connection. 'I feel I know you better now than I ever did before,' she admitted.

If they'd come here three years ago, would it have changed the direction their relationship had been heading? Avoided disaster?

'Me too.' His whispered words sounded like a promise.

She picked up a flower and told herself not to be silly. Luc didn't do promises. Not the romantic kind, anyway. Only to his father and his sisters – and how she loved this about him: he was a man of his word. She twisted the stem between her finger and thumb as she wound a thin piece of wire around it.

He picked up a flower, too, and went back to stripping away the leaves. But even as they got on with their respective tasks, she was still aware of him a few feet away, of the steady sound of his breathing and his long slender fingers handling the flower stems. It must be the late hour, or tiredness, that was making her feel so sensitive to him. She'd do well to remember that what drove Luc Duval was his construction company.

Focusing on the flower in her hand, she tried to sound casual as she asked, 'Are you missing your work?'

'I am, yes. We're busy at the moment. Lots of potential new work in the pipeline.'

'You like this?'

'I love it. Meeting new clients, pitching for new business, there's nothing better . . .'

She listened while he told her about the projects he was hoping to win. He sounded enthused, excited. His eyes lit up as he spoke, and she could see he was looking forward to getting back to his own life once his father had recovered and things were back to normal. It was good to listen to him speak. It was a reminder to her of what was important to Luc, what counted in his life. It wasn't relationships or love. His goals and dreams were nothing like hers.

She counted the wired flowers. Satisfied that she had enough, she laid out some greenery, cut lengths of white ribbon, and began to make individual posies.

'Have you talked to your dad about this?' she asked.

'About my work? No. Why would I?'

'Because he might understand better why you don't want to take over the vineyard if he could see how much you love what you do.'

He shrugged. 'Maybe. And you? Are you looking forward to going back to Willowbrook?'

An unexpected muddle of emotions stirred. 'Very much,' she said automatically.

But even as she spoke she knew it wasn't true any more. Why didn't she long to return home as she had when she'd arrived here? She lowered her gaze and concentrated on picking out just the right piece of greenery as she tried to work out what had changed. Why was her picture of the village fading? In its place she couldn't help but see a bold blue sky and a landscape that shimmered in the fierce heat. Was it possible that Provence had cast a spell over her?

Chapter Fifteen

L uc watched as Natasha picked up a posy and slipped a piece of ribbon around it. He continued to clip leaves, but he found it impossible to resist watching her surreptitiously as she deftly twisted wire, gathered flowers and greenery and laced them together with white ribbon. Her hair fell over her face, her lashes were lowered. She looked calm and content as she worked.

'Here, let me help you with that,' said Luc. She held the flowers in her left hand and was trying to tie the ribbon with the other. 'You can't tie a bow one-handed.'

'I can. It's fine,' she said.

'Let me hold the flowers for you,' he insisted, and took the posy.

She tried to tie the bow, but with two hands she was clumsy, the ribbon slipping. 'I can't do it like that.' She laughed. 'I've always done it one-handed. Give it back to me. I can manage better by myself.'

Reluctantly, he handed it to her, and she tied the bow quickly and deftly, as she'd evidently done a million times before.

'Miss I-Don't-Need-Anyone-Else,' he murmured, with a smile. 'Tell me, were you always so independent?'

Sadness flickered in her eyes before she looked away and laid down the finished posy. 'Being independent is no bad thing,' she said defensively, and picked up the next bunch of flowers. 'No one likes people who are needy or weak.'

'True,' he agreed, with a tip of his head. 'But I wish you would open up to me more.'

He wished he could read her thoughts and feelings and understand her better. He wished she'd trust him enough to share them with him.

Yet why was he wishing for this when he should be keeping his distance? They had just a week left of their charade. Intimacy wasn't necessary. Still, he found he was craving it all the same.

After a few hours, exhaustion struck. The room was filling with bouquets, posies and tall vases of sunflowers, but Luc's energy levels were dipping, and he could see Natasha was slowing down too. He went up to the kitchen and came back with a tray of coffee and food.

She accepted the coffee, with an eager smile, but shook her head at the food. 'I can't. I'd have to wash my hands and there's no time,' she said, and held up her fingers, which were tinged green and sticky with sap.

'Eat. It will give you energy and you'll work faster, be finished sooner.' He picked up a slice of peach.

Her eyes widened with surprise as he fed it to her, and she grinned. 'Mm. That's so refreshing.'

He ate some too. Then he broke off a piece of chocolate cake. 'Try this. It's an old family recipe that's been handed down through my mother's side.' He laughed as she took a big mouthful and her eyes darkened with pleasure. 'Good, isn't it?'

'Mmm.' It was a while before she could speak. 'Delicious.'

He ate some too. It was cold from the fridge, and he savoured the fudgy sweetness as it spread through him. He slipped another small piece between her lips. 'Eat. You need to keep your strength up.'

Desire coiled in him. He tried to ignore it, smiling as she licked her lips. Natasha giggled.

Then something changed. The mood suddenly became serious, the room hushed. His eyes dipped to her lips and desire flared in him. She must have seen the change in his expression because she stilled. The ancient brick walls seemed to move in a little closer. His gaze locked with hers, and somewhere in his mind he was aware of warnings flashing, that this couldn't work, that he should steer clear.

But around Natasha his brain didn't seem to follow logic. He was drawn to her. Like the heatwave that had been building over the last few days, so had his awareness of her.

She reached up and touched her lips to his. There was a heartbeat's pause, an intake of breath. Then their lips met again, and this time the kiss was hungry and urgent. He put the plate down and drew her to him. Their bodies pressed together, and their breathing became ragged.

There'd been times this week when she'd looked so happy, when her blue eyes had sparkled as she smiled. They were the moments he thought of now, and he wanted to make her smile again. For him.

She woke reactions and feelings in him that were

becoming impossible to ignore. And, truth be told, he was growing tired of fighting them. He didn't want to ignore them any more.

A sudden loud crash made them look up. The cellar door banged open, and feet slapped down the steps. Luc and Natasha sprang apart just as Arthur appeared. 'There you are! I've been looking everywhere for you. Oh – wow!' He stopped. 'This is amazing! I've never been down here before. And the flowers – they're everywhere.'

Luc glanced at Natasha, who smiled bashfully but said nothing. Disappointment mingled with amusement that they'd been interrupted. But there wasn't time to think it through properly now. He turned back to his nephew. 'Morning, Arthur. You're up early. It's . . .' he held his wristwatch up to the light '. . . only six thirty.'

'I know. Papa said it's too early, but I want to teach Natasha some more French.' His eyes danced with mischief. 'Today we learn naughty words.'

Natasha resumed cutting flowers and slotting them into a tall vase. 'Do you mean swear words?'

He nodded enthusiastically. 'They're very important. French people use them all the time.'

Luc grinned and lifted the boy onto the table so he could see what Natasha was doing. 'I'm interested to know these words, too. Go on, you can teach us both while Natasha is finishing her work.'

At eight o'clock there was a rap on the door. Natasha looked up and saw Marc's face at the top of the steps.

Arthur groaned, knowing what that meant. Natasha wasn't sure if she felt relieved or anxious at the prospect of being alone with Luc again.

That kiss had come out of nowhere. And yet, at the same time, it hadn't because she was permanently on edge around Luc. The surprise had been how passionately he'd kissed her. She frowned, too tired to make sense of it.

Marc came down the steps. 'Arthur,' he said. 'So this is where you are. I thought I told you to go back to bed. That was nearly two hours ago.'

Arthur grinned cheekily. Natasha tried not to smile but it was impossible.

'I'm sorry, you two,' Marc said, addressing Luc and Natasha. 'I'm sure the last thing you needed was this little one getting under your feet.'

'It's fine,' said Luc, and ruffled the boy's hair. 'He's been a good boy.'

Marc held out his hand for Arthur to take. 'Well, it's time for breakfast now. *Viens.*'

'See you later, Arthur,' called Luc.

Natasha smiled and concentrated on pushing a flower head into the oasis. But once Arthur was gone, she tensed. She reached for another flower and glanced at Luc. He was sweeping the floor, pushing bits of stalks, leaves and petals into a corner. She held her breath, half expecting him to say something about what had happened earlier, but he didn't. He seemed deep in thought. Her fingers squeezed the short stem as she tried to focus on getting the spacing right between flowers: they mustn't look squashed, but she didn't want any gaps, either. However, her mind was only half on the job. Why couldn't she ignore the hum of attraction? Working through the night together, while everyone else had been asleep, had felt special. Cosy. Intimate. And when they'd kissed she'd felt such . . . need.

But she mustn't. She mustn't feel anything. In seven days she'd be gone.

Luc leaned the broom against the wall and came over. The lock of hair had fallen over his eyes again and she fought the urge to push it back, to frame his cheek with the palm of her hand.

'We need to talk about—' he started.

'Do you want to get breakfast too?' she cut in. 'You must be hungry. I don't mind if you want to go.' She waved her hand in the direction of the stone stairs.

He shook his head and stepped closer. 'I don't want breakfast. I want to talk about what happened earlier,' he said, his voice low, his gaze on her lips. 'About why it keeps happening—'

'No!' She jerked back. Fear gripped her. 'I don't want to talk about it.'

'But you can't deny there's something—'

'Luc, stop!' She held up her hand. Surprise made his eyes widen. 'I – I have two hours left until I have to be at the church and there's still so much to do.'

She couldn't understand why her throat felt so tight, why she felt such raw panic at the thought of discussing what they'd done. It had felt so wonderful, so wicked and beautiful and – and dangerous.

So dangerous. If Arthur hadn't burst in when he had, she didn't know where it would have ended. That was what scared her. She'd been so completely out of control.

She must not succumb to this pull. Luc was her ex. He'd hurt her before, he could hurt her again.

His dark eyes searched hers a moment longer, then, 'OK.' He looked disappointed. A little confused, too. 'You're tired, you haven't slept, and you've worked through the night. I understand.'

His quiet acceptance was almost too much. She blinked hard. 'That's all it was,' she said, grasping at straws. 'Tiredness. Lack of sleep.' She turned away and checked off on her list what she'd done, then skimmed over what was left to do. She heard him sigh and his footsteps receded.

She still had her back to him when she heard him stop at the top of the stairs.

'It wasn't tiredness,' he said quietly.

She stilled. No? Her pulse raced. Eventually, she found her voice and asked, 'What was it, then?'

He didn't answer. She turned round.

But the doorway was empty, and he'd gone.

Natasha cast her eye critically over the church. It was a sunny riot of sunflowers and daisies. When she found nothing wanting she was able at last to relax a little.

She'd been up at the crack of dawn to complete the bride and bridesmaids' bouquets as well as the buttonholes for the men, but everything else she'd finished yesterday.

At the château she'd overseen the installation of wine barrels in the garden on which flower arrangements had been placed, she'd strung balls of sunflowers and white lanterns from the trees, and Luc had put up fairy lights all around the terrace where there would be dancing in the evening. There'd been so much to do, she hadn't had time to think, but now her work was done, she welcomed the opportunity to stop and take stock. To enjoy the ceremony. Juliette must have got over her last-minute nerves because she and Philippe had been to the town hall yesterday and were technically married, much to Natasha's relief.

The church began to fill. The air was buzzing with anticipation, and Philippe stood at the front, glowing with undisguised excitement. It was impossible not to share his joy, especially seeing Jean-Pierre in his suit, sitting up in his wheelchair, tall with pride as Caroline's children lined up to show him their bridesmaid and pageboy outfits. Their mother straightened ties and ribbons, then sent them outside to wait for the bride.

Natasha sat quietly in the row behind, alone because Luc was outside waiting for Juliette to arrive. She tucked her hair behind one ear and smoothed the gold satin of her dress. As she began to calm down after the frenetic preparations of the last forty-eight hours, a sharp prickle touched the back of her neck: she was sitting there as if she were part of Luc's family.

But the uncomfortable thought was cut short when the background music abruptly stopped, and everyone turned to look at the back of the church.

There stood Juliette, looking stunning in a sleek and simple ivory satin gown. And beside her, Luc. The proud big brother.

Natasha's chest squeezed. He wore a pale blue jacket with navy trousers, and a smile so genuine it was utterly disarming. She tried not to stare, but she couldn't stop herself. Silhouetted against the bright sunlight outside, he cut a fine figure, tall and dark-haired. Juliette whispered something to him and he nodded, giving her a reassuring pat on the hand she'd slipped through his arm. His skin was bronze next to the white of his shirt, and his eyes gleamed as they scanned the congregation. When they sought out Natasha's and connected, her heart tilted violently.

Then the music started, and he solemnly walked his sister down the aisle towards Philippe, who was waiting for his bride.

Luc felt a ripple of panic. Philippe was coming to the end of his speech, and any moment now, he would be expected to stand up and speak.

Just a few words, Juliette had said, keep it short. He swallowed. It might be very short, because he still didn't know what to say.

What could he say about marriage when, as far as he was concerned, marriage was restrictive, it was binding? People talked about compromise, but from what he could tell, what they meant was sacrifice. Giving up your freedom, tying yourself to one place and one person.

But he loved his sister. He wanted her to be happy and

he certainly didn't want to spoil her wedding day by saying something that would upset her.

Philippe finished, the guests clapped, and everyone hushed. All along the table they turned to Luc, their faces expectant. Well there was no option left but to wing it, he decided, and stood up.

'My sister has never been happier than she is now – with Philippe,' he said. There were murmurs of agreement, and Juliette shot him the same starry-eyed smile she'd had all day. Caroline leaned in to Natasha and quietly translated what he'd said into English for her.

'Philippe brings out her best qualities – her generosity, her sense of fun, her optimism. He also,' he said, winking at his sister, 'accepts her tendency to be dramatic, to get excited, and her impatience with detail.'

The crowd laughed and his mother nodded in agreement, before turning to fuss over his father, who batted her away. If Jean-Pierre hadn't been ill, he would have been making this speech, thought Luc, and he would have done a better job. He would have known what to say. He'd been married for thirty-five years. He knew about duty and love and longevity. His father might not be an easy man to get along with, but he and Marianne had always been a solid unit.

Oblivious to his dark thoughts, Natasha looked up at him and smiled. Her cheeks dimpled, her eyes, smoky with make-up, looked bluer than the summer sky, and his chest constricted. He'd let her down in the past, yet in the last few days they'd got to know each other far better. Coming here, she'd seen so much. She knew everything about him now – his past, his faults, his failings.

He'd laid himself bare. And though that made him uncomfortable, he could honestly say he had no regrets. How could he regret the last eight days when his father had made such a dramatic recovery? How could he regret all the joy Natasha had brought to his family? All the time he'd spent getting to know her better than he'd ever known her before?

'And I guess that's what love is about,' he forged on. 'Taking the good and the bad. Seeing a person as a whole . . .' His voice softened and his gaze remained welded to Natasha's. 'Accepting them for who they are.'

She stared up at him, her hair gleaming gold.

He'd never let anyone so close before. How ironic that the one time he did it was a pretence. A pretence that almost felt real.

Almost.

He broke eye contact and reached for his champagne.

Marriage would never be for him. He'd disappointed enough people already in his life – his father, Natasha. He wouldn't risk that happening again.

'I'd like to propose a toast,' he said, and all around the table glasses were lifted. Luc turned to the bride and groom. 'To Juliette and Philippe. I hope you have a long and happy marriage.'

And he was surprised to find he meant it.

Luc watched Natasha as she sat talking with his father. She was great with him: relaxed, not intimidated. Anyone would think she'd been part of the family for years.

He pushed that thought aside, and began to force his way through the crowd towards them.

'Luc!' she said, when he reached her. 'We were just talking about you.'

He looked at his father. 'Oh dear.'

She smiled. 'We have a proposition to put to you – regarding the vineyard.'

He steeled himself. 'Nat, I don't think this is the place. Juliette will be upset if this degenerates into an argument.'

'It won't,' his father said firmly.

'Jean-Pierre has agreed that when he comes home he'll have to slow down. He can't go back to running the business single-handedly. It's time to plan for his retirement.'

Luc tensed. He could see where this was going and he didn't like it. He'd taken a step back from his company for a few weeks, but that couldn't go on permanently. He was itching to get back to business, to new ventures and negotiations.

'So, we thought you might come to a compromise agreement where Caroline runs the vineyard and you would simply be on hand to help in a strategic capacity, offering advice if she feels she needs it. Isn't that how you run your own subsidiary offices around the world?'

'It is,' he said slowly, and glanced at his father. Who was taking great care to straighten the flower in his button-hole.

'So, what do you say?' Natasha asked. 'We've spoken to Caroline already. The only question now is would you be happy with that arrangement?'

His father finally looked up and Luc saw in his eyes both resignation and hope. Where was the obstinacy? The pig-headed refusal to compromise? Their absence was disconcerting – more so than seeing his father in a wheelchair.

'Yes. Yes, I would.'

She turned to Jean-Pierre. 'See? I told you he'd accept. Right, I'll get us some drinks to celebrate.'

The two men sat in silence, watching her go.

Then Luc said, 'You weren't happy with that suggestion when I put it to you before.'

'Yes – well, as you pointed out, Caro has proven herself over the last few weeks, and . . . things have changed.'

What did that mean? That his father had genuinely been impressed by her work? Or that his illness had weakened him and brought him to accept his limitations? Somehow, Luc didn't think either of those were at the root of this turnaround.

His gaze surveyed the crowd, homing in automatically on the blonde-haired figure who bent to lift Élodie into her arms, then laughed at something the little girl said. She raised her hand for Élodie to see and the two of them peered at the sunflowers painted on her nails.

'It's Natasha, isn't it?' he said. 'She's won you over.'

Jean-Pierre smiled, his gaze also on Natasha. 'She has.'

Luc's head whipped round to him. He couldn't believe it. His father was a man who demanded, who domineered, a strong man, a hard man. And yet the affection in his voice was unmistakable. It must be the wedding – the intensity of the day was getting to him.

'I like her very much. She looks like a delicate little thing but underneath she's strong.'

'Yes . . .' Luc thought of how vulnerable she'd sounded speaking about their baby, of how lost she'd looked when she'd first arrived there, but his father was right. Beneath that vulnerability was a core of independence and determination.

'She's good for you. Make sure you treat her well.'

His father doubted his ability to keep hold of Natasha, and he was right to. She wasn't even his to keep hold of because he'd lost her three years ago.

Guilt began to gnaw at him as he foresaw his father's reaction when he learned the truth. Which he would have to, sooner or later.

'You can't afford to lose a woman like her again. They're rare.'

The blood drained. Luc stared at his father. 'Again?'

'What?'

'Did you say *again*?'

His father looked confused – then tutted in his usual impatient style. 'You're imagining things. I said she's special. But, then, you must know that – you married her.'

There was a long pause.

Jean-Pierre dragged in air. 'I am proud of all you've achieved, Luc,' he said quietly. 'Proud of you.'

Luc stared at his father. Then he asked carefully, 'Is Natasha behind this, too?'

'No. I've had a lot of time to think in hospital. These are my own thoughts.' He took a deep breath. 'You were right to leave. Château Duval isn't the place for you. You are cleverer than me, and you think . . . differently. And Duval would be a millstone around your neck.'

'No,' Luc cut in. 'It's our legacy. We're privileged to be part of it. I just couldn't stay here and . . .' He searched for the words to express how torn he'd felt between duty and desire, how sometimes the guilt of not living up to his father's expectations had been torturous, but he hadn't been able to face the prospect of being confined to this place, 'I can't—'

Jean-Pierre placed his hand on his lap. 'I understand. You don't need to explain.' Luc saw the genuine understanding in his father's eyes and his shoulders sagged with relief. 'I felt it too – once. But I didn't have your courage to push back. I fell into line. I took it on without argument and buried my own dreams.'

'You were a better man than me.'

'Or a coward. I've come to see that what you did eight years ago took courage.'

Luc was silent. It hadn't felt courageous. Those eight years had been hard. If he'd learned anything these last few weeks at home, it was that life was more meaningful with family around you. He leaned forward on his elbows and gazed up at the château, its ancient walls and serene air of history.

'I shouldn't have pressured you so much to take it on,' said Jean-Pierre. 'I should have let you choose – but that wasn't the way I was raised. It was drummed into me that I must continue the line.'

Luc nodded. 'Caro will do that. She wants to.'

'Yes. And you were right – she's good. Organised. In control.' He winked at his son. 'Her father's daughter.'

'She's also open to new ideas,' Luc teased.

Jean-Pierre chuckled. 'Yes, well. Perhaps it is time for me to think about retirement. The doctors are telling me I need to slow down.'

'How does Maman feel about that? Will she want you under her feet all day?'

His father had a mischievous glint in his eye. 'We'll see.'

'I'm glad you appreciate Caroline. I'll help whenever she needs me. I'm not washing my hands of the place, I just have to do my own thing. What I do best.'

'I know,' said Jean-Pierre, and patted Luc's shoulder. 'I was always proud of you – though I didn't show it.'

And Luc knew he'd never forget those words.

The crowd suddenly hushed. Luc looked up and spotted Victor and Laurette Roger. They were clearly a little nervous as they shuffled towards Jean-Pierre, who noticed them too. Surprise was written on his face. 'What is this?' he asked. 'Who invited them?'

'I did.' Luc swallowed. He just hoped he'd done the right thing. If this backfired it would ruin Juliette's wedding day.

Out of the corner of his eye he saw his mother and sister hurry forward. People stepped aside and heads turned to watch as the elderly couple moved slowly forwards, arm in arm, supporting each other. They finally stopped in front of Jean-Pierre and Luc held his breath.

'Jean-Pierre.'

'Victor. Laurette.'

Victor looked at his wife. He gave her a little nudge. Then she spoke: 'I've come to thank you for your gift.'

A short silence followed. 'What gift?' said Jean-Pierre. He looked at Marianne and Juliette, who shrugged, then at Caroline. She smiled guiltily. So did Luc.

Laurette went on: 'I took it to be an apology from you. It was about time, in any case. Neither of us is getting any younger.'

Jean-Pierre opened his mouth to speak, but Victor spoke: 'What my wife is trying to say is that she accepts your gift and she is ready to apologise too.' Then he muttered, 'It was a ridiculous argument. You two should have sorted it out years ago.'

Laurette's chin lifted, her expression tense and wary.

Luc watched his father as puzzlement gave way to understanding, then to something else. His gaze darted suspiciously from Luc to Caroline before he said, 'Is this true, Laurette? You want to put the past behind us?'

She blinked. Her husband nudged her. 'Yes. It is.'

Luc bit his lip.

Jean-Pierre hauled himself to his feet and opened his arms. 'Come here, you silly old bat.'

Marianne gave a delighted cry. There were cheers and clapping as the pair embraced. When Laurette pulled back, Jean-Pierre said loudly, 'Don't go thinking you can worm your way into my will, though.'

'Why would I want your stupid money?' Laurette fired back. 'It's your wine I'm after.'

Jean-Pierre chuckled. 'Good idea. Where's my glass? Let's raise a glass to our friendship.'

It had been a perfect day, Natasha decided, as she sipped rosé and watched the sun sink behind the hills, blurring the distant trees and casting shadows over the fields of vines. A peachy glow settled over the scene in front of her. Juliette and Philippe were dancing, guests milled around chatting, and children dashed in and out of the trees and bushes, blurs of pretty dresses and ringlets and unbuttoned shirts. She hadn't followed much of the church ceremony but, judging by the laughter and tears, it had been moving, and Juliette and Philippe had shone with love for one another. Back at the château the meal had been relaxed, the wine – Duval's most prized vintage – was flowing, and the atmosphere was one of warmth and love.

Her eyes sought out Luc among the crowd. He speared his fingers through his hair, and his eyes creased as he smiled. She couldn't stop thinking about the way he'd looked at her when he'd made his speech, as if he'd been silently communicating something to her, as if his words had held meaning for him and her. Her heart clenched. Had they?

He appeared by her side now and put his arm around her, dropped a light kiss on her cheek. The weather was too warm for that kind of thing and she knew he was only doing it for appearances' sake, but it felt good all the same. She slipped hers around his waist, too, as yet another pair of guests she didn't know stopped to speak to her.

'The flowers are beautiful. *Incroyable*. Is it true this is your work, Natasha?'

Her cheeks flushed. 'Oh, it was nothing. I was happy to help.' She glanced at Luc, who beamed back at her, his expression one of pride.

'You're too modest,' he told her, before turning to the couple and saying, 'My wife is hugely talented.'

Warmth flowed through her. His fake wife, she had to remind herself sternly. His temporary wife for two weeks only. She sipped her drink, aware that none of this was hers to enjoy. She was an interloper.

'They look so modern and *naturelles*,' said the lady, 'so in keeping with the local landscape.'

Natasha and Luc exchanged a look. No one knew about Luc's adventure in the night to pick the flowers, and she had to bite her lip to stop a giggle. 'This is the look Juliette asked for.'

'We'd better circulate,' Luc said firmly, and steered her away to the other side of the garden, where they dissolved into laughter together. People were dancing nearby. The sun had disappeared now, the sky was a dusky mauve, and the lanterns and fairy lights had been switched on. They reflected in Luc's eyes, making them glitter and gleam.

'Will you dance with me, *chérie*?' he asked, his voice deep and low.

'I'd love to.' She smiled and let him lead her to join the others.

The music was slow and romantic, the air growing rapidly cooler, which was a relief after the heat of the day. But it was also blissful to lean into him and feel the warmth of his body next to hers. She relaxed, enjoying the gentle pressure of his hand in the small of her back, their hips touching, legs brushing. He smelt of aftershave and Luc. Such a familiar scent, it was as if the last three years apart had never happened.

Luc looked over at his parents. 'My father's enjoying himself. I'm hoping he won't be too tired at the end of it. If he carries on recovering as fast as he has, the doctors say he should be able to return home soon.'

She followed his gaze. Jean-Pierre was smiling and batting away Marianne as she tried to tuck a blanket around his knees. When she bent to kiss him, he reached up and touched her face. Marianne smiled. Natasha looked away quickly, feeling as if she'd intruded on a private moment.

'Really? That's wonderful.' His mother would be so pleased. Natasha knew all the travelling to and from the hospital had taken its toll on Marianne, who just wanted her husband home and well again.

She rested her head on Luc's shoulder and let the music carry her, savoured the warmth of his hands on her waist and at the base of her neck. The evening air was deliciously scented with flowers.

'Juliette looks happy too. All in all, it's been a good day.'

She heard the smile in his voice. 'It's been a lovely day.' She sighed dreamily. 'Relaxed, not too formal, romantic. Just how I'd like my wedding to . . .' Why had she said that?

Luc missed a beat, then continued to dance. 'What happened between us didn't put you off, then?'

She sensed tension in him, but she put it down to his feelings on weddings and marriage. 'No, it didn't,' she said honestly.

Though it had made her cautious. Cautious in the extreme. Perhaps that was why she hadn't found her Mr Right yet. She'd dated a few men in the last three years but none had made her senses tingle, none had lit sparks in her. 'I still hope to marry and have a family – when I meet the right person.'

He stopped dancing and held her far enough away so he could see her face. 'And who is the right person, Natasha? How will you know when you've found him?'

He stared into her eyes, searching them, and she swallowed. His gaze was distracting. It was making her mouth dry, making her body tense against his.

She shrugged and tried to make light of it when really her heart was clattering, though she didn't know why. 'Oh, there'll be a bolt of lightning, music in the air, and – and I'll just know.'

The corner of his mouth lifted, but his smile was indulgent rather than mocking.

His gaze lingered on hers, then dropped to her mouth, and she felt a surge of desire so strong it made her flush. She'd spent the last few days fighting it, but it was like trying to hold back an incoming tide. Every time his arm brushed hers or their eyes connected, the air became charged, the fire burned.

'You really believe in *coups de foudre* and all that?' he asked.

Her chin lifted. 'Yes, actually. I think when the right man comes along there will be a connection. Maybe not love at first sight, although that would be good, but everything will just click into place. It will feel . . . right.'

Luc's dark gaze bored into her, making her skin tingle as if she'd stepped inside a hothouse. He searched her face, but his own expression remained inscrutable. She ran her tongue across her lips.

Then he dipped his head to kiss her slowly. Tenderly.

The music swirled around them as he pressed his hand into the small of her back and drew her against his body. For a moment she was lost in the deliciousness of it, swept up by its intensity. She couldn't stop this: she wanted him, still.

Then he drew back. Breathless, she watched his lips curve.

'A connection like this?' he asked, eyes glittering with mischief.

Yes, she thought.

'No,' she said.

And frowned, her head spinning.

She knew what he was doing. He was mocking her, questioning her romantic ideals because he knew she was attracted to him.

But that attraction was just physical. It had always been there between them and it hadn't prevented the divorce. On its own it wasn't enough.

'We both know you're not the right man for me,' she whispered, though she didn't know why she said it out loud. He resisted all ties. Whereas she wanted this – all she saw around her now. The wedding, the confetti, the lifelong commitment.

She craved it more than anything.

The sound of Juliette clearing her throat broke them apart.

'Love is in the air,' she said, and it was clear she'd been watching them because she smiled fondly, as if she'd just witnessed a touching moment.

Natasha looked at Luc, who had turned away to speak to another guest, and smiled. 'Not so nervous any more?' she asked.

'Not at all. It feels one hundred per cent right. Thank you for reassuring me the other night. I don't know what got into me.'

'It was nothing.'

Juliette hesitated. 'I haven't told Philippe.'

'Don't worry. I won't breathe a word to anyone.'

'Thanks. And for the flowers, too. They're even more beautiful than I imagined they would be.'

'I really enjoyed doing them.' Natasha's cheeks flushed as she remembered Luc's kiss in the cellar. And Arthur's timely interruption. She still wasn't sure if she'd been relieved or frustrated that he'd arrived when he did. The more time she and Luc spent together, the more the connection between them seemed to be growing, the lines between real and pretence blurring.

Juliette took her hand. 'I'm so glad you came. The wedding wouldn't have been the same without you. You're part of the family now.'

Natasha stiffened, and guilt slid down her spine.

Then, when Juliette was whisked away to speak to

someone else, Natasha was left watching her with a growing sense of unease. The same unease that had been trailing her all day.

You're part of the family now.

When she'd arrived a week ago she'd been worried that Luc's family wouldn't believe she was his wife – but they had. His mother, his sisters, the children, his father – they'd all accepted the pretence that she and Luc had put on of being a loving couple. They'd welcomed her and she'd grown to feel part of their family.

And wasn't that worse than being found out?

Her insides twisted. She couldn't think of another time in her life when she'd deceived anyone like this, on this scale. Especially people she'd grown close to. She glanced about her, taking in the noise, the smiles. She'd watched the celebrations conscious of her outsider status, acutely aware that she was deceiving everyone.

But she'd also been deceiving herself, because she would miss them when she left. Miss them so much. She loved it here – the children, the house, being part of a big family. There was always someone around, someone who needed help with something, someone to talk to. What would it be like to have Marianne for her mother-in-law? Caroline and Juliette for sisters? What would it be like to come here each summer and Christmas, perhaps other holidays too? To have children of her own who'd splash about with their cousins in the pool, share a room, have day trips to the seaside, picnics and family games of cricket on the beach? Her heart quickened. In less than a week she'd be saying goodbye.

For good.

A lump lodged in her throat.

She slipped away from the celebrations, and once she was out of sight, she followed the narrow path away from the garden and towards the vineyards. She needed space to clear her head. Gravel became hard soil underfoot, and leaves rustled as she passed. The moon was a coral-tinged crescent, the sky studded with diamanté pinheads. Away from the party, the temperature dropped a little, but her lungs felt tight and hot.

What would Luc's family think when they learned the truth? How would they feel when they knew she'd deceived them? She touched Luc's ring. When had it started to feel so familiar, so comfortable on her finger? She even had a white mark where it had shielded her skin from the sun.

'Nat?'

Luc's deep, low voice made her start. She spun round.

He placed his hands on her shoulders and his tall frame loomed over her. In the pale glow of the moon she saw his dark eyes were filled with concern.

'You're upset,' he said. 'What's wrong?'

This was what was wrong, what she'd tried to get away from – the electric charge, the relentless buzzing when she was around him. Her inability to think rationally, but instead to feel – oh, to feel too much.

'Nothing,' she said.

The lift of his brow told her he didn't believe her for a second. 'Tell me.'

He kept his hands on her shoulders, not letting go,

keeping her prisoner, and yet she didn't feel trapped. His touch was firm and reassuring. It steadied her.

'They really believe us.'

'Believe us? Who?'

'Your family – that we're a couple.'

He looked so handsome: dark hair, strong jaw, gleaming eyes. He was film-star perfect, but he was also human. He worried about his relationship with his dad, cared for his mother and sisters. She realised she'd barely known him when they were married. At first she'd had him on a pedestal, then, when she'd become pregnant, she'd demonised him. But he was just flesh and blood with weaknesses and insecurities like everyone else. Now she understood him too well. She should have stayed detached and then she wouldn't care so much.

'That was the idea, remember? That's why you're here.'

She shook her head. 'I can't do it any more.'

'Do what?'

'Keep up the charade. Your family are so kind. They've been so good to me. I can't deceive them like this any longer.'

Chapter Sixteen

Luc saw the anguish in her eyes and heard it in her voice; this was tearing her up inside.

Panic ripped through him and he gripped her shoulders – but he also felt a flood of admiration. Because Natasha wouldn't feel like this if she was not honest and good-natured.

She was right, what they'd done was wrong, but his father wasn't strong enough yet to learn the truth. It had been one thing to tell him Caroline was running the vineyard, but if he learned Natasha was no longer his wife he'd be devastated. His father adored her. All his family did. He had to keep her here a few days more – until the wedding festivities were over, at least.

His mind worked fast to find a solution. He could remind her of the cottage. After all, that was what had hooked her into this in the first place. He could threaten her with losing it if she backed out now—

But he didn't want to blackmail her.

He couldn't explain it, but the determination with which he'd gone into this had been replaced with something more complicated.

It hit him then, in the darkening night: this wasn't just

about his father's health any more. It was about him and Natasha, and what had developed between them these last few days. Perhaps it had never gone away.

'Don't go, Nat,' he said.

She looked up at him. Her shoulders were tense beneath his hands and he tried to relax his grip but couldn't.

'This isn't about my family or my father any more. It's about you and me.'

Her eyes widened, and she wasn't the only one who was surprised. He was laying himself bare.

But the idea of letting her go was unthinkable. 'Please – stay.'

The sound of laughter, of music, travelled through the night to infiltrate the stillness of the vineyard.

She swallowed. 'Why?'

Her lovely eyes, dark smudges in the moonlight, searched his face, and he registered the hope in them, saw them drop to his mouth, then hastily lift again.

'Because you want to?' he suggested softly.

Because he wanted her to. Though the words remained trapped inside his throat and he couldn't bring himself to promise more than he could give. He had too much respect for her to do that.

She shook her head and her blonde hair caught the silver light of the moon. 'This isn't just about wanting,' she said, and stepped back. 'That's what got me pregnant the last time.'

She looked small and lost, and he was shocked at how that made him feel. He wanted to draw her to him, fold her into his arms and wipe away the pain. He stepped towards her and cupped her cheek with his hand. His body tightened, remembering how good it had felt to hold her in the dark of their room. Her eyes closed briefly at his touch and seeds of hope cracked open inside him.

Then she looked up at him. 'It won't work,' she said. 'We've been here before.'

He felt a punch to his centre.

'No!' he said. 'Last time we got married in a rush, I was a suspicious bastard and shut you out, and then we lost a baby. It was bound to fail. But that was then.'

She drew in breath. 'And now?'

He could hear the frayed edge of desire in her voice, he could feel it in her body. She was barely breathing, and her pulse was hammering beneath his fingertips. He stroked the hair back from her face. 'The last few days have changed everything,' he said honestly, though he was walking a tightrope. Alarm bells rang. He'd spent all his adult life warning women not to get close to him.

But he wasn't proposing a lifelong commitment here. Simply a willingness to try again.

'Now we have this.' He traced her bottom lip slowly with a finger. This connection. 'And it works.'

God, he'd missed her. No one he'd met during the last few years had come even close to drawing this response from him. He'd told himself it was because he'd changed, but now he knew he'd been wrong. It was Natasha who woke the fire in him. Only her.

'But, Luc, there has to be more . . .'

His skin puckered as if a cold breeze had just blown in off the hillside. *I still hope to marry and have a family,* she'd told him, *when I meet the right person.* He didn't know why her words had sliced through him, but even the simple memory of them roused the jealous beast in him. He moved in closer and dipped his head to kiss her neck where her skin was pale and soft, where she tasted of perfume and sunshine and that sweet peachy scent that was simply hers. She sucked in air and shuddered beneath his touch. His body kicked to life and he kept on dropping kisses, his hands slipping around her waist. He knew she felt it too, this energy between them, this pull. He'd seen it in her eyes – he felt it now as she leaned in to him.

She might regret their marriage, she might have other plans for the future that didn't involve him, but she wanted him.

'Why fight it, Nat?' he asked, his mouth so close to hers he could feel her breath, quick and shallow, against his lips. 'Can't we just take it one day at a time?'

She stilled.

Natasha's gaze flickered from his eyes to his mouth. One day at a time. The same words she'd said to Juliette when she'd been frightened. And today Juliette was married and radiant with joy. Natasha swallowed. The fight was being sucked out of her, barriers were cracking and collapsing.

She tipped her head up a little more towards his.

Every rational part of her brain screamed against it but – oh, the look in Luc's eyes. She couldn't name what she saw but she felt its effect. It wrapped her in heat. It made her feel desperately needed.

And wasn't that exactly what she'd been searching for all these years?

'What do we have to lose?' he murmured.

Ever since he'd held her in the night, she'd been coiled tight, thirsty for his touch, and now that his lips were just a whisper away from hers, temptation reeled her in.

If they let their relationship become real again, it would be like putting right all the wrong they'd done in deceiving his family. Her guilt could be assuaged. This burning need too.

But what about her heart? Their relationship hadn't worked last time – why should it now? She bit her lip. Last time they had been younger: they hadn't known each other as well as they did now. Coming here had shown her who Luc was. She understood him better now, and he understood her. Maybe that was what he'd been saying in his speech earlier when he'd stared at her with that look in his eyes.

The same look she saw now. *Don't go. Please – stay.*

Her chest swelled and hope blossomed. Perhaps it could work. Perhaps they'd both changed enough to make a future for themselves. She lifted onto her toes and their lips met. She tangled her fingers in his hair, her hips pressed against his, creating friction, sending sparks firing through her. He gathered her to him, softness against strength.

When they broke off, panting for air, she saw joy in his eyes and knew it mirrored hers.

'Shall we go inside?' he asked, his voice rough.

She nodded at the garden and the lights and the noise. 'What about the others?'

'They won't miss us.'

He led her by the hand to the side of the house where it was quiet. They slipped inside and climbed the stairs in silence. When they got to their room, he shut the door.

Leaning back against it, he paused and something in the way he searched her face – warily, fearfully – told her he was giving her a moment to reconsider. Though it looked as if it was paining him to do so, he wasn't taking anything for granted, and that made her heart squeeze.

She stepped towards him. 'Luc,' she whispered, and wrapped her arms around his neck.

He groaned, and her fingers moved across his chest, splaying over tense muscle, tugging at his shirt. Within moments his chest was bare.

Her breath caught in her throat.

'Nat . . .' he began, then shook his head as if words were hopeless, and when he kissed her, it was as if chains had been cast aside.

She responded as feverishly, as hungrily. She undressed him in clumsy snatches, and he did the same, then carried her, naked, to the bed.

'I want to stay with Natasha!'

Élodie stamped her feet and clenched her fists, her small face red with exertion. One thing was for sure, she'd inherited the Duval gene of stubbornness. Luc hid a small smile and Caroline sighed with exasperation at her daughter.

'Élodie, you need to have a bath and go to bed. Your brothers and sister are up there already.'

But the little girl, red-faced and exhausted, just shook her head and clung to Natasha's legs.

'Élodie,' Natasha said softly, and pulled the child onto her lap. 'Why don't you go with Maman? After you've had your bath I'll come and read you a story.'

Élodie considered this. Her thumb was in her mouth, exhaustion catching up with her. Luc was watching Natasha with his tiny niece. She would make a fantastic mother, he thought. Patient, loving, devoted.

The thought left him confused so he shoved it aside. All that mattered now was that these last few days had been good. Better than good. He was glad they were giving it another go, though he was going to take it slowly this time – what they had felt so fragile and he didn't want to mess up. There would be no rushing their relationship, no making promises he wasn't a hundred per cent certain he could keep.

Finally, Élodie gave a small nod and climbed down to take her mother's hand. Caroline, visibly relieved, gave Natasha a grateful smile, then led her off into the house. He and Natasha were left alone outside. She smoothed her skirt: the green cotton was creased where Élodie had been curled up.

'Your family are so lovely,' Natasha said.

He laughed. 'I don't think that was Élodie at her best, do you?'

'She's just tired. The last few days have been emotional and intense. A lot for a little girl to process. She'll be fine after a good night's sleep.'

'I hope you're right. We don't need any more tantrums. We were six adults but none of us was able to calm her down. Except you, of course.'

She smiled bashfully and gazed at the door through which his sister and niece had disappeared. 'It's nice that you're all so close. You're very lucky.'

He topped up their wine glasses. 'You sound envious.'

'I am,' she admitted, and threw him a weak smile. Her dimples appeared, and her cheeks flushed a little, though the colour was less noticeable now her skin had turned honey-gold.

'What was your great-aunt like?' he asked, trying to remember what little she'd told him before.

Her eyes clouded. It wasn't the reaction Luc had expected. 'Ancient,' she said. 'Or, at least, that was how she seemed to me then, as a child.'

'Tell me more.'

Natasha shrugged. 'She had her own interests, her friends. She played cards and bowls. I suppose she was very active for her age.'

Her deadpan tone didn't sound right. Natasha was warm – he'd just seen her murmuring affectionately to Élodie. Why was she speaking about her great-aunt in such a dull, flat way?

'Were you close?'

'No.' She looked down at her fingernails, which she'd painted cream with pink roses. 'No, we weren't. She wasn't the maternal type. She never married or had children and she was very Victorian in her attitudes. "Children should be seen and not heard." She didn't want to take me in.'

Luc's eyes widened in surprise. 'She didn't? Why not?'

She shrugged. 'I don't know, but she was my only living relative. I think social services pressured her into it. That's why she made me feel like . . .' she searched for the right words '. . . like I was a burden to her.'

'A burden?' He felt a tug of sympathy for the child who'd lost her parents so young.

He'd assumed she'd been raised by a loving relative, but it seemed her loss had been only the beginning of a difficult time.

'Oh, she wasn't cruel or anything like that. She fed me, clothed me, housed me . . . But everything she did, she did because she had to. Not because she wanted to. There was something vital missing.'

'Love?' he asked softly.

She nodded.

He noted how carefully she kept her expression neutral, her tone flat. Yet beneath it there must be an ocean of hurt that she'd learned to cover up. Anger stirred in him. 'How could she be so cold when you'd lost both your parents? How could anyone treat a child like that?'

She picked up her wine glass and squeezed the stem. 'She wasn't a . . . warm person. I remember Mum begged her to keep Poppy Cottage, but she sold it. I suppose she didn't want to move house or have the inconvenience of an empty property.'

'She wanted the money, you mean?' he said.

'That too. Perhaps. I don't know.'

A bat darted around high above them flitting between the trees and the roof of the château. 'When did she die?'

'After our divorce. The lawyers tracked me down because I was her only living relative.'

Not because Natasha was named in the will, he thought. 'So you inherited her estate?'

'Yes. It wasn't much, but I used it to set up my shop.'

'What happened to the money from your parents' cottage? Did that come back to you too?'

'No.' She stared into the bottom of her glass. 'I guess she must have spent it.'

Her tone was resigned, but Luc was furious on her behalf. The injustice of it, the cruelty. 'How long did you live with her?'

'Until I was sixteen. I left home as soon as I could, and I didn't keep in touch. I swore I'd never allow myself to be in that situation again . . .' Her eyes were dull with remembered sadness, and she met his gaze directly as she finished '. . . being with someone who didn't want me.'

She'd had the same hollow look in her eyes when they'd been married, and she'd been so quiet, so withdrawn. A draught of cold air touched the back of his neck. He wondered if that was how she'd felt with him. Unwanted? The idea disturbed him.

But the past was history.

Right now, things were going so well between them – the proof being that she was confiding in him, sharing with him things she'd never shared before. He felt a rush of satisfaction, of optimism.

'Is that why you're so independent?' he asked.

'Probably.'

He reached out and touched her cheek. 'I'm glad you told me about her,' he said quietly.

Caroline poked her head out of an upstairs window. 'Natasha?' she called.

Luc watched as Natasha hurried off inside to read to Élodie, her green skirt swinging around her bare legs. He frowned and gazed thoughtfully at the flickering tea light on the table. He mulled over all she'd told him, piecing it together with the other fragments he'd gleaned about her childhood. Christ, the pain, the trauma she must have gone through. His chest constricted with indignation, which roused in him the urge to protect her from all harm in future. He was thrilled at the way they'd managed to rebuild their relationship. Holding her in his arms, making love to her had rocked his world.

But he had to tread carefully. He was more conscious than ever of the pain in Natasha's past, and determined that, no matter what, she shouldn't suffer again.

Natasha woke up to the sound of tapping. She opened one eye. Luc was sitting up in bed, his laptop on his knees, typing. He wore reading glasses and his hair was ruffled and messy.

'You're working?' she asked.

He nodded. 'Bit of a crisis with my US team.'

She waited for him to expand but he didn't. For a split

second she was reminded of three years ago, when his work had come before everything else. Before her.

But she had been timid then. Perhaps she'd even believed she wasn't lovable enough to be someone's priority. Now she smiled to herself, remembering last night. And the night before. It had been hot, it had been endlessly satisfying. And now she was greedy for more.

She shifted under the light cotton sheet, but the ache wouldn't go away. Not when Luc was sitting so close. She propped herself up on one elbow to watch him.

'What?' he asked, glancing at her, then returning his attention to his computer.

'Just watching you.' She smiled. 'I love the glasses. They're sexy.'

'Really?'

'M-hm.' She ran her tongue over her lips.

He smiled, shook his head, and continued to type.

She drew herself up and looked over his shoulder. He was typing an email, issuing instructions. She dropped kisses on his shoulder and the tops of his arms. She loved how the muscles tensed beneath his skin.

'Are you trying to distract me?' he asked.

'M-hm.' She brushed her lips over his biceps and across his naked chest.

'You know this is important, right?'

'So you said.' She smiled mischievously and reached up to kiss his neck, behind his ear.

'Nat, I really need to deal with this.'

'Now?'

'Yes, now.'

'Carry on, then. Don't mind me.' She planted another kiss on the side of his neck where he was most sensitive.

He released a slow breath, then turned to her, his eyes dark, his smile indulgent, and she captured his mouth with hers. It was a slow, lingering kiss.

God, she wanted him so much. His breathing quickened.

'I thought you had to deal with it. What's stopping you?' she asked innocently, her voice low, her mouth near his. She threw him a teasing smile and his eyes darkened even more.

He gave a rough growl, put the laptop to one side, and pushed her on to her back. 'You minx,' he said, and she laughed as he pinned her down with his body and pressed urgent kisses on her.

Then she closed her eyes and allowed the delicious sensations to carry her away.

Natasha sipped her drink, glad of the chance to rest in the shade. She and Luc had been sent to do some shopping at the market for Simone. They'd bought lots of fruit, as well as a basket full of aubergines for a *gratin*. Marianne had decided that, after all the rich food and wine of the wedding, they should have a couple of days of light meals. They'd stopped at the café for a quick drink before the drive back to the château. It was a relief to get away from the crowded market stalls and do a spot of people-watching. Everyone seemed to know everyone else in the small town, and paused to chat, comparing baskets full of produce. Across the road an old townhouse was being renovated, and a couple of men in hardhats scooped rubble into a long tube, which fed into a skip at the bottom. The house appeared to have been gutted: only the roof and the outer walls remained.

'What work does Poppy Cottage need doing?' asked Luc.

Natasha laughed. 'Hopefully it won't be as drastic as that, but it does need a lot. The last owner was elderly and became very ill. He let it fall into disrepair, and when he died there was a dispute over the inheritance. It stood empty for years until recently.'

'Does it need structural work?'

'Yes. The roof's leaking quite badly, there's a bit of damp. The orangery was all glass and wooden frames, but the wood has rotted. Oh, and it needs rewiring, too. I could go on.' Her smile faded. She had told herself she'd tackle these jobs one at a time, but listing them made her realise the extent of the undertaking. She stirred her *diabolo menthe*, a refreshing drink of mint syrup and fizzy water, absently watching the ice cubes spin.

'Will you live there while the work's going on?'

'I'm not sure. I'm planning to get more detailed surveys done before I decide.' She grinned. 'I can always pitch a tent in the garden.'

He frowned. 'There's no need for that. You could stay in your current flat until the house is ready, couldn't you?'

'It was a joke. I can't wait to move in there.' She turned away, dreamily picturing the place as she hoped it would be one day.

She was aware of Luc watching her before he remarked, 'You have fond memories?'

'Very.' The cottage gave on to fields at the back and she remembered long walks with her parents, picnics by the stream, a house filled with music, laughter and love. Her pulse picked up at the thought of bringing the place back to life. Giving it the care it deserved. 'It's hard to believe, but it was beautiful once. Dad always made sure the paintwork was immaculate and the garden was full of flowers. And Mum decorated the place. I remember her making curtains, and we grew fruit and veg in the back garden among the flowers. Peas and strawberries. I used to enjoy picking them and eating them when I was about Arthur's age.'

Luc didn't reply. He was watching her with a curious look in his eye that she couldn't decipher. He'd left most of his drink untouched.

She added, 'It will be wonderful to bring life back to the place, to fill it with noise again. Make it a home.'

A long silence followed.

'With Mr Right?'

She looked at him. Her hopes rose, thinking of how blissful the last few nights had felt in his arms. She realised she was longing for him to say something more, to paint himself into that picture of her future.

But he said nothing. He remained stern and waited for her to answer. He didn't want to share in her future.

'Yes,' she said. 'With Mr Right.'

The temperature had cranked up a notch since the wedding four days ago. The flowers were wilting, the paper lanterns torn and fraying, and the fairy lights hung forlornly from the tree branches. It was time to take down the decorations, and since Luc and his family were all at the hospital, Natasha decided she might as well make herself useful and spare them the task.

She climbed up the stepladder and began to unhook the lights. She wore a camisole and white shorts, but her skin prickled in the sun, and she knew it wasn't just the intense heat that was making her feel uncomfortable and on edge. The last few days had been wonderful – she thought of the moments she and Luc had shared in their bed, the joy of waking up beside him, of feeling his heartbeat against her cheek when he wrapped her in his arms – but the festivities were over. It was time for normal life to resume, and she had to ask herself, apart from the sex, what had changed in their relationship.

This isn't about my family or my father any more. It's about you and me, Luc had said on the night of Juliette's wedding when the air had been so charged with magic and hope that the vines had seemed to tremble and glow in the moonlight. Today, in the fierce glare of the sun, they seemed dry and lifeless in their regimented, military lines.

What do we have to lose? Luc had asked. As if the answer was: nothing at all.

But now she'd had a few days to think, she could list all the things she had to lose, such as her pride, her peace of mind and the fragile happiness she'd managed to find in Willowbrook.

There was so much at stake.

A loud crash from the kitchen made her jump. The clatter of metal on stone was followed by a string of curses from Simone. The cook peered through the window and called, 'It's just a pan. *Rien de grave.*' Relieved it was nothing serious, Natasha went back to unhooking the lights. But her heart thumped. Getting involved with Luc again, being physically intimate, was the most dangerous thing she could have done – so why had she let it happen?

She'd been seduced by the romantic mood of Juliette's wedding, the incredible setting, the love that had suffused the air more potently than the lavender that edged the garden paths of this beautiful château. And she'd been seduced by Luc's words. *The last few days have changed everything.* They had indeed changed everything for her. She loved it here. She'd learned so much about him, and now she felt she knew the real Luc. But had he meant what she thought he'd meant? Had he been talking about love and marriage, or had she simply heard what she wanted to hear?

She climbed down from the ladder and began to gather up the cable of lights. The last few days had been blissfully sensual, but he hadn't given any hint that this was more than a short-term arrangement. One day at a time was all well and good, but he hadn't spoken about her departure in a couple of days or what would happen after she returned to Willowbrook.

And he hadn't mentioned love.

She breathed hard, fighting the crushing sensation in her chest. But, then, she'd been a fool to hope even for a second that he would. *Now we have this . . . And it works.*

It had hardly been a pledge. She had looked into his eyes and seen what she hoped to see – rather than the stark reality. And now she had only herself to blame because he'd always been honest with her. He didn't do commitment. He'd never made a secret of that. She even understood his reasons: coming here had taught her so much about the man and what had shaped him.

But in growing to understand him better she'd let barriers fall and bonds form. Her fingers gripped the cable of fairy lights. Where there had been acrimony and distance, now there was closeness, warmth – and something else.

For her, every touch, every kiss, every night together had nurtured seeds of feeling. Her pulse fired like a machine gun. She couldn't allow those feelings to develop. He was the man she'd divorced: he'd hurt her before and she couldn't go through that much pain again.

Yet even as she thought this, she was aware of emotion taking root, of tiny new shoots springing up inside her and buds of growth on the verge of unfurling. She tried to stop them, to hold them back. She mustn't fall in love with him again. She had to fight it.

But a feeling of dread settled on her, heavy and inevitable. Her eyes squeezed shut because although she knew she mustn't fall in love she had the feeling it might already be too late.

'I'd like to buy Poppy Cottage from you, Luc.'

He had been idly stroking her hair. Now his hand

stilled. Sunlight streamed in through the half-open shutters, bathing their bed in warmth, and as she lay with her head against his chest, he sensed the tension in her. Was she bracing herself for a fight? And why did she want to buy the cottage when it was hers already?

'There's no need,' he said.

'I insist. I can't afford to match what you paid, but I can give you the asking price now, and arrange to pay you the rest as soon as I have the money.'

'Forget it, Nat. The place isn't worth that much. I only paid it to get you here.'

She flinched, and he realised how his words had sounded. But it was true. And he didn't regret it: buying the cottage had brought her back into his life.

'Luc, I've given it a lot of thought, and I really want this.'

He heard the truth in her voice and it made him rethink. He rolled her on to her back and looked down at her. 'It's important to you?'

Intense blue eyes gazed up at him. 'Yes,' she said. 'I need to feel the cottage is mine.'

'It *is* yours.' He reached across to the bedside table and slid open a drawer. 'Here, take the keys.'

She looked at them, then at him. 'It won't feel like my home as long as I haven't paid for it.'

Something in him yielded. The money he'd spent meant nothing to him, he wanted her to have the cottage – but he could see she felt strongly about it. The place was of great importance to her and he knew she was proud to pay her own way. So he agreed – to please her.

Besides, now they were back together, what did it matter who had paid for what? They hadn't discussed it, but for the last few days they'd been sharing a bed and he was hopeful that this might develop, that this was a new start for them, a second chance. And if it worked out, it would become irrelevant who had bought the cottage.

But perhaps she saw things differently. It was difficult to know what she thought or felt. When they'd discussed the renovations, he'd hoped she might ask for his opinion or recommendations, since construction was his speciality. But no. Her plans didn't involve him.

Still, he hoped that soon she might begin to trust him, to open up. They had all the time in the world, and it was impossible not to feel optimistic when the last few days had felt so natural, so right. So perfect.

'We didn't pay you for doing Juliette's flowers,' he reminded her, one brow lifted.

'That isn't worth much compared to what you paid.'

'You took time out from running your business. You can't put a price on that. And it was invaluable to my family.'

Her lips flattened as she considered this. 'I suppose that could make up some of the difference.'

'All of it,' he said dismissively.

She concurred with a small nod. 'So I'll pay you the asking price for the cottage and then we'll be quits?'

His eyes held hers. 'Agreed. But let me arrange the renovation work for you. I know the right people – they'll do a good job.'

She smiled and nodded. 'Thank you.'

He dipped his head and closed his eyes to savour the soft warmth of her lips.

Then he heard the kitchen door creak open and the clatter of quick footsteps on the gravel, the children's squeals and shouts.

He pulled away reluctantly. 'We should get up.'

'Yes,' she said. Then she asked quietly, 'Should I book a taxi to go to the airport tomorrow?'

He frowned. 'Tomorrow?'

His mind raced to catch up – the end of the two weeks.

'You don't have to leave tomorrow,' he reassured her. Since Juliette's wedding everything had changed between them – the agreement they'd made was null and void now their relationship was real again.

She looked at him with the cautious expression of someone about to break bad news. 'I do,' she said carefully.

Shock rattled through him, making his head spin. 'I know that was what we arranged, but given how things have developed, why not reconsider your plans?'

He expected to see her eyes light up, her cheeks dimple as she smiled back at him. Instead, she slipped out from under him and pulled on her bathrobe, belted it tight with a sharp tug.

'No. The deal was two weeks. I need to go home.'

He stared at her, but she was avoiding his gaze. He didn't understand. 'Why? Your shop is in good hands. Why not phone your staff and arrange to stay here a little longer?'

'Debbie's not just staff. She's a friend and she's pregnant and – and it wouldn't be fair to do that . . . Besides, it's not just about my shop.'

A prickle touched the back of his neck. 'What, then?'

'I want to go home,' she said, with a tiny shrug.

He sat up in bed and watched as she pulled her case out of the wardrobe and began to pack. She was serious. He'd thought it was going so well that she'd at least consider staying, but she seemed determined as she folded skirts and dresses and laid them neatly in her case. He didn't know what to say, didn't know how to stop her. She wanted to leave?

'But, Natasha, it's working so well between us.'

'It's been good sex –' he stiffened, feeling the insult like a blow to his body '– but it's not real. We both have our own lives to get back to.'

Outside, the children were calling to each other. He heard shouts of excitement and laughter. A far cry from the mood in this room.

'I could come with you.'

She shot him a disbelieving look. 'To Willowbrook?'

He nodded. 'My position is more flexible than yours.'

'Because you're the boss of a multimillion-dollar business, you mean?' She laughed, then said dismissively, 'You wouldn't do that.'

'I would,' he said unsteadily.

Would he?

He silently cursed his own uncertainty. Why hadn't he thought this through? If he'd anticipated this, he wouldn't have been caught on the back foot. But he'd been taking each day as it came, optimistic that their relationship was working, that she felt the same – and he felt betrayed because she hadn't given him any indication that she was unhappy. That it was only 'good sex'. His hands curled into fists. Was that really how she saw it?

For him it had been way more than just sex, it had been . . .

What had it been exactly?

He frowned, unsure of the answer. All he knew was that he'd wanted to take things one step at a time, see how they progressed. Evidently she didn't want the same thing.

'You see?' she said. 'You're not even sure yourself.' She paused from folding clothes. Then she said, 'It wouldn't work, Luc. This,' she pointed to their bed, 'was good for a few days while it lasted, but it's not going anywhere.'

There was a long silence as he tried to impose order on the whirl of emotions that whipped through him. His teeth were clenched so hard his jaw ached. 'Why – why do you say that?' he asked finally.

The irony of the situation wasn't lost on him. How many times had he told women he couldn't give them anything more than the here and now? Hundreds. He'd even said it to her once.

And yet now he was hearing it, it was like a knife to his ribs.

She was leaving him. Again.

He looked at the crumpled sheets. How could two people who'd shared something as intimate and as special as they'd had these last few days view the situation so differently? He didn't want her to go. He desperately wanted her to stay – he was certain it could work . . .

But he wasn't certain, was he?

That was the problem.

None of his relationships had worked in the past. Relationships were the one thing he was no good at, and if he failed in this, Natasha would get hurt.

'Luc, we were married before, remember? It didn't work last time. Why would it now?'

He got up and pulled on a pair of soft shorts. They'd been through this already. 'Because it's different this time. We've both changed, and . . .' He thought of the pregnancy, the miscarriage, and his memories of that time were like vinegar on the tongue. Painful. Sharp. '. . . and the circumstances are not the same.'

'It's precisely circumstances that brought us together – your father's illness. You didn't come and find me because you wanted to, but because you had to. If this was really meant to be, you would have thought of me sooner.'

The words gushed from her, breathless and fierce, as if she'd been bottling them up for a long time and the truth had unexpectedly bared itself.

'That's not fair,' he said. 'You were the one who left me, who filed divorce papers as soon as you got away.'

And he *had* thought of her. He'd never forgotten her in the three years they were apart. He'd compared every woman he'd dated with Natasha and had found them all wanting. He'd signed the divorce papers, but in his mind, they'd made a commitment and he couldn't undo that. Perhaps that was why he'd kept the wedding ring she left behind. And the giant panda, he thought wryly.

'And you signed them! You didn't stop me leaving. In

fact, you carried my bags down to the taxi as if you couldn't be happier to see the back of me!'

'That's what you think?' He stared at her, appalled.

How could they be on such different wavelengths? She'd completely misinterpreted his every action. He thought that during the last two weeks she'd got to know and understand him better, and that he'd come to know her better too.

It seemed he was wrong.

So maybe she was right. Maybe there was no hope for them. Maybe this was going nowhere.

Chapter Seventeen

Natasha watched his shocked expression turn to a dark scowl. He pushed the hair back from his face and strode across the room to the window. He shoved his hands into his pockets and stared down at the garden. He looked as if he was battling to control his temper, though she couldn't understand why: they'd had a deal and she'd believed they would stick to it. That was how Luc operated: unemotional, a man of his word. She reached for the last of her dresses from the wardrobe, but it was tangled up with one of his shirts. Impatiently, she tugged the dress free and shook it before folding it.

All she was certain of was that she mustn't cave into the temptation of believing that their story would have a happy-ever-after. She had to be strong and remember what had happened last time. The last two weeks had been a holiday with good sex, very different from love or marriage. He hadn't said he loved her or spoken about the future even once. Her heart gripped. Now she had to go – before she got sucked in any further. Back to Willowbrook and her friends, her shop, the cottage – where she belonged. This was the right thing to do, the sensible thing. This way she wouldn't get hurt.

'For your information, I was not happy to see the back of you,' he said.

His voice was a deep rasp, his accent so unusually strong that she stopped what she was doing and turned to him. He was facing her. It would be easy to feel intimidated when he looked like that. Fierce. Dark-eyed. Angry.

'I was worried about you, Nat, I was shocked – you took me completely by surprise with your decision to leave.'

The look in his eyes made her hesitate, because she could almost believe he'd been hurt.

But she knew better. Their marriage had been hell – for both of them. She didn't doubt that he was surprised when she'd left so soon after the miscarriage, but anything else he'd felt had simply been wounded pride.

'Was it so bad,' he went on, 'being with me that you had to leave the moment you came out of hospital?'

She remembered how fragile she'd been. She couldn't eat, could barely hold a conversation because her thoughts were so chaotic – and bleak. So bleak she could have drowned in them.

'I just didn't see the point in staying. Our marriage was doomed, Luc.' What would he have done – nursed her? He put his multinational construction business before everything else. He didn't do love.

She knew who he was. And she knew she loved him. Which was why he had the power to hurt her.

Around him she was vulnerable, and that terrified her. No wonder she'd run from him last time. It hadn't just been losing the baby that had driven her away, she saw that now. She'd run to protect herself, and she had to leave tomorrow for the same reason.

'When a relationship isn't going anywhere, why delay the inevitable?'

Her words hung in the air, loaded with reference to the present as much as the past.

She turned away and began to slot her bottles of nail varnish into their plastic box, avoiding his gaze, though she could feel it burning the back of her neck.

'This is how you feel?'

She swallowed. A part of her was tempted to stay. Really tempted. After all, the last few days had been idyllic, and for a fleeting moment she pictured him coming to Willowbrook, spending weekends there, helping her to restore the cottage, romantic evenings by the fire, holidays here with his family . . .

But then the automatic brake inside her was activated and the dream cut short.

It was fantasy, nothing more. Luc's life was in London and travelling the world. He was a free spirit. Being tied down would make him unhappy, which would take them straight back to where they'd been when they were married. She didn't want to be tolerated. She wanted to be cherished and loved.

And if she couldn't have that, then she'd rather be alone.

'It is,' she said, feeling as if she'd been teetering on the edge of a cliff and had just stepped back to safety. 'I'm happy with my life, Luc. Willowbrook is my home now. I feel I belong there. I have friends, I have . . . plans.'

Silence stretched. 'Plans to marry?'

'Yes,' she said honestly. 'One day. I want a family, love – the long-haul.'

He didn't say anything. He didn't need to. He couldn't give her those things: he didn't want them.

She dropped the last bottle of varnish into its slot and snapped the box shut, feeling awful that it had to end like this. After all, what they'd shared the last few days had been special, and the thought of never seeing him again . . .

She'd miss him. She'd miss him terribly.

So, although it went against the plans she'd made to cut all ties with him, she said, 'Perhaps we could meet for dinner some time.'

'Dinner?' He laughed incredulously and she realised – too late – that she'd really wounded his pride now.

She wished she could take her words back.

He crossed the room to tower over her, his dark eyes flashing like deep water. 'Did you really just say that?'

'We never had a normal relationship,' she blustered, 'just a few weeks before a shotgun wedding, then this.' She waved her hand, indicating the bizarrely intimate situation of having shared his family's crisis and wedding all in two short weeks. 'And I'd like to keep in touch. To hear how your family are doing . . .'

'You're offering me a consolation prize of dinner so you can get updates on my family,' he said, and turned away, his jaw like rock.

'Luc, I didn't mean – it's really not like that . . .' She reached out to him, but he shook her hand off his arm.

'Isn't it?' He whirled back round. 'Isn't it? The way I

see it, now you've got your cottage, your interest in me – in us – is over. Isn't that the truth, Natasha?'

His words pierced through her. She was already feeling fragile, but this was the knock-out blow. Did he really believe that she'd use him for sex and then mercilessly turn her back on him the moment she'd got what she wanted?

'I'm just sticking to the original agreement we made, Luc. Nothing more, nothing less.'

He was silent during the family meal that night. He'd made himself scarce all day, using the excuse of visiting his father and having errands to run, and when dinner was over and Natasha excused herself to go to bed, he didn't follow. Instead he stayed outside, glowering into a glass of wine.

She tossed and turned, unable to sleep. If only she'd handled it differently. She didn't want to part on such bad terms.

When he finally came upstairs she lay rigid on her side of the bed, trying not to move or make a sound. Only when he fell asleep could she relax and doze off.

Then in the night she woke to find herself in his arms.

Luc had been lying sleepless for a while. Her breathing changed as she woke, and he felt her tense as she realised his arm was wrapped around her, and her legs were entwined with his. He didn't know who had reached for whom, but it seemed that unconsciously they'd gravitated back to each other. Now he wondered if she'd pull away when she remembered their argument.

But she didn't.

'Luc,' she said. 'It's not true that now I've got the cottage, my interest is over.'

His chest lifted as he dragged in air. 'I know.'

The night was quiet. He could hear only his heartbeat and the rustle of the sheet as she moved her leg.

'You do?'

'Yes,' he said. 'I lashed out earlier. I didn't mean it. I know I hurt you the first time and I'm sorry.'

'You already apologised. And we were both to blame. We both made mistakes. It doesn't matter now.'

'It does matter. Natasha, I . . .' He wanted to tell her how he felt, but how could he trust his feelings? How could he be sure that, in a few weeks, they wouldn't have faded, that he wouldn't get itchy feet again and want to move on? His world was one of fast-paced business deals, and he was hungry to get back to the buzz of his demanding schedule.

Natasha's reason for leaving was watertight. She was hoping to meet her Mr Right and marry him, and how could Luc even audition for that role when he didn't do commitment? She'd told him how painful their marriage had been for her – he'd been the cause of that pain. He couldn't risk hurting her again.

He gave up trying to find the words. He let out a rough sigh and kissed her.

And they made love.

Fiercely. Tenderly. Slowly.

Knowing it would be the last time.

Chapter Eighteen

Natasha placed the last jug of sunflowers in the window, then went outside to check the finished result.

Standing in the street she absently brushed petals off her blue dress and surveyed her work. Thick squares of lavender contrasted with the bold yellow flowers, and she'd deliberately overfilled the window with plants so the effect of solid colour was even more striking.

'Hey, good work,' said Debbie, who'd come out to have a look. 'It's really eye-catching.'

Natasha nodded thoughtfully. Colourful, noticeable, it was exactly what she wanted from her shop front, and yet she felt only a tiny sense of satisfaction at her work. Instead, she was remembering the drive back to the airport, which she and Luc had made in silence. Her chest ached, as if she'd left a part of herself in Provence among the vineyards. She could visualise the bold blue sky, smell Simone's delicious cooking and feel the sun on her skin.

She wondered what they were all doing: if Jean-Pierre was growing stronger, if Juliette and Philippe had booked a honeymoon yet. Was Caroline still enjoying running the vineyard? Had Xavier learned to dive? Did Luc miss her?

Tears pricked the backs of her eyes. Of course he didn't.

He'd sent her a few texts, phoned her a couple of times – but he'd kept the conversation factual. Asked her how the renovations were coming along, if she was happy with the builders he'd sent in.

She was. They were doing a great job. They reckoned the cottage would be ready to move into in a few months. Soon she would have made good her promise to her mum, and the cottage would once more be a home. And it was rightfully hers now because Luc had accepted her payment for it. Her shoulders slumped.

'Hey – are you OK?'

Debbie had turned to look at her, and Natasha quickly tried to hide what she'd been feeling with a forced smile. 'I'm fine.'

'Listen, Nat. I don't know what happened in France, but I'm worried about you. You haven't been yourself since.'

She stared at her friend, dismayed that her efforts to appear cheerful had failed so miserably. 'Haven't I?'

When she'd left Château Duval she'd believed she'd return to Willowbrook and normal life, that she'd be happy, just as she had been before – even more so now she had the cottage. But those two weeks in France had changed her.

Debbie shook her head. 'Maybe it would do you good to talk about it. Get it off your chest.'

'No,' she said. 'I mean, I'm not ready.'

'Then maybe you should arrange to see your ex again,'

she suggested gently, 'because whatever happened between you two, you clearly have unfinished business.'

Natasha swallowed. Yes, they had unfinished business. She hadn't been honest with Luc, hadn't told him the truth. That she loved him. She'd let him believe she didn't care because protecting herself from hurt was engrained in her, but what could possibly hurt more than this?

Being with him when he didn't love her, she reminded herself.

'It's definitely finished,' she said quietly.

She just had to get used to that.

Luc stared out of the glass office walls at the view over London, words washing over him as a discussion took place around him.

After Natasha had left, he'd stayed with his family a couple of weeks longer, flying out for a few business trips to the US, Malaysia and eastern Europe. But when his father had come home from hospital, Luc knew he wasn't really needed any more. He had to get back to normal life, so he'd forced himself to board his plane to London and open the negotiations for a new development site.

But the buzz wasn't there.

All the things that had excited him before – new ventures, growth opportunities, sales projections – suddenly seemed unimportant. Even irritating. The meeting was happening in front of him but he couldn't focus. The man he was doing business with was a cheerful guy, prone to cracking jokes. But Luc couldn't bring himself to smile. Instead, he was wondering what Natasha was doing. He was picturing the dimple in her cheek when she smiled, remembering how she'd curled up against him in her sleep, her blonde hair brushing his chin, her peach scent weaving itself around his senses.

And he had the feeling he'd let something very precious slip out of his grasp, yet again.

He'd never met another woman like her and knew he never would. He didn't know how he was so certain – she'd talked about bolts of lightning, but he'd never believed in all that stuff. All he knew was that those two weeks with her had changed him: he was a different man, someone who saw the world more clearly, who had reorganised his priorities in life. Who was lost without her.

He sighed and leaned back in his chair. His assistant, John, threw him a worried look.

He couldn't think of anything but Natasha. He couldn't concentrate. He needed her. He loved her.

At first he hadn't been sure whether to trust this feeling – what was love, after all, and how could he be sure it would last?

But as time had passed, his certainty had grown.

The only problem was, there was nothing to suggest that Natasha felt the same.

He pushed his chair back. 'Excuse me, something's come up,' he explained to the others in the room. 'Something important.'

Eyes widened as he walked out of the meeting. A shocked silence followed. His assistant caught up with him in the corridor.

'Luc, what is it?' John asked urgently. 'What's wrong?'

'Nothing's wrong.' Luc strode towards the lift. He should have done this sooner. He just hoped it wasn't too late.

John was almost running to keep up with him. 'You can't just leave. You know how crucial these talks—'

'I can. I have to.' He reached the lift and stopped. Looked the other man in the eye. 'You deal with it. I know you're capable.'

'But – but what about the other side? What will they think, you just leaving like this?'

'I don't care what they think.'

There was only one person whose opinion Luc cared about now.

Natasha picked her way through the weeds and over-enthusiastic hardy geraniums that sprawled across the path to the front door. In her hand she held the key, as if it were made of gold.

She liked to visit each night after work. She told herself she was keeping tabs on the work the builders had done, but really she found it comforting. She enjoyed exploring the rooms, and she was making plans too, prioritising the work that needed to be done once the structural repairs were finished. As she moved through the hall, memories flowed. In the kitchen she felt a tingling sensation as she remembered her mother standing by the window with a tray of empty glass jars. She used to keep beehives in the field next door and Natasha remembered watching her boil the honey to make it set. When it was cool, she used to help to stick labels on the jars.

Natasha went upstairs. Her childhood bedroom was so tiny, but her parents' old room had a lovely view of the back garden and the fields beyond. That would be hers, she decided. She'd choose sunny shades for it, and she saw in her mind patterned wallpaper and gauzy curtains that would let in the light. There'd be room for a king-size bed with a cast-iron frame painted cream, and if she positioned it near the window she'd be able to see the fields from her bed. She looked out on to the garden behind. It was overgrown but the apple and pear trees that had made up the orchard were still there and she could picture how it would look when everything had been pruned and tidied, the house fixed and cleaned. Made homely again. It would be beautiful, welcoming.

She'd made good her promise to her mother, she thought, trying to push Luc's dark-eyed face out of her mind. It might have cost her emotional heartache, but the cottage and her parents' memory would be well preserved.

Her phone rang. She reached into her pocket and saw Luc's number. Her heart hiccuped and she made herself take a deep breath before answering; 'Luc, hi.'

'Natasha.'

His deep voice was so familiar it rumbled through her. It transported her back to those long, warm nights in the château, and her skin tingled. 'How are you? How's your father?'

'He's fine. Well, he was this morning when I called them.'

'Right. Well . . . that's good.'

A pause followed. 'What are you doing Friday night?'

'Friday? Er – nothing. Why?'

'Have dinner with me.'

She heard the smile in his voice and her breath caught. Hope lifted in her like butterflies taking flight on a summer's day. But immediately she clamped down on it. She asked warily, 'Why?'

'Do I need a reason?' His voice had an edge and she couldn't tell if it was impatience – or hurt. He added gently, 'It was your suggestion, remember?'

Her fingers squeezed the phone. 'I remember.'

Her heart swelled with feelings she tried to fight down, but it was impossible. Seeing Luc again, hearing what was going on in his life would bring the same intense combination of torment and longing.

But not seeing him would be harder. 'Yes,' she said finally. 'I'll see you Friday.'

She was going through the motions of making beaded rings and bracelets to sell in her shop, but Natasha had positioned herself by the window of her flat, and really she had one eye on the street below, watching for Luc, who should be here any minute. She had on the blue satin dress she'd worn on her first night in France and she'd spent too long blow-drying her hair, too long putting on make-up, then toning it down so it didn't look like she was trying hard to impress.

Her fingers were unsteady and, when she dropped a

bead, she sighed and wondered for the hundredth time since he'd called if this wasn't a terrible mistake.

Despite Debbie's advice that she should see him again, every sensible part of Natasha warned against it. It would be agony hearing all about Luc's life when she wished she were a part of it. And yet she hadn't been able to resist the opportunity to see him again, hadn't been able to say no, just like she hadn't been able to say no when he'd come here asking for her help.

The sound of a car pulling up outside made her head turn. But it was an inconspicuous black family car. Not Luc, then, she thought.

However, a few moments later a head of dark hair caught her eye. Her heart jumped and she looked again. It *was* Luc.

'No sports car?' she asked him, when she opened her door.

'I thought it was time I got something more sensible,' he said.

'Oh,' she said, unsure how to respond to that. What had changed? Her heart lurched. Oh, God, perhaps he'd met someone new already.

He frowned. 'What's this?' he asked, lifting her left hand and running his fingers over the multi-coloured beaded rings.

They were the only colour. Her nail polish was called silver glitter, but really it was pale grey – which was exactly how she'd felt recently.

'I made them,' she said. 'To hide the white mark your ring left. Which reminds me – I have it here.'

She reached into her bag and retrieved the box in which the platinum ring was safely stored. She didn't tell him her finger felt too light without it, and she was reluctant to hand it over. She didn't say what she secretly hoped – that he'd tell her to keep it.

But he smiled and took it. 'Thank you.'

He slipped it into his pocket and, as she watched it disappear into his jacket, the last of her hopes died.

'So where are we going?' she asked, once they were in his car. He looked calm and completely composed, whereas she was a bundle of nerves, filling the silence with anxious chatter. 'There aren't many places round here, you know. Willowbrook is tiny. Nothing like the places you're used to in the city.'

'It's a surprise,' was all he said.

Chapter Nineteen

'Why are you stopping here?' she asked, as they drew up outside Poppy Cottage.

The answer should have been obvious: he wanted to see how the renovations were coming along. After all, he'd organised the builders, who were carrying out the work. Dusk was falling, though, so he'd have to hurry because there were no lights in the place yet.

'This is where we're having dinner,' he said.

'Don't be silly! We can't. The builders told me not to come near the place today. They're doing some dangerous work and there'll be dust and rubble and . . .'

Luc was smiling. Creases fanned from his beautiful chocolate eyes. 'There was no dangerous work. Just a couple of men with tools and hardhats helping me get things ready,' he told her.

'Helping you? What were you . . .?'

'Come.'

He took her hand and led her inside.

They walked straight through to the back of the cottage and the old orangery. She'd passed through this room just a few days ago and she was certain that the glass structure had been pockmarked with broken panes and peeling paint.

Now it was fully restored. Not only that, but someone had strung up tiny lanterns with tea lights flickering inside. There were potted plants all around them, vases filled with bouquets, which she recognised, and a glass table in the centre of the room set for dinner for two, music playing softly.

'I made those bouquets. How did you get them?'

'I sent someone.'

She tried to think but she couldn't remember anyone coming into the shop.

'Debbie served him,' Luc explained. 'It's a little too cold to be outside, but you said you used to sit with your parents and watch the stars,' Luc said, looking up through the glass ceiling to the darkening sky. She followed his gaze and stared. He'd remembered that? She was stunned.

'Sunset is not for another hour,' he said, 'but the forecast is for a clear night so I hope you'll see stars. If you're willing to wait.'

'Oh, Luc, it's beautiful . . .' Emotion choked her words. The happy memories rushed to the surface, and the thoughtfulness of the gesture was overwhelming. He'd gone to the trouble of preparing all this? She was touched beyond words. Why had he done it? Her pulse beat unsteadily. Could it be that he loved her, after all?

No. If he loved her, he would have come sooner. He would have missed her and ached for the sound of her voice, as she had for his.

'Glass of wine?' His deep voice came from behind her.

She turned and nodded, unable to speak, and he placed a glass in her hand. 'Sit down. Dinner's nearly ready.'

She looked towards the kitchen. 'Is someone else here?'

'No one but you and me,' he assured her.

'But you can't cook.' He must have bought food in. It smelt delicious.

'Actually, I can. Simone has been teaching me a few of her recipes. I decided it was time I became more domesticated.'

Her heart pinched. First the sensible car, now he'd learned to cook. He must have met somebody special to have changed so much. She felt a stab of pain that he'd moved on so fast. What had she been thinking of, suggesting they meet for dinner? It was only making her yearn for what she couldn't have.

'I hope you're hungry,' he said.

'Very.' Her gaze met with his and held.

'We're having tomato tarts to start with, then *navarin* of lamb.'

They sat down and the food was lovely. They made small-talk about his work and hers, but Natasha was too much on edge to relax and enjoy it.

Luc brought in Mont Blancs for dessert, delicious bowls of sweet chestnut purée, ice cream and cream. She tried to make hers last, not wanting this precious time with him to end, but the ice cream melted, hurrying her along.

As Luc stirred sugar into his coffee, he said, 'I've missed you these last few weeks.'

His quietly spoken admission took her by surprise. 'H-have you?'

She thought of all the days they'd been apart and how,

for her, they'd been so unbearably long, and there'd been so little communication from him.

'Yes. I've been working on a new business deal . . . but my mind wasn't on it.'

He was watching her intently, but she wasn't sure what he was trying to tell her. It didn't marry with his actions, with the distance he'd kept from her these last few weeks.

Then again, she'd left him. She'd told him she wanted to go home and she'd hardened her heart to his protests when he'd suggested she stay in France.

'That's strange,' she said. 'Your work used to mean more to you than anything else.'

'Used to.'

She waited for him to elucidate, but that was all he said.

'Maybe it's your family you were missing – your sisters, the children . . .'

'I saw them. Last weekend we went to the beach.' His eyes glittered fondly. 'No, what I've missed has been having you by my side, somebody to talk to, to share things with, to laugh and smile with . . . and to make love to.'

Colour scorched her cheeks. She felt a tug, but she ignored it. Though she missed it, too, making love wasn't enough.

'Well, the wife thing was a pretence.'

'The rest wasn't. Those two weeks were the best and the worst of my life. The worst because my father was so sick and I pray we never have to go through anything like that again.' His voice dropped. 'The best because you were there with me. And this is what tonight is all about. I have to tell you how I feel. Even if you don't feel the same, you need to know.'

She blinked. Her hopes lifted like a hot-air balloon. She pinned them down, restrained them by reminding herself of how hard the last few weeks had been. 'Why didn't you come sooner?'

Behind him the sky had turned inky dark and the candles made shadows flicker across his face, emphasising all the hard angles, the whites of his eyes and his teeth.

'Because I needed to be sure of my feelings.' He put his spoon down and looked into her eyes. 'I know I hurt you before. I couldn't risk doing it again. But I've had time to reflect and now I'm certain I love you, Natasha.'

Her heart became a crazy drum. Her mouth dried.

'I know you don't love me any more, but I don't want to have any regrets this time.'

There were so many questions spinning in her head it was difficult to know where to start. 'You had regrets last time?'

'Many. But the biggest was that I let you go. When my father said he wanted to meet you, I had to swallow my pride to come here and ask for your help – but I also jumped at the chance to see you again.'

Her heart folded. Outside an owl called softly from across the fields.

'What makes you think I don't feel the same?'

'You have plans,' he said, and nodded to the magical décor he'd arranged. 'You're looking for Mr Right to share this with you.'

She took a sip of her coffee, thinking she needed to wake up because she must be dreaming. 'You don't think you can be him?'

He stilled. She saw hope flare in his eyes, and the corner of his mouth twitched.

'Actually, I do. I hope. I'd like to. If you'll have me.' His eyes gleamed, and his smile made her stomach tighten.

She tried to temper her excitement and be practical, realistic. 'But you travel all over the world with your work.'

'And I want to come home to you here,' he said softly. Definitively.

'What about your family?'

'What about them? I see them regularly now. I still would if I was with you. They adore you – they think we're married anyway.'

Her eyes widened. 'You haven't told them yet?'

'I wanted to speak to you first.' He leaned forward. 'Nat, I want to be part of your life, take care of you, be the father of your children.'

Her heart stuttered. Tears stung the backs of her eyes and she blinked hard.

'I've told you what I want, but what do you want, Natasha?'

Him. She'd only ever wanted him.

She took a deep breath, feeling like she was laying herself bare. 'I love you, Luc.'

His eyes shone. His throat worked.

Then he pushed back his chair. 'Nat,' he said roughly.

She got up and went into his arms.

'I love you,' he whispered into her hair. Then pulled away so he could see her.

He removed a beaded ring from her left hand and slipped his ring back into its rightful place.

'But I have to warn you,' he said gravely, 'this time it will be for ever – because I'm never going to let you out of my life again.'

Epilogue

'So it was a test?' asked Luc.

'Yes,' said his father.

It was exactly a month since Juliette's wedding and the temperature was still high, even for August. The late-morning air was scented with lavender, and a host of cicadas were feverishly scratching out their song in the pine trees. Luc and Natasha had come to Château Duval to confess the truth and announce their plans to his family.

But before they could, Jean-Pierre had dropped this bombshell of his own. Luc and Natasha looked at each other.

'It wasn't hard to find out the truth,' his father went on. He was sitting in the shade of the plane tree, a newspaper on his lap. He'd regained some weight, although not too much – he was on a strict diet now – and looked healthier, more like his old self. Yet Luc noticed that his demeanour had changed. There was something gentler about him, as if his illness had rubbed away the hard edges, the insufferable pride, the arrogance. It had made him more approachable. 'I made some enquiries and learned you'd been divorced.'

'And you thought that bringing two divorcees back together was a good idea?' Luc asked, incredulous to learn that his father had known all along they were pretending to be a married couple.

'Yes,' his father insisted firmly. 'I heard you were devastated after Natasha left. That your marriage changed you – you hardly dated, you worked even more ridiculously long hours . . . I was concerned.'

'So you thought you'd play Cupid.' Luc felt betrayed. He wasn't sure who had been more deceitful – him or his father. One day, he knew, they would look back on this and laugh. 'Did everyone know? Maman, Caro, Juliette?' He looked around, as if they might step out from behind the oleander bush. Of course, they wouldn't. Juliette and Philippe were on honeymoon, and Marianne, Caroline and Marc had taken the children to the beach for the day. Only Simone was here, tasked with making sure Jean-Pierre didn't leave the house and go to the office, he'd explained, when they'd arrived ten minutes ago.

'No. Just me.'

Natasha looked confused. 'Why was it a test? A test of whom? Of what?'

Luc took her hand. 'Of me,' he explained. 'To make me realise what was important, what my life was missing. And also to see how far I would go for him. Isn't that right, Papa?'

His father had the grace to look ashamed of himself. 'You passed with flying colours,' he said softly.

Natasha's brow puckered. 'You shouldn't test people like that, Jean-Pierre. You should trust those closest to you. Luc would have done anything for you – you must have known that without putting him to the test.'

Luc wrapped an arm around her, smiling at her gentle reprimand.

'You're right,' said Jean-Pierre.

She shot him a stern look. 'Promise you won't pull a stunt like that again.'

'I promise.'

'We'll tell everyone else the whole story tonight,' said Luc. He reached for Natasha's left hand. 'And we'll announce our wedding too.'

Excitement made her eyes sparkle like the Mediterranean. They wanted a simple wedding, smaller than Juliette's, but here in the grounds of the château too. He couldn't wait. This time he'd make sure Natasha got her every wish. He was determined she should have the day she'd dreamed of. He planned to spend the rest of his life making her dreams come true . . . and making sure she knew how completely and unreservedly he loved her.

'They'll be pleased,' said Jean-Pierre. 'As am I.'

Luc smiled, savouring his father's approval, relieved that the truth was finally out. 'Right, then. How about we unpack then go and cool off by the pool while we wait for the rabble to return?'

'Don't call them that,' Natasha said fondly. 'Your family are wonderful.'

They stood up to go inside.

315

'You have to admit, I did you both a favour, though?'

Jean-Pierre's words made them stop in their tracks. They glanced at each other, then back at him. The old man's lips curved, his eyes sparkled.

Luc smiled. 'You did.'

Recipes

The recipes mentioned in the story are all dishes I cook at home, and many were handed down to me from my French *grandmère*, who grew up in the north-east of France but loved the flavours of Provençal cooking. The recipes are shown in the order they appear in the book.

Roast Lamb with Garlic

Don't be put off by the amount of garlic that goes into this. Of course you can use less, but I promise the garlic flavour is much milder once cooked, and it cuts through the fattiness of the lamb beautifully.

The French are not huge fans of roast potatoes but, having lived most of my life in the UK, I can't imagine a roast without them. I serve this with roast potatoes, flageolet beans (tinned are fine) and green beans, plus the juices from the meat.

Oh, and keep any leftovers and the bone for the *navarin* recipe on page 328.

  2 tablespoons olive oil
  1 leg of lamb (on the bone)
  1 bulb of garlic, cloves separated and peeled
  Salt and freshly ground black pepper

Preheat the oven to 180°C Fan/Gas 4. Reserve about half a tablespoon of oil, then pour the rest into a large roasting tin and lay the lamb on it. Rub the remaining oil over the top of the meat. Using the end of a sharp knife, poke small holes, about 1cm deep, into the lamb and insert a clove of garlic into each one (if the cloves are especially big, cut them in half). Repeat until the lamb is studded all over with garlic, then season well. Roast for 1–1½ hours depending on how well done you like it.

Gratin Dauphinois

  150ml milk
  150g crème fraîche
  100ml vegetable stock
  1kg Désirée potatoes, peeled and very thinly sliced
  1 clove of garlic, sliced
  50g grated Gruyère or Cheddar

Preheat the oven to 140°C Fan/Gas 2. Make the stock and let it cool while you peel and slice the garlic and potatoes. Put the milk and crème fraîche into a jug and mix until smooth. Add the cool stock and season. Layer half the potatoes in a gratin or other ovenproof dish (approximately 20 x 30cm), then sprinkle over the garlic. Pour over half of the milk mixture. Add the rest of the potatoes, the remaining milk mixture, and scatter the cheese over the top. Bake for 75 minutes or until golden.

Paté de Crabe

This was a dish Grandmère kept for special occasions. It's not a soft paté, but we eat it in the same way with bread or crackers. Grandmère used to make her own mayonnaise to accompany it, but I'm too lazy so I buy the best I can afford instead (the organic ones are usually very good).

200g crabmeat

70g shrimps

4 eggs

100ml double cream

75g tomato purée

Salt and black pepper

Preheat the oven to 200°C Fan/Gas 7. Line a small (500g) loaf tin with baking parchment. Put the crab and shrimps into a blender and pulse. Add everything else, season, pulse again, and pour into the loaf tin. Put the tin into a large roasting tin and pour in enough water to come halfway up the loaf tin. Bake au bain-marie for 65 minutes. (Check after 40 minutes: if the top looks like it's darkening you can cover it with foil. I don't bother because it doesn't affect the taste.) Let it cool, then refrigerate.

Once the paté is cold, serve it with bread, mayonnaise and lemon wedges. Be warned, it's very filling!

Ratatouille

Another recipe that has been handed down through generations of my French family, but this one has been adapted by each cook: my aunt leaves out the tomato purée and the tin of tomatoes and uses fresh instead, my mum uses less garlic, and I tend to add more courgettes because we always grow too many on our allotment. I urge you to make it your own, too, using whatever quantities you fancy because I'm sure it will taste delicious however it's made.

I tablespoon olive oil
I onion, peeled and chopped
3 peppers, core and seeds removed, flesh chopped
4 cloves garlic, peeled and crushed
3 courgettes, sliced
I aubergine, cubed
I tin tomatoes
3 tablespoons tomato purée
I bay leaf and I teaspoon mixed herbs or thyme
Salt and black pepper

Heat the oil in a large, deep saucepan and fry the onion on a gentle heat for 5 minutes or so until it has softened. Add the peppers and garlic and cook for 2 minutes more. Put in all of the other ingredients with a splash of water (not too much because the courgettes give off water as they cook) and season well. Cook for 45 minutes with the lid half on, stirring every now and then. Add more water if it looks too dry. It improves in flavour if left until the next day, and it freezes really well.

Tarte aux Abricots

When we stayed at my grandparents' villa in France, my bedroom was next to the kitchen. Grandmère used to get up very early and I remember the soothing sounds of her quietly moving about the kitchen cooking before the sun rose and it became too unbearably hot to work. By the time I got up, there would often be a tart or two cooling on the kitchen table and Grandmère would have left for the market. The smell was delicious, but we knew better than to nibble. However, if there were any leftovers, they made a delicious breakfast the next day.

This recipe is so simple. No blind baking, no glaze or stewed fruit to prepare. And I make no apology for that. This was the dessert Grandmère made for every family gathering in summer, using either apricots, or plums from the tree in the garden. Its simplicity showcases the delicious sweet fruit and they become the star of the dish. I urge you to seek out the best possible apricots you can get hold of (I go to Marks & Spencer for them). And don't worry about a soggy bottom – as the apricot juices soak into the pastry, this only adds to its syrupy deliciousness.

> 500g shortcrust pastry
> 1kg apricots (or plums), halved and stoned
> 4 tablespoons granulated sugar

Preheat the oven to 170°C Fan/Gas 3. Line a 30-cm tart tin with the pastry. Prick it all over with a fork, then chill for 30 minutes. Arrange the apricots over the pastry, cut side up, and pack them in tightly because they shrink as they cook. Then sprinkle with the sugar and bake the tart for 35 minutes. Serve at room temperature with cream or ice cream, if you wish, or simply as it is.

Soupe au Pistou

A light, summery soup, this recipe is typical of Provençal cooking for its simplicity, and not a million miles away from Italian minestrone. I've found that each family has its own variation on the ingredients of this soup (you can add tomatoes, potatoes, turnips – the choices are endless) and even the cooking method: some boil the beans and vegetables separately, others start with the *pistou* and add the soup to it. I prefer to sweat the vegetables before the stock is added at the end: I think this preserves their flavours better. And I like to add the *pistou* sauce as I serve: its punchy garlic flavour really livens things up.

For the soup

2 tablespoons olive oil

2 onions, peeled and diced

4 cloves of garlic, peeled and crushed

2 courgettes, diced

2 carrots, diced

200g green beans, cut into 2cm pieces

2 bay leaves

Salt and freshly ground black pepper

1 x 400g tin haricot beans (or cannellini)

150g frozen peas

100g small dried pasta

2 litres vegetable stock

For the pistou

3 cloves of garlic

1 x 30g bunch of basil

4 tablespoons olive oil

A pinch of salt

For the soup: heat the olive oil in a large, deep pan and soften the onions on a low heat. Once they're translucent, add the garlic, courgettes, carrots, green beans, bay leaves and a little seasoning. Cook for around 15 minutes until the vegetables are soft. Drain the tinned beans and add them with the peas, pasta and vegetable stock. Bring to the boil, then simmer for 10 minutes or until the pasta is cooked.

Meanwhile, place all the *pistou* ingredients in a blender and whizz to a smooth paste (or pound them using a pestle and mortar).

Once the soup is ready, check the seasoning, and serve, adding a heaped teaspoon of *pistou* to each bowl.

Grandmère's Chocolate Cake

This is such a special recipe to me. It's been handed down through my mother's side of the family and it's the cake Grandmère always used to make for us when there was a birthday or other celebration. I've never tasted another chocolate cake quite like it (believe me, I've tried many). Whatever you do, don't overcook it. Five minutes too long in the oven and the middle will dry out. Like American brownies, you want the centre to be sticky and squidgy and a little sunken. It will glue your mouth closed and taste heavenly.

200g dark chocolate (not too bitter – I use Bournville)
100g butter
5 eggs, separated
200g sugar
100g plain flour
Icing sugar, to dust

Preheat the oven to 170°C Fan/Gas 3. Grease and line the base of a 20-cm round cake tin. On the lowest heat melt the chocolate and butter, stirring all the time. Remove from the heat and add the egg yolks, sugar and flour. Whisk the egg whites until stiff. With a metal spoon, gently fold the beaten egg whites into the chocolate mixture. Pour the batter into the tin. Bake for 30 minutes.

When cool, dust with icing sugar.

Gratin d'Aubergines

This recipe divides opinion. I love it. It's light, it's delicious, and unlike any other aubergine dish I've tasted. But my boys won't go near it. Their loss. That leaves all the more for me.

For the topping, Grandmère used to mix breadcrumbs with *biscotte* (cracker) crumbs to give extra crunch. Personally, I prefer chunky breadcrumbs, and you could also add grated cheese. It makes a light supper served on its own with crusty bread. Alternatively, you can serve it as a side dish alongside your roast or main course.

1.5kg aubergines (approximately 6)
5 tablespoons olive oil
2 onions, peeled and finely diced
2 cloves of garlic, peeled and crushed
1 tablespoon anchovy paste
1 tablespoon fresh parsley, chopped

Salt and freshly ground black pepper

4 eggs, separated

1 tablespoon plain flour

70g Gruyère, grated

4 tablespoons chunky breadcrumbs

Preheat the oven to 190°C Fan/Gas 5, and grease a gratin or other ovenproof dish (approximately 20 x 30cm).

Peel the aubergines and cut each one into quarters. Boil them for 10 minutes. Drain and mince them in the food processor. (I pulse them gently because I like to leave a few chunks rather than puréeing them.)

Heat 1 tablespoon of the olive oil in a large stockpot and fry the onions on a low heat until soft. Stir in the garlic, anchovy paste and parsley. Add the minced aubergines and season with salt and freshly ground black pepper. Remove from the heat, then stir in the egg yolks, flour and Gruyère.

Beat the egg whites until stiff peaks form, and gradually fold them into the aubergine mixture. Check the seasoning again, adding more salt if necessary. Stir the remaining 4 tablespoons of olive oil into the breadcrumbs. Tip the aubergine mixture into the oven dish, scatter over the breadcrumbs, and bake for 20–30 minutes, until the top is golden.

Diabolo Menthe

This is a lovely refreshing non-alcoholic drink, which you'll often see served in French cafés during the summer months. It might make you look twice because it's pea green!

Mint syrup (Teisseire is the top brand in France and is stocked in my British supermarket)

Sparkling water

Dilute the syrup, according to the bottle's instructions, with water, stir well, and add lots of ice.

Oven-baked Tomato Tarts

375g ready-rolled puff pastry
2 cloves of garlic, peeled and crushed
4 tablespoons sundried tomato paste
5–6 tomatoes, thinly sliced
Salt and freshly ground black pepper
½ teaspoon dried oregano
75g mozzarella, diced
1 egg, beaten

Preheat the oven to 180°C Fan/Gas 4. Line a baking tray with baking parchment. Using a saucer as a guide, cut 6 circles out of the puff pastry, each approximately 12 cm in diameter. Lay the circles on the baking tray and lightly score a 1-cm border around the edge of each, being careful not to cut all the way through. Use a fork to prick the centres of the circles. Mix the garlic and tomato paste together, and spread over the pastry, leaving the borders clear. Lay 3 tomato slices over each, season, and sprinkle with oregano. Dot the mozzarella over the tops, and brush the edges with egg. Bake for 20–25 minutes until the pastry is golden. Serve at room temperature.

Navarin of Lamb

Don't worry if you haven't much leftover roast lamb: this stew is delicious with very little meat and lots of vegetables. The flavour comes mainly from the bone, so do hang on to it. If I have a glass of white or rosé wine handy, I add that to the stock, but it's not essential.

2 tablespoons olive oil

1 onion, peeled and diced

3 cloves of garlic, peeled and chopped

400g-ish roast lamb leftovers and bone (or use neck of lamb)

2 heaped teaspoons plain flour

6 carrots, cut into large chunks

3 small turnips, cut into large chunks

500g new potatoes

2 bay leaves

1 litre chicken or lamb stock

Salt and freshly ground black pepper

Heat the oil in a large stockpot and fry the onions on a low heat until translucent. Add the garlic and meat (if you're using raw meat, brown it quickly in another pan, with a little olive oil). Sprinkle in the flour and stir well. Add the bone, carrots, turnips, potatoes, bay leaves, stock and seasoning. Cover and bring to the boil, then simmer for 1½ hours, stirring every now and then. (Alternatively, you can cook it in the oven at 180°C Fan/Gas 4.) Remove the bone and the bay leaves. Serve hot, with crusty bread.

Mont Blanc

This isn't really a recipe so much as an assembly job, but it was my favourite dessert as a child so I'm keen to pass it on. When we used to drive to France for the summer, we'd always return with a car boot full of wine and tins of *crème de marrons*. The finished Mont Blanc is like an ice-cream sundae, but it's supposed to mimic the mountain with a snow-topped peak.

> 1 x 250g tin sweetened *crème de marrons* (chestnut purée)
> Vanilla ice cream
> Whipped cream

Spoon the chestnut purée into individual bowls, top with a ball of ice cream and a dollop of whipped cream. That's it. I know. You're welcome.

Acknowledgements

Thanks to Hodder for giving me the opportunity to add more depth and detail to this book which was originally much shorter when it was first published. Kim and Madeleine, your editorial advice is always so helpful, and you make the process so easy with your professionalism and positivity. Thanks too to my wonderful agent, Megan Carroll.

I'm grateful to all the friends and family who helped me brainstorm extra scenes – there are so many of you! But special thanks must go to the Novelistas, Maureen and my husband Ian who, after a bottle of wine, was unstoppable with his suggestions.

Thanks to Lynn Evans who chatted to me about flowers and gave me some real gems of information about owning a florist's shop.

And finally, thanks to my mum, Brigitte, who checked my French spellings and answered many questions about all things French. And to my dad, Jim, for his knowledge of wine-making and for all the wine-tasting trips we've made in France – they gave me the inspiration for the Duval family's vineyard. I feel very lucky to have such happy memories of the family holidays we spent in

France when I was a child. (Is it too late to apologise for my teenaged self who complained it was boring to go to the same place every year? Sorry.)

Read on for an extract from
The Christmas Holiday
by Sophie Claire

Chapter One

Evie had a bad feeling about the place. Or perhaps it was simply the chill in the air as she hurried from her car to the Old Hall, carrying her heavy load. The forecast tonight was snow. She prayed it would wait until she'd finished what she was there to do and had driven back down the hill to the village. It should take her an hour, tops, and once she was home in her little cottage, it could snow as much as it liked: she'd be tucked up in bed with a warm quilt and a hot-water bottle. Tomorrow she'd email her invoice. The sooner she collected payment, the happier her bank manager would be. Maybe he'd even stop breathing down her neck.

She unlocked the door of the big house and flicked on the lights, accidentally knocking the coat stand. She caught it before it toppled, then scurried on towards the dining room. Two chandeliers lit it, and she saw her reflection in the tall, naked windows – her red coat was a beacon glowing brightly in the doorway. Carefully, Evie laid the curtain she'd made on the grand dining table. She flicked her long plait over her shoulder, then went back to her car. Floor-length, in a burgundy and gold damask that caught the light, the curtains would look perfect in that room, but they were so heavy she had to carry them in one at a time, all four of them.

As she scuttled back from her car for the last time, the first snowflakes began to fall. She smiled as they tickled her cheeks, but quickened her pace and closed the solid oak door, shutting out the icy air. Not that it was much warmer inside the huge empty house: her breath left a thin cloud in the air as she marched along the corridor. Perhaps the place would come to life once the new owner moved in.

Her foot caught something hard and she stumbled. A metal doorstop lay on its side. With her toe, she pushed it under the dining-room door to prop it open. She put her heavy parcel down with the others, stopped and listened.

Funny. She'd thought she'd heard barking.

But, of course, that couldn't be. Hers was the only car on the drive, and when she'd arrived the house had been in darkness. The owner wasn't due to move in for another week.

Evie brushed aside the thought and carried her stepladder to the window. It squeaked loudly as she unfolded it. She unwrapped the first curtain from its plastic cover, lifted it expertly over her shoulder, and climbed up to the highest step. These windows were tall, and it was a balancing act as she supported the weight of the fabric with one hand and hooked the curtain with the other. She had finished one and was starting on the second when she heard barking again – louder this time. Perched on the stepladder, she stilled. It wasn't the tinny yap of a small dog, but a deep, loud bark.

The Christmas Holiday

Her heart thumped. What if a guard dog was patrolling?

Surely not. She'd been given a key by the owner's PA, and tradespeople had been coming and going for weeks now.

Still, the owner might assume she would only seek access during the day. She looked at her watch. It was nine thirty now.

She heard footsteps approaching and the deep tones of a male voice. The dog's bark made her jump this time, and she heard the scrabble of paws as an animal – several, perhaps? – raced down the corridor. Frozen, she watched the open door, not daring to let go of the curtain, which was attached by only three hooks. Her eyes widened as a large Dalmatian bounded in and leaped up at her. She screamed and clung to the stepladder, which wobbled violently. The curtain was wrenched from her hands, she heard a creak – and looked up to see that the curtain pole was now hanging at a crooked angle.

'Smoke! Down!' the man shouted.

The dog ignored him, barked and jumped, knocking the ladder again. Evie gasped as it wobbled, then tumbled in a clatter of metal, fabric and barking.

She blinked. She and the curtains were in a heap on the floor. Instinctively, she lifted her arm to protect her face as the dog went for her, but instead of teeth, she felt only a warm wet tongue licking her hand.

'What the . . .' Shocked, she put her arm down and stared at the dog. It tilted its head to peer at her in turn, then whined affectionately. Evie laughed. 'After all that, you want your ears scratching? You silly dog!' She rubbed the Dalmatian behind the ears, and it made happy noises in return.

But her smile faded as she spotted the holes in the plaster where the curtain pole had been ripped from the wall. 'Oh, but look what you've done . . .' She tried to extricate herself from the curtains but she was well and truly tangled in them, and the combined weight of the ladder and the dog pinned her to the floor.

'Look what *he*'s done?'

She and the dog turned their heads at the sound of the disapproving male voice.

Now Evie got a proper look at the tall, unshaven man standing a few feet away. She guessed he was somewhere in his mid-thirties, though she couldn't be sure. He stepped closer to inspect the heap of ladder, metal pole and curtain in which Evie was trapped, and she caught a strong whiff of alcohol. The stubble on his chin gave him an air of menace, his hair was dishevelled, and when he turned his sharp gaze back on her she saw his eyes were bloodshot.

'He was simply protecting my property. The question is, what were *you* doing here?'

Not an outstretched hand to help her up, she noticed. No 'Are you hurt?' Just an accusing look, as if he'd caught her trespassing.

Her heart beat double-time. No one knew she was here – alone with this angry stranger and his dog. Suddenly she felt vulnerable.

'What does it look like I was doing? Breaking and entering?' He continued to glare down at her. She sighed and spelled it out for him: 'I was fitting these curtains, of course.'

'Of course,' he said drily. 'Because that's a perfectly normal thing to be doing at –' he looked at his watch, which glinted in the light of the chandeliers '– almost ten in the evening.'

Indignation bubbled up inside her. 'I have a key!' She wrestled to free herself from the fabric, but with no success. The Dalmatian stepped forward and nuzzled her hand. It was difficult to stay angry with the horrible man when his dog was so adorable.

'Really.'

His sarcasm was cutting. A picture of her ex flashed into her mind, but she pushed it aside to concentrate on the here and now. 'Yes!' She felt about for her pocket, but the tangle of curtains made it impossible. 'Heidi gave it to me.'

The flicker of recognition in his eyes reassured her that Heidi's name meant something to him. 'And did Heidi invite you to come here in the middle of the night?'

'It was the only time I could make it,' she said, through gritted teeth, as she finally managed to pull herself free and clambered to her feet. Pain shot up from her left ankle, making her gasp and lose her balance. She grabbed the nearest object – a chair.

'What's wrong?' he asked, sounding exasperated rather than concerned.

'Nothing.' She rooted in her coat pocket. 'Here's your damned key. Satisfied?'

He shot the medieval-looking piece of metal a cursory

glance, then turned his gaze back on the pitiful heap of curtains.

'Satisfied is hardly the right word. Have you seen the damage you've done?'

She followed his eyes to the holes in the wall where the curtain pole had been attached. Her jaw tightened as she bit back several possible retorts. She was aware that if he was the owner he was also her client, but she'd just been doing her job. She didn't deserve this treatment and he was by far the rudest customer she'd ever dealt with.

Although he wasn't the first man to make her feel small and wanting. Her ex, Tim, and this man were definitely cut from the same cloth. But if she'd learned anything from Tim, it was not to let another man walk all over her.

The dog ran excited circles around her, by turns sniffing at the curtains and rubbing his head against her leg. Evie gripped the chair and tried her best to keep her balance while not putting any weight on her left ankle. 'So, rather than apologise for your dog's behaviour, you're turning this back on me? I might ask who you are and why you're here.'

'This is my house. I don't have to justify my presence to you.'

Ah. So he *was* the client. And these curtains had cost a fortune in fabric alone. She couldn't afford for him to refuse to pay or she'd be in even bigger trouble with the bank.

'But – but Heidi told me you weren't moving in until next week!' If she'd known he'd be here she'd have called first.

And how she wished she had.

'When I move in is my affair,' he said brusquely. A strange expression flashed through his eyes before he looked away.

'Well, this is unfortunate. But I was just doing my job.' She lifted her chin. 'Perhaps if you'd kept your dog under control, there'd be less damage and I wouldn't have had the fright of my life.'

And she wouldn't have been hurt. She reached down to touch her ankle and the dog licked her hand.

'Smoke!' the man said sharply. 'Come here!'

The dog looked up at the sound of his name but ignored the command. The man glared at the animal as if it were a traitor, then sighed and set about righting the mess. He picked up the stepladder and propped it against the wall. The smell of alcohol grew stronger as he approached, and Evie watched him warily. He was angry and inebriated, and no one knew she was there.

She reached for the curtains, brushed off a small piece of plaster, and inspected them for damage. 'They seem to be fine, thank goodness. It took me hours to make them.'

She draped them carefully over the table so they wouldn't crease.

The man was picking up chunks of plaster. 'Tell me again why you're delivering curtains in the dark.'

Her fists curled in her pockets. Tim used to take the same disparaging tone with her when they were out with his colleagues and she spoke too much or said the wrong thing.

'I run a shop in the day,' she said, 'so I always deliver

my curtains in the evening.' Most clients appreciated this service, knowing that other suppliers expected customers to collect and hang their own curtains.

'You couldn't wait until tomorrow, given the weather?'

'No, I couldn't. Tomorrow is my friend's birthday and . . .' This red-eyed man wouldn't understand her cash-flow problems. He owned a hall, for goodness' sake. Not a house, but a hall!

'And?' he prompted.

She decided to admit the truth. 'And I needed to get them finished and delivered so I could invoice for them.'

Instantly, his eyes narrowed, as she had known they would. 'So, this is about money?'

'No! Well . . . yes.'

His bloodshot eyes became two red slits.

She added quickly, 'I've done nothing but work on them for the last week, and the cost of the material was in the hundreds – which creates cash-flow problems. I'm just a small business. I need to collect payment for them as soon as possible or my bank account will go into the red.'

'You couldn't send the invoice, then deliver them? You knew the place was empty.'

She looked at him in horror. 'I never invoice a customer until I've delivered the curtains and I'm satisfied they're the perfect fit.'

'Surely if you've measured correctly they'll fit.'

Spoken like someone who had never hung a pair of curtains in his life. 'It's not that simple – which is why I like to put them up myself and make sure they hang right.'

He raised a brow. 'Make sure they hang right?'

'Yes.' She was infuriated by his condescending attitude.

'What did you think – that the laws of gravity might not apply here in this house?'

If it had been anyone else, she'd have thought that was a joke. But he was just plain mocking. 'Clearly you know nothing about curtains.'

'You're right. Please enlighten me, because I've yet to see curtains that don't hang but float horizontally instead.'

She ground her teeth. 'Curtains can be the perfect measurements but if they aren't hung correctly with the pleats in the right places, they'll look stiff and – and awkward.'

'Awkward?' The corners of his mouth twitched with derision, which only raised her blood pressure even more.

'Yes! Which is why I like to dress them personally, so they look their best.' In her sewing bag she had extra weights she could slip into the lining if necessary, but usually it was simply a case of rearranging the pleats and fabric, and that was something experience had taught her how to do.

Somehow his silence was more damning than his caustic words.

'You can leave now,' he said eventually, with a nod towards the door. 'You've done enough damage. Your services are no longer required.'

Evie stared at him, a rush of jumbled thoughts filling her head. He was throwing her out after his dog had attacked her? And no longer required? Did that mean he wasn't going to pay her? Her heart raced as she thought of the grim warning the bank had issued. There would be no mercy if her account went into the red again.

'Now look here! You can't not pay for those curtains – especially when your dog was responsible for the damage, not me!'

'I'm not talking about the damn payment. Is everything about money with you?'

'No! But you said—'

'I asked you to leave. The door's this way.'

She glared at him, then snatched up her sewing bag and reached for her ladder.

'I'll take those,' he said, lifting them out of her hands.

She didn't have the fight to refuse. She hobbled after him, but every time she put weight on her left ankle pain ripped through it. She blinked hard. What a horrible, horrible man. The Dalmatian trotted happily beside her, occasionally nuzzling her hand as if to comfort her, bless him.

'What about the rest of the curtains?' she asked, glancing back at the pair still in their protective covers.

'I'll have to get someone in to repair the damage first,' he said, without so much as a glance in her direction.

'When they've been, I'll come back to finish the job.'

'That won't be necessary. I'll let you know if there's a problem – with gravity or otherwise.'

Evie shrugged. 'Suit yourself.'

A rush of cold air gusted in as he opened the front door, and Evie's eyes widened. Her car was sitting under a sparkling duvet, and snow spiralled down in a shimmering dance that lit up the night. It was coming thick and fast. At any other time it would have been beautiful – even magical – but tonight her heart sank. 'Oh, no . . .'

'Didn't you hear the forecast? They said it would snow.'

'I know. But it's the first of December. I didn't think there'd be so much of it!'

Snowflakes continued to float down like feathers and the air was eerily silent – although that was probably always the case up there on top of the hill. Evie was used to living in the village, with friends and neighbours close by.

'Where do you want that?' he asked, indicating the stepladder.

'In the back, please,' she said, and stepped outside to open her car. The snow crunched beneath her feet, and she was relieved that it hadn't got too deep yet. 'It fits in the footwell.'

He slid it inside, then regarded the car gravely. 'I'll help you clear the snow.'

His expensive-looking brogues were half submerged in it. Thank goodness she'd worn knee-high boots, Evie thought. 'There's no need,' she said quickly. 'I can manage.' She just wanted to get away from him. She'd be home soon, she reassured herself, as she scraped snow off the windscreen.

'Right. I'll be off, then. My name's Evie, by the way,' she said, and held out her hand. 'Evie Miller.' It was a bit late for niceties, but it felt wrong to drive away without introducing herself, particularly as tomorrow her invoice would be winging its way to him.

He looked at her hand, then shook it. 'Jake Hartwood.'

His hand was as cold as her own, but his grip was firm and strong. Close up, though, the stench of alcohol made her recoil. How sad that such a good-looking young man had turned out so embittered and unpleasant. He might have been attractive – if he'd had a different personality.

Still, at least she'd stood up to him. In fact, she'd surprised herself. Why couldn't she do the same with Tim? And her parents, for that matter?

'Drive slowly and stay in a low gear,' he warned, as she got into the car.

'I'll be fine. It's not deep.' She shut the door and looked at the long drive that snaked away into the snow-speckled darkness. In the doorway of the Old Hall the man and his dog watched as she started the car.

'Low gear indeed,' she muttered to herself, and pressed the accelerator. She couldn't get away fast enough. Goodbye and good riddance to him and his sour-faced advice.

The car moved quickly, and Evie smiled to herself. Thank goodness the snow wasn't too deep . . . but as the car gathered momentum, her smile slipped. She was turning the wheel to no avail. And the car was heading not down the drive but to the right. It was difficult to see, but she thought she remembered a steep slope down into the gardens. She pressed her foot hard on the brake. The car simply lurched forward. She turned the wheel as the drive wound to the left, but nothing happened. She touched the brake again. Her pulse revved up in panic. She braked harder, but the car only skidded, and the steering wheel felt loose in her hand.

'No!' she murmured, gripping the wheel harder. The car was picking up speed as it moved downhill. Muttering a prayer and a curse, she tried again and willed it to cooperate. 'Stop!' she cried, stamping on the brake pedal, and lifting the handbrake in desperation.

The car rolled faster. She yanked the wheel, pressed all the pedals, took it out of gear, put it back in – but still it gathered speed and slid uncontrollably. Her heart thumped crazily. Should she jump out and abandon it? No – she couldn't afford to pay for the repairs if it crashed. Then again, she wasn't in any position to prevent it crashing. She glanced back. Was Jake still watching? She couldn't see – and, anyway, at that moment the car left the drive and plunged down the slope.

Evie gasped as it stopped. She blinked.

The car was wedged at an angle, but she was unhurt, thank goodness. She tried to reverse, but nothing happened. She tried to go forward – it was optimistic, but if she could just turn the car, perhaps it could climb the hill back to the drive. She wound the window down, looked out, then tried the accelerator again. The wheels spun and the car sank deeper into the snow. She closed her eyes in despair. She had to face it: she was well and truly stuck.

The Christmas Holiday is available to buy now

Bookends

When one book ends, another begins...

Bookends is a vibrant new reading community to help you ensure you're never without a good book.

You'll find exclusive previews of the brilliant new books from your favourite authors as well as exciting debuts and past classics. Read our blog, check out our recommendations for your reading group, enter great competitions and much more!

Visit our website to see which great books we're recommending this month.

Join the Bookends community:

www.welcometobookends.co.uk

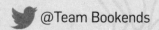 @Team Bookends   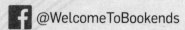 @WelcomeToBookends